A Doctor BILLIONAIRE for the COWBOY

dobi daniels

Luxhaven
Publishing

ISBN paperback, 978-1-958987-16-2

Interior Design by Luxhaven Publishing

Cover Design by The Book Brander Boutique

Proofreading by Lisa Lee Proofreading

To JC, Grandma D, and DC, whom I love more than life itself.

Her Billionaire Nemesis (short story)

SEE ALL OF DOBI DANIELS BOOKS

at https://dobidaniels.com

AUTHOR'S NOTE

Thank you for choosing A DOCTOR BILLIONAIRE FOR THE COWBOY. I enjoyed writing the story of Simone Addison and Jax Dexin, two very interesting and lovable characters!

Sometimes we make the wrong choices out of love, and when we realize we've derailed, it can be difficult to ask for forgiveness or accept the same for ourselves. I pray A DOCTOR BILLIONAIRE FOR THE COWBOY gives you hope to believe you can find love again, despite your mistakes.

Please continue this journey with me with a detour back to Dexington with LOVING THE BILLIONAIRE ROYAL DOC, a royal billionaire story in which a wonderful royal surgeon, Dr. Roman Sinclair, finds love. You can grab your copy at https://dobidaniels.com.

Would you like to be notified when the next Dobi Daniels book releases? Sign up at https://dobidaniels.com.

Once again, thank you so much for purchasing A DOCTOR BILLIONAIRE FOR THE COWBOY and for meeting Simone Addison and Jax Dexin. If you enjoyed it, please consider leaving a review at your favorite retailer or recommending it to a friend.

Thanks again for your support!

Dobi Daniels

A Doctor
BILLIONAIRE
for the COWBOY

CHAPTER 1

ax Dexin had guessed she was special from the first time he'd laid eyes on her. But he'd been wrong, dead wrong. Simone Addison was so much more. She was the last person he ever wanted to set his eyes on ever again.

She'd eroded his heart, made it her own, and then smashed it into pieces five years, six months, and seven days ago. Not that he'd been counting. Simone had cut him off without a word, and every attempt to reach her had been futile.

It'd been the day he'd received the news that had blindsided him. The one that had left him gasping in pain.

Dr. Simone Addison, the only woman he'd let in and cherished with all his heart, his angel on earth whom he'd believed loved him in return, had betrayed him.

Mercilessly.

He, Jax Dexin, had been thoroughly fooled.

His world had fallen apart, and only with a herculean effort had Jax woken up each day and continued like nothing happened, burying himself so deep in his work he wasn't sure how he'd been able to breathe. He'd forced himself to forget her, which'd been hard, since he hadn't yet recovered from the sudden disappearance and betrayal by his twin brother Rex. Soon, the years had passed, and he'd thought he'd moved on.

Until today.

In the spacious barn set up for the evening's singles' mixer event with the aromas of fresh air, nature, and aftershave competing for prominence, Jax stood rooted on the spot, his traitorous heart betraying him and beating wildly like a bird trying to free itself from its cage as soon as he'd spotted her a few feet away. She flashed that quiet but confident smile that had always taken his breath away and later haunted his memories at night.

What was Simone doing here in Dexin, his home-town of all places?

Dexin wasn't a popular town on the map by any

means, so it wasn't one of those places people could say they accidentally showed up at. And at a fall singles' mixer event, no less? Wasn't Simone supposed to be married by now, after what she'd done to him? So many questions raced through his mind like speedy trains on rail tracks.

Jax watched, his heart squeezing with hurt, as she replied with a smile to a remark from a young man standing by her side, the adoring look on the man's face a telltale sign he was already smitten with her. Jax wasn't surprised—Simone had that effect on people.

He forced out a breath, which helped to loosen his frozen limbs. He couldn't stay any longer, even though he'd promised his foster mother, Maggie, he'd be there for the whole event—Maggie was keen on him marrying and settling down soon, and Jax had humored her only to get her off his back.

But then she wouldn't have imagined he'd meet Simone here. Not that Maggie had known her—at Simone's request, Jax hadn't told his family about the relationship when they'd started dating, which had seemed reasonable at the time. However, it meant he'd had to weather the devastation that had followed alone, tucking the secret deep down in his heart.

A harrowing experience, and one he never planned to repeat.

Jax was a man who preferred to face any difficult situation head-on, but matters of the heart were unpredictable, and another beast entirely. His head now told him it was time to flee this place and get as far away from Simone as possible. She'd stomped his heart to the ground the first time, and nothing good could come from being around her now.

Tearing his eyes away from her, he made to leave, but then another thought stopped him in his tracks.

None of these innocent folks at the event, most of whom he'd grown up with, knew who Simone truly was, no matter her reason for being here. Jax couldn't stand by and allow this female wolf-in-sheep's-clothing to devour yet another gullible young man— Jax could already see a few of them gravitating toward her like bees to a shallow blossom.

The muscles in Jax's jaw tightened. This was his town. He had to protect them somehow. Here in Dexin, folks looked out for each other, and he'd be remiss in his duty if he left just like that. Jax had to confront Simone and get her away from here, even if it meant ripping open the scars that had healed over his heart.

Which was the last thing he wanted to do.

Because even though he'd survived the wounds the first time, what guarantee did he have that he'd heal again?

Jax watched as yet another unsuspecting young man headed in Simone's direction and then waited in the wings to chat with her.

I can't let Simone fool them, he thought to himself. *I can do this. For everyone.*

Jax let out an exhale, squared his shoulders, and forced his reluctant limbs to head in her direction.

It was time to face his nemesis and put a stop to whatever mischief Simone had up her sleeves.

Even if it meant reliving the bitter truth of what had happened many years ago.

CHAPTER 2

SIX YEARS AGO

Simone Addison hurried down the corridor that May afternoon, her flats soundless on the hospital's marble floor, and her heart pounding in her chest. How could this have happened? She'd just left the grounds for her medical school graduation ceremony when she'd gotten the call about her boyfriend's accident, and had flown to Vegas in a private jet as soon as she could.

With her busy schedule and Ethan's extended out-of-town work trip, they'd seen little of each other in the past few months. Video chatting on the phone hadn't had quite the same effect, and they'd been too busy to spend more than a few minutes at a time. Simone had missed him a lot. Ethan had promised to be back in town in a few days, even though he couldn't make her graduation, and they'd planned to take a brief vacation together once he'd returned. So news of his accident in Vegas had been a shock.

Wait! Wasn't he supposed to be in Arizona for work? How had he ended up in Vegas?

She shook her head. That wasn't important for now. Ethan just needed to be okay. Every other question could wait.

Simone had first met Ethan Morrison at a gala fundraiser she'd attended while in her first year of medical school. Ethan had been in charge of the charity auction—on behalf of the private equity firm he worked at—and Simone's family friends had roped her into helping.

Somehow, they'd gotten talking, and Simone had found Ethan to be down-to-earth, a rarity in the world in which she moved. Chatting with him had been a breath of fresh air. He'd asked her out for coffee the next day, and the rest had been history. Ethan had become her best friend, her soulmate, her heart, and nothing could happen to him now.

She halted as she spied the room number the nurse at the VIP central station had given her.

Simone took a deep breath and let out an exhale. Ethan was going to be alright no matter what. She had to believe that. She wasn't certain what condition he was in—the nurse hadn't told her. Regardless, she couldn't let him see how anxious she was.

Simone needed to remain calm for his sake.

She could do this.

So she pasted a smile on her face, let out one more exhale, and knocked on the door. Without waiting for a response, she slid it open and stepped in.

Into an alternate reality where her world came crashing down.

Simone's smile froze, and her breath caught in her throat at the sight before her. She hadn't seen this coming.

This isn't real, she told herself. *It can't be what it seems.*

She pinched her arm and flinched, but the throbbing pain confirmed her eyes weren't playing tricks on her.

Ethan, the love of her life, the man she was looking forward to spending the rest of her life with, had his so-called assistant on his lap, and they were making out.

Her heart felt like someone had dropped it in an ice bucket. In that moment, Simone wished she'd never come to Vegas.

"What's going on here?" she asked in an icy

voice, even as she fought to maintain her composure as her heart cracked and shattered into shards.

The petite assistant, Vera, jumped to her feet at the sound of Simone's voice. "I'm so sorry, I'm so sorry," she said as she hurried to button up her open blouse and smooth her skirt. Ethan's shirt was in a similar disarray.

Simone ignored her, her eyes meeting Ethan's instead. How could he betray her like this? She thought she saw a flash of pain cross his handsome face, but then his eyes went blank as he held her gaze.

Right as he grabbed Vera's hand and pulled her to his side.

Simone almost buckled from the pain that hit her at the sight. How dare he do this in front of her? She'd guessed Vera had a crush on Ethan since the first day Ethan had introduced her to Simone at his office, but so did the other females who worked there, which was why Simone hadn't thought it was a big deal. Besides, it took two hands to clap, and Ethan hadn't seemed like the cheating type.

Or so she'd thought.

"How could you, Ethan?" Simone said. He faltered for a moment under her steady gaze, but then seemed to straighten.

"The real question is why did you have to be such an uptight prude?" he replied, each word slung like arrows at her.

Simone wilted on the inside at his words. She couldn't believe what she was hearing. Was this the same Ethan she knew? "What?"

He let out a sigh, his arm tightening around Vera. "I'm a man, Simone, and men have needs. Since you weren't helping, I had to get my needs met elsewhere."

Unbelievable! Was he being serious right now? It wasn't like she'd forced him to be in a relationship with her. "You've always known my stance from the beginning, Ethan. I made that clear when you asked me out, and you said you were fine with it."

He adjusted until he rested against one of his hospital pillows. It was like he'd regained his confidence the more he spoke. "Yeah, yeah, you did. But I thought you'd change your mind and open up with time. It didn't help that you were always so busy with medical school, with this exam, or that exam. You were never there when I needed you."

But he'd said nothing all these years. How dare he blame her? "If you weren't happy with our relationship, you could have broken it off ages ago instead of doing this behind my back!" She took a deep breath and fought to stay calm. Getting all worked up wouldn't do her any good at this point. "It's been four years, Ethan. Has this been going on the entire time? Why bother deceiving me when we could have gone our separate ways?"

Ethan gave a disbelieving laugh, as if Simone was a moron for even asking. "Why else? For the money, of course. It's not everyday I get a chance to marry a billionaire heiress."

Simone flinched like he'd slapped her. Was this the same Ethan she'd loved, the same one who'd hinted at a proposal a few months ago? How had she been so blind not to see he'd only loved her money and not her? She'd thought he differed from others who'd tried to take advantage of her. Except now it was clear it'd been a mistake and had only been wishful thinking on her part.

She, Simone Addison, had been played for a fool.

But no longer. Simone couldn't allow herself to fall apart here, even though her heart was in a million pieces, the same way her grandma's treasured china had shattered a few years ago when the neighbor's poodle crashed into it. She was Simone Addison, granddaughter of two leading Boston families and a freshly minted MD. She was made of hardier stock than most people imagined.

Simone straightened her shoulders and looked Ethan right in the eye. "It's over, Ethan. Good luck with your assistant." She whirled around and strode out of the hospital room, head held high and blinking back the tears that burned at the back of her eyes. She didn't pay attention to where she was going or the curious eyes that stared at her as she passed, only nursing a desperate desire to get away from Ethan as fast as possible.

Soon, she stood in front of a set of glass double doors that led to what looked like a garden.

Simone pushed one door open and stepped outside. The potent scent of honeysuckle and fresh grass hit her nostrils as she hurried down the stone pavement lined with trees interspersed with shrubs of sunflower and cacti, searching for a spot where she could be all alone. Thankfully, the garden appeared deserted. Soon she spied a long stone bench tucked into a corner of the garden and she collapsed on it, dropping her large purse beside her, and gripping the edge of the seat as if afraid that letting go would disintegrate her already fragile composure.

Simone forced herself to take a few deep breaths of the Saturday afternoon's gentle breeze. Fresh scented air rushed into her lungs, yet it couldn't loosen the tightness in her chest. She leaned forward, hoping for a respite from the unpleasantness she'd just experienced, and dropped her head into her hands.

How could this have happened to her? She'd loved Ethan and had thought they were meant for each other. But more than that, they'd been good friends. Though it hadn't been easy for her to let down her guard, Simone had opened up to him, and he'd become one of the few people she'd been herself with in the past few years.

How could it have all been a lie?

She fought back the tears that threatened to fall. She would not cry because of that bastard—he didn't deserve it. But what was she going to do now? Where would she even begin to pick up the pieces of her life? Her head ached from just thinking about it, and she rubbed her temples.

"Are you okay, ma'am?" a warm, masculine voice asked.

Simone stiffened and looked up to see a tall, attractive young man in a blue shirt with rolled-up sleeves and jeans, a cowboy hat perched on his head, standing a few feet away from her. He appeared to be in his late twenties, not much older than her. Soft grey eyes met hers.

"I'm fine," she said in a flat voice, wishing he

would just go away. She didn't need an audience to her pity party and wasn't in the mood for any flirting, either.

But he settled on the other end of the bench instead and said nothing else to her.

After waiting a few minutes to see if he would leave, Simone snuck a look at him. Sure, she couldn't miss the fact that he was a feast for sore eyes, but why did he have to sit here, of all places? He didn't have to be a genius to know she didn't want company.

But then she noticed the slump of his broad shoulders and the grief mirrored on his handsome face. What had happened to him?

She shook her head. *Get a hold of yourself, Simone.* Many a time, friends and family had accused her of being too empathetic. Sure, she was guilty as charged, but this was not the time to get into anyone else's business. She already had enough worries of her own as well as nursing a broken, vulnerable heart. Besides, he was a stranger in an unfamiliar place. What if he meant her harm?

Then the stranger let out a long sigh, a sound that her heart seemed to recognize. Had someone shattered his heart, too? One miserable heartbroken person was more than enough for the day.

"Are you okay?" she couldn't help asking.

He turned his head to look at her and gave her a small embarrassed smile, revealing a left dimple. "I'm sorry if I disturbed you," he said. "But there's no other bench here, and I just needed a moment."

Why did she have to be a sucker for dimples? Now, Simone couldn't stay out of his matter if she tried.

"Is everything alright?" she asked.

CHAPTER 3

ax Dexin stared back at the stunning young lady sitting a few feet away from him on the garden bench. She'd asked him a question, but he was at a loss for more words, blindsided by how graceful she looked, even dressed in a loose-fitting blouse and skinny jeans.

The lady also had the most beautiful hair he'd ever seen—luscious wavy black hair pulled into a ponytail with tendrils at the nape. He'd never known why anyone would want to run their fingers through a woman's hair, but now he understood it, really got it. She was like a regal queen perched on her throne— that was how fantastic she looked.

"Are you okay?" she asked again, with a trace of

a cultured Bostonian accent coming through. It seemed she was not from these parts, just like him.

"Sorry. I hope I didn't disturb you," he said.

"Maybe," she responded with a hint of a smile, one he hoped to see again. But then he remembered his brother, Max, lying on the hospital bed.

Jax let out a long sigh. "I've had better days." He ran a hand through his hair. "And unless I'm wrong, I guess that might be the same for you."

"Maybe. You have someone at the hospital?"

Usually, Jax liked to keep his matters private, but somehow, he felt comfortable opening up to her. Maybe because she was a stranger, and he'd never see her again, though a part of him seemed to rebel at the very thought. "My brother had an accident and is admitted here."

Concern filled her face. "Is he alright?" she asked.

Jax had always thought Max invincible, so getting a call about the accident had shaved a few years off his life. Max had only travelled to Vegas to attend the rodeo at his brothers' insistence. They'd thought the trip would do him good—Max's fiancée had jilted him at the altar, and he hadn't been taking it well.

But it'd turned out to be a mistake, since Max

was now lying asleep on a hospital bed with a bad concussion. The doctor had reassured Jax that he'd be fine, but Jax hated seeing his strong brother this way. Max was the best of them all and didn't deserve what had happened to him.

Since he could only tolerate being in the hospital for so long, and Max would be asleep for some time, Jax had left his brother's bedside and come down into the garden to get some much-needed fresh air.

"The doctors said he'll be," Jax replied. "But he's lost some of his memory." Thankfully, Max remembered Jax and his other brothers, Dex and Rex, but Jax was worried there might be other side effects that weren't visible yet.

"I'm so sorry to hear that. I'm sure he'll get better. Memories can also return after a while."

"Thanks." Her words made him feel better, even though the doctors had pretty much said the same thing. "What about you? You have a loved one here?"

"Used to," she replied. The shadows on her face darkened.

"I'm sorry. Did the person pass away?"

Her slim, manicured fingers played with the zipper pull of her purse. Back and forth, back and forth. It was dizzying to watch, he had to admit, and he worried an item might fall out. "I wish he would," she muttered.

That was unexpected. What did that even mean?

She let out an exhale. "Forget I said that."

It seemed whoever it was had hurt her deeply for her to wish him dead. A father? Or a boyfriend? "You don't have to talk about it if you don't want to," Jax said. It was best to respect her space if she didn't feel like opening up.

She stayed silent for a while, so it startled Jax when she finally spoke. "A jerk who used to be my boyfriend until a few minutes ago. He got into an accident, and I flew over to see him, only to catch him in the arms of his secretary." Even though she tried to hide it, it was clear she'd been hurt.

"Ouch." Jax couldn't stand cheaters of any kind.

"Ouch indeed."

"He's an idiot for losing you," he couldn't help saying.

That seemed to lift her spirits as her face brightened a little. "That's a nice thing to say, even though you don't know me."

"I'm generally a good judge of character. I don't think you're all bad."

The corners of her lips lifted into a smile. "Thanks for the compliment."

"You're welcome. Besides, no one deserves to be cheated on."

She said nothing in response to that and instead stared out in front of her.

They stayed in companionable silence for a few more minutes. In that time, Jax's worries and concerns began to fade away. The sky appeared more cornflower blue, and he felt like he could breathe easier. With her soft scent of fresh florals mixed with subtle notes of sandalwood filling the air between them, Jax wished for the first time in his interactions with females that they could keep sitting there. Together. He'd never felt this comfortable with any other woman before.

Finally, she got up. "I have to go."

Jax rose to his feet as well. A part of him wished she could stay longer. She was a total stranger, yet he felt like he'd known her forever, which just seemed insane. But what could he really say? That he wanted to see her again and would like her number? Jax would look like a douchebag, especially since the lady had just lost her boyfriend, for crying out loud. But he wondered if they'd ever cross paths again. "It was nice meeting you," he said instead.

"Same here. Good luck with your brother," she said. "I pray he recovers fully."

"Thank you."

Then she picked up her purse and strode away.

Jax stayed for a little longer after she'd left, hesitant to leave the bench they'd shared. But then he remembered his brother all alone in his hospital bed, and he jumped to his feet.

That was when he noticed the rose-gold-encased phone lying at the other edge of the bench.

CHAPTER 4

Jax picked up the phone and examined it. This probably belonged to *her*—it was funny he'd shared such a wonderful moment with her, yet didn't even know her name.

Since she appeared to be from out-of-town and had just had a disappointing encounter with her boyfriend, chances were she was headed out of Las Vegas soon. He had to get the phone to her fast.

Jax sprinted out of the garden, burst through the glass doors, and hurried down the hallway. Soon he reached the hospital lobby.

The crowd was thicker than at a local western horse show, with medical staff, patients, and their caregivers all headed in scattered directions. Jax was head and shoulders taller than most folks, yet he couldn't find the beautiful mystery lady.

He navigated his way through the throng of people while searching for her, and soon he reached and exited the hospital through one of the revolving doors.

The cacophony outside the hospital entrance from blaring horns of cars in long queues waiting to discharge their occupants and sirens from departing ambulances was even worse than when he'd arrived. But Jax ignored it all, scanning the area and hoping and praying for a glimpse of her.

Finally, he spotted that beautiful, luscious hair. *Thank You, God.*

Jax took off in her direction, keeping her in his sights even as she retrieved her car keys from a valet in a red attendant jacket and entered the driver's seat of a white BMW coupe. The car had just started rolling down the hospital driveway when Jax darted in front of her vehicle.

The sound of squealing tires filled the air as she slammed on her brakes. Jax rushed to her window, ignoring the gasps and curious stares from folks in the immediate vicinity.

"What were you thinking?" the lady said, fury

written all over her face as she lowered her car window. "I could have hit you!"

But what did that say about him if he thought she looked hotter than ever? "Sorry about that, ma'am," he said, "but you dropped this." He extended the phone to her.

Her eyes widened in surprise. "Oh." She accepted the phone. "I didn't notice it was missing. Thank you. Still, that was dangerous, rushing in front of the car."

Somehow, he didn't mind being scolded by her. She was right, after all. "I didn't think you'd run me over," he replied.

She looked at him like he'd sprouted horns on his head. Jax was sure she wondered if he'd taken leave of his senses. "Daring," she said after a moment, a small smile playing at the corners of her lips. "But thank you."

"There's a better way to thank me," Jax said boldly. She was the first woman to catch his attention, and he had a feeling he'd regret it if he let this chance slip away.

"What do you mean?" Her smile faded, and a wary expression replaced it.

A loud blare from the car behind hers told him he had to hurry. Jax made a quick gesture of apology to the driver before turning back to her. "Can I have your number?" he asked. Would she think he was some sort of playboy for requesting it? But hadn't they just bonded over shared broken memories? Well, sort of?

He watched a myriad of emotions cross her face as she remained silent. In that moment, Jax was willing to pay a thousand bucks just to know what she was thinking. Would she say yes, or would she throw him off, like a bull bucking a rider off its back?

"You didn't get it already?" she said as she shook the phone in her hand.

Jax grinned. Now, that was a reaction he hadn't expected. He'd noticed the phone had been unlocked. "That would be an invasion of privacy, ma'am."

She stared at him for a moment and then, surprisingly, rattled off her digits.

Jax memorized them. "Thank you," he said. "I'll call you soon." A second angry blare from behind reminded him it was time to let her go.

He stepped back and tipped his hat at her. "Have a safe trip, ma'am," he said.

She looked at him like an equation she couldn't figure out, rolled up her window, and drove out of the hospital.

Jax apologized again to the annoyed driver and

then watched as her car headed down the driveway, turned left, and disappeared into the traffic.

There was something about her that called to him, an electric pull toward her that made him want to see her again.

Even though he knew next to nothing about her, even her name.

Just thinking about it made him feel excited and upbeat for the first time since the news of Max's accident.

But it was time to check up on Max. He could be awake by now.

Jax adjusted his hat and hurried back into the hospital.

CHAPTER 5

Simone couldn't get used to how opulent the formal dining room at the seven-bedroom Addison mansion was with its original Gilded Age detailed moldings, marble fireplaces, and a statement crystal chandelier that towered over the table. Yet it gave off a modern vibe with its open living spaces complemented by gorgeous floor-to-ceiling windows.

She hadn't grown up in this home—Simone had spent much of her elementary up to her sophomore year in high school with her maternal grandmother, whose home was more down-to-earth, warm, and inviting. Sure, the Addison home was elegant and sophisticated—a designer's dream and the envy of the neighborhood—yet Simone found it cold like a museum.

While she'd never understood why she'd lived apart from her parents, Simone had been grateful for it. She'd only moved back to the mansion after her grandma had passed away and had ended up stuck with the once-a-week required Sunday family dinners, even all through her college and medical school years.

But as much as she disliked these evening Sunday dinners, she had no choice but to show up—her father only exempted her on call days at the hospital, and even then, Simone was certain one of her father's many assistants had called the hospital to confirm each time. She'd thought inheriting her grandma's billion-dollar fortune would have given her the freedom she desired, and so she'd once missed the dinner on a whim, but there'd been consequences, an experience she had no plan of repeating anytime soon.

Not that she hated her family, but they were like strangers she couldn't get used to: a larger-than-life father whose stern glances were sharp enough to cut like glass, a mother who seemed absent-minded and more like a wallflower for the most part, and a younger brother who preferred to be immersed in video game worlds rather than reality, yet never seemed to do any wrong as far as the family was concerned.

Unlike Simone.

She couldn't remember when either parent had ever complimented her. Simone's father was always critical of everything she did, while her mother never said anything, good or bad.

This was why she missed her grandma each time she stepped into this room. The woman had been a force of nature, one that her father hadn't dared to cross, yet she'd adored Simone. If she was alive, there was no way her father would have shackled Simone to these meaningless dinners.

Soon the clinking sound of silverware was all that filled the air as Simone took dainty bites of her grilled lobster tail. Though she was certain the food was delicious, it tasted like ash in Simone's mouth, and she couldn't wait for the meal to end and for her to make her escape.

"Now that you have some free time, I've set up some dates for you," her father's booming voice cut through the air from where he sat at the head of the table. "It's about time you got married and did your duty for the family."

Sebastian Addison was a handsome man even in

his late fifties with his salt-and-pepper hair, but a quick eye contact with his blue enigmatic eyes was enough to let anyone know he wasn't a man to trifle with. His ever-present executive assistant, Derek, handed a sheet to Simone, which she dropped, without a glance, on the table in front of her. She didn't have to look at the list to know they'd filled it with names of the same boring young men she'd met over the years at various society functions her father had forced her to attend.

"I'm in no hurry to marry," Simone replied. "Besides, this is my first vacation in a long time, one that I need before residency starts in July." And she needed time to get over Ethan's betrayal.

Her father waved her concern away like it was a buzzing fly. "I don't care what you do with the rest of your time as long as you show up for these dates."

"I'm not interested." Well, she used to love dating, but after what had happened with Ethan? No way.

"You'll have to get married soon. It's the least you can do for this family."

Family? The only family member she'd truly had had been Grandma, and she was gone. No one else had any right to dictate to her when or who she should marry. "My marriage is my business. Besides, now isn't the right time."

Her father dropped his cutlery and leaned back. The pulse ticked at the base of his throat, a telltale sign things might go south if she wasn't careful. But this was one area of her life she couldn't give up.

"I don't understand why you always have to make things so difficult," he said. "Michael would have just gone along with it."

She hated being compared to her brother. "Then you can ask him to go on those dates. I'm sure he can handle them."

"Simone!" her mother's whispered caution carried through the air. As much as it pained her to disregard her mother's warning, Simone couldn't back down now. Her father could make her perfect brother go to them if it was that important to him.

"This isn't a debate, and I'd prefer you use the places I've selected."

It sounded like a suggestion, but Simone knew it was an order, which she also detested. "I'm not going on these dates." The mere thought of them put bile in her mouth.

The tension in the room rose as daughter and father stared at each other, neither refusing to back down.

"They're only dates, Simone," her mom said softly with a sigh. "Please."

Simone glanced at her mother. She looked just like she always did—beautiful, flawless, with her wavy kinky hair in an elegant side-swooped bun. Most people commented that Simone and her mother, Annabella Addison, looked more like sisters rather than mother and daughter.

Simone's fingernails bit into her palm. As much as she hated it, the discussion was over. She could never deny her mother's earnest plea. "Okay."

By now she'd lost her appetite and couldn't stand being in the same room as her father for another minute.

Simone rose to her feet. "I have to go." She grabbed her purse from where she'd placed it on the seat beside her.

"Don't forget the list," her father reminded.

She grabbed the paper like one would grab a viper. Simone wished she could just set it on fire and be done with it. Instead, she tucked it into her purse.

"See you next week, sis," her twenty-four-year-old brother, Michael, said without looking up from his phone where he was likely playing a game.

Like she needed the reminder. It was incredible how he managed to stuff food in his mouth at the same time, and how their parents never reprimanded him for playing with his phone at the dinner table. But that was how it'd always been at the Addison home: her brother was perfect, while Simone was the black sheep.

"Bye," Simone said.

Then she slung her purse over her shoulder and made her escape.

Simone leaned her back against the wall as she sat on the window bench of her penthouse and stared out at the beautiful Boston city view. She'd bought this apartment as soon as it'd come on the market, and even though it'd been expensive, the view alone had been worth it.

No matter how rough her day was—whether from demanding patients or dealing with her family, Simone could feel the burden lift just from enjoying the panoramic view of the city and its surrounding landscape—a juxtaposition of steely skyscrapers and picturesque brownstones, narrow cobbled streets, and traditional gas street lamps.

But its effect on her wasn't working tonight as she rested her head against the floor-to-ceiling glass.

Memories of times with Ethan assailed her mind even as she pondered about tonight's dinner at the Addison mansion.

How sad that her heart had just gotten broken, yet she couldn't even open up about it to any of her family. Given how her father controlled and monitored their lives, there was no way he wouldn't have known by now. Instead he'd only jumped in to stuff more dates down her throat. Her mother probably didn't care enough to even notice. Her brother... well, it was best to leave him out of the equation. She ran her hand through her long, loose hair as she exhaled a deep sigh. How could she be part of the Addison family yet be so different from them?

It was at times like this she missed her grandma the most—if nothing else, Simone would have had a warm shoulder to cry on. But even if her family couldn't help, why couldn't they—her father specifically—just let her live her life how she wanted? She'd go mad soon if she didn't find a way out from under his domineering control.

Her phone rang, the melodious tone a welcome reprieve from her disquieting thoughts.

Simone rose from the window bench and picked up her phone from the glass coffee table with gilt bronze legs she'd picked up at Sotheby's. She glanced at the phone screen—it was an unknown number. Who could it be?

"Good evening," she said on answering the call.

"Good evening, ma'am," a soothing, low voice replied.

Now where had she heard this voice before? "Who's this?"

"The Vegas cowboy, ma'am."

Simone couldn't help the smile that touched the corners of her lips. What an apt way to describe himself. She'd totally forgotten about him.

She carried the phone back to the window bench and settled herself on it. "Interesting."

"You thought I wouldn't call? I'm a man of my word," he said.

It was nice he'd called, but he was still a stranger, albeit a handsome one. "So, to what do I owe the pleasure of this call?" she asked.

"Just calling to find out how you're doing."

Her heart couldn't help warming at the thought. He was the first person today to ask her how she was. "I'm good. How's your brother?"

"He's much better. He should be discharged in a few days, and then we head back home."

"And where is that?" She wasn't probing, just making polite conversation.

"Dexin Valley. A little town not far from Boston and Dexington."

Simone knew of Dexington, but Dexin was a new one. "Dexin? Never heard of it."

"Most folks haven't, but then it's more cowboy country, and we like the anonymity. Life there is also slower than in the city."

Simone had always been a city girl, so she couldn't imagine life on a ranch. But he had to like it if he lived there. "Sounds nice," she said politely.

He chuckled. "I bet you've never been on a ranch."

Could having her own horse stable count? It was located a short drive from Boston and she'd inherited it along with a team that ran it. Given she no longer rode as much as she'd once loved to, due to her busy schedule, Simone had worked with the team to develop and open a program for low income kids and children with disabilities to learn how to ride at little or no cost. The program had been running successfully for the past few years. "No, I haven't," she replied.

"It may not be life-changing, but I bet it'd be fun for you. You strike me as an adventurer."

"From the thirty-second conversation we had?"

"More like twenty minutes."

So he'd been counting. *Huh.*

"What about you, ma'am? Where do you call home?"

She could afford to be general. "Boston."

"So we're neighbors."

Simone fought back a smile. She didn't think the towns were *that close*. "If you can call it that."

"Sure we are. And I'd like to take my neighbor out to lunch."

Woah! Hold your horses, cowboy! Or was that the right saying? Anyway, as much as she thought he sounded cute, she had no desire to date him or anyone. "Not interested."

"Ouch. Way to kick me to the curb. Why not?"

"Dates are not on my radar right now."

"It's not a date. Just a chance for two neighbors to chat. Just interested in making a new friend."

"Really?"

"Really. Cross my heart and hope to live."

Simone chuckled. "I'm sure that's not how the phrase is worded."

"I have no plans to die, only live. And I'm certain you got my meaning. Besides, it would be insensitive of me to ask you out on a date."

So he got her. But still, it wouldn't be… wait.

Simone straightened as inspiration struck her.

Since she was stuck with her father's boring dates, what if she had a chance to make those times more fun? The more she thought about it, the more she liked the idea. "Give me one second."

Simone hurried to her room, opened her purse on the bed, and fished out the list her father's assistant had given her. On it, she could see there were six dates, one per week, with the first one two weeks away. Thankfully, all were lunch dates. This could work.

She sat on her bed and dropped the list beside her. "Here's the deal," she said to the Vegas cowboy. "I'm stuck with a series of blind dates I don't care for, courtesy of my father. How about we meet after each date and have lunch as neighbors? Does that work?"

"You want me to crash your blind dates?" he asked in an incredulous tone.

"You wouldn't be crashing them *per se*. The blind dates would be over by then, but I'm pretty sure I won't get to eat much during them, and I'll probably like a nice lunch after."

"What if you enjoy the blind date, and it doesn't end as quickly as planned?"

Simone snorted. "As if that would happen. I know the guys involved, and they're so not my type."

"Hmmm…"

"You'll be helping out your neighbor. But you don't have to if you don't want to."

"When is the first one?"

"In two weeks."

The cowboy was silent for a moment. "Okay, it's a deal."

Simone let out a breath she hadn't known she'd been holding. "Great. I'm Simone Addison by the way."

"Nice to meet you, Simone. I'm Jax Dexin."

"Your town is named after your family?"

"Something like that."

"So, Jax Dexin, see you in two weeks. I'll send you a text later with the details."

"It's a non-date."

Simone laughed. That was *certainly not* how that phrase went. "See you then, cowboy."

"Have a wonderful evening, ma'am."

"You too." Then she ended the call and flopped back on her king-sized bed.

Only a few minutes ago she'd been feeling down and sorry for herself. But now? She felt more light-hearted and peaceful. Jax's call couldn't have come at a better time.

Jax. Such an unusual name, but she liked it. She was surprised he'd accepted her offer, given how unusual it was. But it was really only going to be lunch. Simone had no plans to open her heart again, not even for a handsome cowboy, though she could use a friend right now. Besides, she got a kick from the thought of having lunch with him on the same days her father had booked the dates for. *Take that, Father*.

Simone closed her eyes, her lips drawn into a smile.

Now she couldn't wait for the first date to come.

CHAPTER 6

$\mathscr{A}$ smiling hostess greeted Simone with a warm smile as she entered the restaurant for her first date, dressed in a cream blouse and slacks—she'd had an appointment with one of her mentors at the Harvard Medical School earlier that morning before the short drive to the restaurant and had seen no reason to change.

"Good afternoon, ma'am," the hostess said. "Welcome to Mooo...."

The Mooo...., a restaurant in the luxurious boutique XV Beacon Hotel in Boston's Beacon Hill, was famous for their steaks. Simone had been there a few times over the years for dinner, but never for early lunch.

"Thank you," Simone said. "I have a reservation

for Simone Addison." The list stated all reservations were under her name.

"This way, ma'am," the hostess said and led Simone through the breathtaking sophisticated ambience of the modern steakhouse with its gold-beige theme, tree branches styled as tree art on the wall, cobblestone flooring, and covered chandeliers, and down to the next level to one of the *Parlor Suites*.

An intimate, elegant room featuring a grand mahogany dining table, a lounge area with its own gas fireplace, and large windows that allowed for natural light, fresh air and views of Beacon Street, Simone could appreciate why her father had selected it for the privacy it offered, but the more formal upstairs dining area would have been more appropriate and comfortable for this date. Thankfully, she didn't expect the date to last long.

Simone checked her time. She'd arrived on time as planned, but she guessed her date didn't get the memo that said he had to do the same.

"Can I get you anything?" the hostess asked.

"A glass of ginger ale would be fine for now, thank you. I'll order when the other party gets here."

"I'll send it right away."

"Thanks."

"You're welcome."

The hostess excused herself and left the room. Simone settled in one of the dining chairs as she waited for her date to arrive.

A server soon appeared with her drink and a cast iron pan of Parker House rolls sprinkled with sea salt. These were her favorite from the restaurant, and they were warm to the touch, soft, and buttery like she'd expected.

Time ticked away as she chewed the soft rolls, yet Oswald Abington the III was nowhere to be seen. The heir to one of the largest hedge funds in the country, Simone recalled him as a pompous and opinionated young man from her few encounters with him. She checked her phone as well—there were no missed calls from an unfamiliar number.

The door finally opened again, and the young man in question walked in, dressed in a fitted blue pinstripe power suit paired with a red tie. He must have used a generous amount of pomade with the way his blond hair stayed slicked down in a modern side part.

"I'm so sorry I'm late," Oswald said, though Simone could tell from his facial expression he wasn't apologetic one bit. The frown on his forehead indicated he'd expected her to stand up and exchange greetings with him, but since that didn't happen, he'd covered it up by pulling out the opposite seat and settling in.

"Would you like something to drink, sir?" asked the server who'd come in with him.

"Do you have a 1985 Dom Perignon Brut Rose?"

"Yes, we do."

"I'd like a bottle."

Simone couldn't believe her ears. What did he need an entire bottle of expensive wine for when he was supposed to be back at the office after this date? A glass would have been just fine. For one, she hated unnecessary wastage.

"We'll send it right away," the server said. "Would you like to order now, sir?"

Oswald waved him away. "In a few minutes."

"Okay, sir." The server exited the room.

Oswald leaned back in his high-backed chair. "How've you been, Simone?" he asked.

"It's Miss Addison," she said with a deadpan face. *No, Oswald, we're not friends.*

A lazy smile played on his face. "Miss Addison? There's no need for formality between us."

Was he implying there was something between them? *In his dreams.*

"I heard you're now a doctor," he continued. "Congratulations."

"Thank you."

"So, what are you planning to specialize in? Pediatrics? Family Practice?"

Why did most men assume women doctors preferred specializations that had to do with the family and home? It was an antiquated way of thinking, and a school of thought Simone rejected.

"Dermatology," she replied. One of the hardest residencies to get into, given its lifestyle advantages, salary attractiveness, and limited availability, but Simone had been fortunate enough to snag a spot.

His nose crinkled like he'd smelled a decaying rat. "Skin care? Well, I can see how that can be helpful."

Simone let out a sigh. This was why she couldn't see herself getting involved with the young men her father chose. Sure, they were great at managing their family business or whatever, but they seemed to lack intelligence in anything else.

She glanced at her watch and perked up. "I have to go," she said as she rose to her feet.

"What?" Oswald asked with a confused look.

"My time's up." She picked up her purse.

"What do you mean? I just got here."

She glared at him. "Then you should have come

on time or informed me if you were running late for whatever reason. Have a good day, Mr. Abington."

Simone strode out of the room, leaving Oswald with his mouth opened in an "O" and a bill for him to settle. Simone was sure no one had ever ditched him at a date, but she couldn't care less. *Serves him right.* It was basic etiquette to respect the other party's time.

She pulled out her phone from her purse and set it in silent mode. Oswald would complain to her father any minute from now, and he'd call her to demand an explanation. Simone didn't need the distraction, especially since she was excited about her next appointment.

It was time to meet her Vegas cowboy.

CHAPTER 7

Simone arrived at the Scampo restaurant in the famous Liberty hotel in Cambridge a few minutes before her scheduled lunch with Jax. She parked her car, checked the mirror to make sure her hair was still in place, and then pulled out her lip gloss.

Hold on. Now why was she checking her makeup? For goodness' sake, this was only lunch and not a date.

There was a rap on her window.

Simone jumped at the sound and looked up to see a familiar figure with a cowboy hat standing outside her door.

Her shoulders relaxed. It was only Jax. It warmed

her heart to see he'd arrived and had been waiting for her.

Simone lowered her window. "Hello, Jax." She couldn't help but appreciate how tall he looked, how his broad shoulders filled his shirt, and how his cedarwood and masculine leather scent tickled her senses.

He tipped his hat at her. "Good afternoon, ma'am," he said in a low voice with a faint Western drawl she could listen to all day.

"It's Simone," she said as she replaced the lip gloss in her purse and unlocked her doors.

"Yes, ma'am. Let me help." He pulled the door open for her. It was nice to know chivalry wasn't dead.

"Why thank you, sir," she said as she stepped out with her purse in hand, then rolled the window back up, and locked her car.

Jax smiled at her. "It's nothing."

Now why did she have this sudden urge to fan herself? The weather was already hot and could do with some rain showers, and Simone didn't need Jax's smile adding to the heat. She resisted the impulse. "Have you been here for a while?" she asked instead.

"No. Just got here about ten minutes ago."

Warmth spread across Simone's chest. This was what she liked—a man who kept to time, not like that fool Oswald. "I hope the restaurant wasn't hard to find."

"Not at all. The place looks just the same," Jax said.

Interesting. "You've been here before," she stated.

"Yes. It's the famous restaurant in what was once a jail."

"I know, right? It freaked me out the first time I heard about it, but then it got me curious about the place. Now I love coming here whenever I can."

"It's unusual, that's for sure. But that's also part of its charm."

"True. Shall we go in?"

"After you, ma'am." He gave her an appreciative scan. "You look beautiful, by the way."

Ah, this was a man who knew what women liked. Compliments galore all the way, especially when Simone had worn nothing special and had only put her hair up in her regular messy bun.

"Thanks. You look handsome, too." He really did with his blue and brown plaid shirt tucked into close-fitting jeans and wearing what looked like high-end cowboy boots with their polished look and understated intricate stitching on his feet—a pair of boots she wouldn't have minded for herself. Then the hat to top it all off.

"Thank you."

Soon, they reached the doors of the restaurant and entered.

"Good afternoon," a cheerful hostess said to them. "Welcome to Scampo."

"Thanks," Simone replied. "I have a reservation for Simone Addison."

The hostess checked her list. "This way, ma'am," she said and steered them through the bustling restaurant decorated with brown and beige luxury furnishings with shiny copper lamps. Simone looked up and couldn't help being wowed and fascinated again by the high ceilings of the former-jail-turned-restaurant juxtaposed against red brick walls.

A huge open kitchen with a gorgeous copper canopy sat in the center of the restaurant, and Simone could see chefs preparing pizzas and what looked like naan in the brick oven, giving the place a lively yet warm and cozy feel, while the smell of freshly baked bread hung low in the air. The restaurant was Italian, though it certainly drew influences from both the Mediterranean and Middle Eastern regions.

Soon they reached their table at the back—

Simone had requested for a private spot when she'd booked the reservation—and Jax pulled out a chair for her.

"Thank you," Simone said. She liked it when men did that. Jax settled into the opposite chair.

Then he pulled off his hat and placed it on the empty chair beside him.

Oh my. Now how had he kept that beautiful blond hair all perfectly tousled under that hat? She suddenly itched to run her fingers through it. *Get a grip, Simone*, she cautioned herself. What was with all these reactions to Jax?

Thankfully, a male server appeared right before she could dwell further on her thoughts. "Welcome to Scampo," he said warmly. "I'll be your server for today. What can I get you to drink?" He handed them the wine and cocktail lists.

Simone perused them. She wasn't a cocktail person, but she wanted to try something different today. "Can I have the *Bartender's Mocktail* but with a splash of ginger?"

"Sure. What about you, sir?"

"Do you have sparkling apple cider?"

"I believe we do."

"I'll have that."

"Great. Would you like to order now as well?"

Jax looked expectantly at Simone. "Sure," she replied. Simone appreciated he'd deferred to her. She perused the menu the server now handed to her. "I'd like the miso clam chowder, and then the grilled salmon with steamed coconut basmati rice."

"Would you like some dessert too?" the server asked.

"Not sure yet. Maybe later."

"Great. How about you, sir?"

"I'll have the clam chowder and the scampi burger."

"What kind of cheese would you like with it?"

"Mozzarella."

"Our mozzarella is fresh and made in-house. Would you like to try our mozzarella tasting menu?" Simone had had it before at the mozzarella bar in the restaurant, and it'd been wonderful.

"Not at this time, thank you," Jax replied.

"No problem, sir. I'll have your orders ready shortly. Ma'am, sir."

"Thank you," Simone said. They both handed back their menus to the server, who then left.

"You don't drink?" Simone asked.

Jax leaned back. "No, I don't."

"Me neither."

Jax gave her a warm smile. "Something we have in common."

"True. Now I wonder what other interests we share. What school did you study at?"

"Harvard." At her surprised look, "You don't think cowboys go to school?"

Simone waved his concern away. "That's not it. I've always assumed cowboys were mostly interested in horses, animals, or land, and I didn't think Harvard offered anything related to those interests."

The server arrived with their drinks, and Jax waited for him to leave before responding. "They used to have a vet school, but not anymore. However, cowboys have interests beyond those areas. We can study law, management, medicine, or other courses and apply them as they relate to our business."

"Fascinating." Simone took a sip of her drink. The combined flavor of cranberry, lemon, cucumber, and mint hit her taste buds all at once, and it worked. She savored another small mouthful before setting the glass down. "So, which did you study?" she asked.

"Economics. But I also have an MBA."

"Wow. So you use those for the ranch or farm?"

"Ranch. My family runs a small ranch. I oversee its financial operations."

"That sounds interesting."

"It is, though I know some people might consider it non-sexy for a cowboy."

"I don't think it makes you any less sexy," Simone blurted out. Now why did she say that?

Jax fought back a smile. "Thanks for the compliment."

Simone could feel her ears warming. This was so embarrassing. Thankfully, she didn't get red in the face so easily.

"So what about you?" he asked. "What did you study?"

She took a sip of her drink to calm herself before answering. "Pre-med undergrad, and just became an MD."

"Oh wow! Congratulations. That's a huge achievement."

"Thank you." For some unknown reason, it meant a lot coming from him.

"So you're starting residency soon?"

Simone's eyes widened. "How did you know?" Most non-medical folks rarely understood the residency timeline.

"My brother, Max, the one that had the accident? He's a doctor."

"You're kidding! Now I feel bad that I never said

hi to him."

"No need to feel that way. It wasn't a good time."

"How's he doing now?

"Much better. Already hankering to get back to work."

"Do you know his specialty?"

"He's an ER attending at Dexington Medical."

"That's so cool. I haven't been, but Dexington Medical is a well-known tertiary hospital. So he commutes?"

Jax nodded. "About an hour each way without traffic. It's not as bad as most people might think."

"That's not bad at all. You can spend that much time alone in Boston traffic."

Conversation flowed so easily between them Simone lost track of time. Soon their order arrived, and they dug into the meal. It was as delicious as Simone had expected.

She leaned back once she was done. "I'm so full." She patted her stomach. "I don't think there's room for dessert."

"Glad you enjoyed the meal. I like a woman who eats."

"I'm definitely not the nibbling type. Thankfully, I'm fortunate enough not to gain weight from it."

"I can see that. You look great."

"Thank you. You don't look so bad yourself." Which was an understatement. From the cords of muscle peeking out from under his rolled sleeves and his lean build, it was obvious Jax was a man who stayed fit through honest labor.

"How about coffee? Any room for that?" Jax asked.

"I can do coffee."

Their server appeared as if called, took their orders, and cleared their table. Soon, he returned with their coffee.

"So you never answered my question," Jax said.

"Which one?"

"Your residency."

"Oh. Dermatology."

He gave her a look of admiration. "Isn't it one of the tough ones to get a spot in?"

Simone's heart warmed at his response. Now why couldn't all the guys on her date list be like him? She loved a man who was curious and attentive to matters beyond their immediate interests. "Yes, it is."

"Beautiful and smart. A heady combination."

"Thank you. You can keep the compliments coming."

Jax laughed, the sound tickling and warming her insides. If she wasn't careful, she could fall for this cowboy soon, which she couldn't afford right now. "You're definitely not bashful," he said.

"Is that a terrible thing?" Simone asked, though she was comfortable in her own skin.

"Absolutely not. Women can be confident or shy if they want. It's more important to be true to yourself and love yourself the way you are."

Simone raised her coffee cup to him. "Amen to that."

They continued chatting, and soon they'd finished their coffee. Jax called for the check.

"I think we should split it," Simone said.

He glanced at her. "I'm okay with paying for it."

"We're neighborly friends, remember? Friends split the bill." It would be difficult to think of it as just lunch and not a date if he paid the bill alone, which would make it harder for her to meet with him again. And Simone wanted more of this.

Jax studied her for a moment. "You'd prefer it?" he finally said.

"Yes."

"Okay."

The server returned with the check, and Jax handed both their cards over to him.

"Thank you," Simone said as soon as the server left.

"Why? It's not a big deal."

"I know cowboys like to take care of those around them, so that mustn't have been easy."

Jax chuckled. "We're not that fragile. And I get why you prefer it."

"You do?" Was he reading her mind?

"Hmmm."

The server returned with their cards, and Jax left a generous cash tip.

"Thank you for the wonderful meal and conversation," Simone said as she rose to her feet.

Jax stood as well and placed his cowboy hat back on his head. "I had a good time," he replied.

Even though she'd meant this first meeting as a test, there was no way Simone was going to turn down a chance to meet with him again. "I look forward to our lunch next week," Simone said as they walked out of the restaurant.

He'd slowed his stride to match hers. "Can I decide where we go next?"

Simone looked up at him. "I'm open to suggestions. But I'll have to get back to you on the exact location of my next date. It'll be easier if the place you choose is within its vicinity."

"It'll be somewhere in the Boston/Cambridge area."

"Okay, that should work. Last time I checked, all the locations were in the Boston Copley area. Why don't I send you the information later and you can plan accordingly?"

"That'd be perfect." By now, they'd arrived at her car.

Simone unlocked it and made to open the driver's door, but Jax beat her to it.

"Thank you," she said and slid into the car seat. A gentleman and a nice handsome guy? She was all for this friendship.

"You're welcome." He closed the door after her.

"See you next week," she said after rolling down her window.

"Have a great day, Simone," he said and tipped his hat at her.

Simone's heart gave a jolt, and she bit back a gasp. Now why did he say her name like that, all low and sexy, and almost give her a heart attack? She could have had an accident if she'd already taken the car out of parking mode.

"You too, Jax," she managed to say. This man was doing unfamiliar things to her, and it was time to leave before she really did have the heart attack.

Simone pulled out of the parking spot, then gave him a quick wave before driving off.

CHAPTER 8

Jax inhaled the fresh late afternoon country air right before he entered the Dexin main house back at the ranch. This was home, and he'd miss it if he ever left. Jax had left once for college and graduate school in Boston, but he'd been back ever since. He'd had no interest in working on Wall Street, though he'd been top of his class, and had chosen instead to return and handle the ranch's financial operations.

He and his brothers had always dreamed of turning the ranch into one that raised show horses and cattle, and with Dex handling the day-to-day operations, and Max chipping in whenever he was free from work at the hospital, their dream had come true with a ranch set on what he considered the most beautiful place on earth. And now he'd spent time with the most beautiful woman, too.

Jax whistled to himself as he passed through the front door. The tune was a song his ma had loved, and somehow it seemed right for this moment.

The lunch with Simone had gone better than he'd hoped. For a second, he'd doubted whether he was doing the right thing by pursuing her, especially since she'd just come out of a relationship, but now he was thankful he'd followed his instincts.

Simone was funny, smart, and a straight shooter. He could tell she came from money from her mannerisms, but she hadn't put on any airs, which he loved. And a woman who enjoyed her food? That was the icing on the cake. Now, he was all the more excited for their next lunch date, even if she refused to call it one.

"What's with the goofy smile on your face?" a familiar voice asked, jerking him out of his reverie. "If I didn't know better, I'd say you've got a lady on your mind."

Jax turned to see his older brother, Dex, coming out of the kitchen with a plate of cookies in his hand.

"What are you talking about?" Jax said, reaching for a cookie.

"Oh, no, you don't," Dex said, slapping his hand

away and raising the plate high enough from Jax's reach. This was one of those times Dex's height gave him an advantage over Jax. "It's for Max, and Maggie will have my head if one of them is missing."

Maggie had raised Jax and his brothers after their ma passed away. She'd been their ma's best friend. "So Maggie only loves Max now? Ouch, that hurts," Jax said, faking a pained expression.

Dex grinned. "Then you're in for more torture. All the dishes for tonight's dinner are Max's favorites."

Jax thought about it for a moment. "Well, that's not so bad, since several of those are my favorites, too."

Dex smacked his own forehead. "Now, how could I forget you used to be a Max groupie?"

"Hey, don't call me that! As if you didn't used to tag behind him like a dog everywhere."

"I think you need some smacking to come to your senses. Come here."

Jax chuckled as he dodged Dex's hand. "You'll drop the cookies at this rate."

Dex straightened. "That's your lucky save."

Jax adjusted his shirt. "It's not my fault. I can't help being blessed." Then his face turned serious.

"But Max deserves all the love and attention right now."

"Yeah. I'm just glad he's alive, and we didn't lose him."

"Me too. I can't even imagine a world without him, you know?"

"Especially after Rex..." Dex wore a contrite look. "I'm sorry. I shouldn't have mentioned his name."

Just the topic Jax needed to sour his mood. All these—Max going to Vegas, getting hurt—it was Rex, Jax's twin brother's fault. If only he hadn't run off with Max's fiancée right on the day of the wedding. Of course, it was common knowledge Rex had nursed a crush on Tammy, but who did that to their own brother?

Worse, he'd turned his back on Jax, his twin, and the other half of his soul. They'd been tighter than brothers since birth, made big plans together, and there'd been no secrets between them, or so Jax had believed. As the ranch had signed its one hundredth agreement to supply show horses to yet another horse operation in faraway Croatia, they'd realized they'd arrived.

But it appeared Jax had only been deceiving himself, because Rex had left all that behind without a thought. Rex, who'd loved horses more than all his brothers combined, had gone, just like that. They'd searched frantically for him but had found no trace. It'd hurt more than words could express, and Jax wasn't sure if he'd ever get over it.

"I'm sorry, Jax," Dex said.

Jax gave him a small smile. "No worries. I know you didn't mean to. And he's your brother too."

"He deserves a beating whenever he comes home."

"Will he though? Come home, I mean."

"I don't know. But one thing I do know is that you and I will be fine eventually. You know what? Have a cookie." Dex handed one to Jax.

"Thank you," Jax said as he accepted it. Then he gestured in the direction of Max's bedroom on the main floor. "So how's he doing?"

"Much better and less cranky," Dex said. "And insisting on going back to work."

Jax chuckled. "Not going to happen, even if I have to tie him to a tree," he said.

"I'm with you on that one. Maggie has already given him the third degree, and that's the only reason he's stayed in bed."

"Thank God for Maggie. I think it's really true

what they say about doctors being the worst patients."

Dex nodded. "Definitely true."

"I'm guessing now is not a good time to see him. He's probably sulking."

"Hence the cookies." Dex raised the cookie plate. "But I'm sure he'll be fine at the end of the day."

"I pray so." Jax's eyes scanned the living area, including the kitchen. "What about Maggie?"

"She's taking a nap. It seems dealing with Max has tuckered her out."

"She needs to take more breaks."

"I agree. But you know how mothers are. You can't stop them from doing everything for their children. She even shooed me away from the kitchen when I offered to help with the cooking. And you know I'm a good cook."

Maggie must have been anxious about Max if she'd turned down Dex's help. She kept herself very busy when she was worried about something. "Okay, I'll check on Maggie later." He'd give her a hug if needed.

"I think it'll help. The last thing we need is for her to break down, too." Then Dex's mouth softened into a teasing smile, his eyes holding a trace of humor as he leaned in and clasped Jax's shoulder. "So what's got you all sappy and smiley?"

Jax knocked his hand off. "Mind your business."

"Really, who's the lovely lady?" Dex asked, undeterred, in a conspiratorial tone. Jax loved his family, but sometimes he wished he could wring Dex's neck. Most people wouldn't guess, but Dex could be super nosy when he wanted to be.

Jax gave him a blank look. "Whoever said there was a lady?" He had to leave before Dex probed his way to the truth. "I'll see you later. Got some accounting to take care of." Jax headed to the winding stairs that led to the second floor of the log-stone house.

"You do now?" Dex called out. "Let me tell you: you can't hide it, no matter how hard you try or how much you deny it. The truth will come out soon!"

Jax smiled. Dex had to be kidding. There was no way he was letting his meddling family in on this new friendship with Simone.

CHAPTER 9

Simone set down the pencil she'd been using and leaned back to study her creation. It was done. The image she'd worked hard at for the past few hours after her lunch with Jax looked perfect.

She'd gotten into coloring in her final years in college. A friend had invited her to a coloring party—the first she'd heard of one—and Simone had been hooked ever since. Coloring had become a great stress reliever for her, and she enjoyed the feeling of accomplishment she felt whenever she finished a piece.

Simone had started off with regular coloring books, but now she worked on large pieces on her easel. She'd since migrated to creating her own draw-ings, coloring them, and sharing snapshots of her creations on social media. A few of her pieces had even caught the eye of a fabric maker who'd licensed some of her designs for a special collection. Simone had donated the proceeds to the horse riding program.

She studied the artwork with a critical eye. This piece showcased a style different from her usual geometric-inspired creations, and she could already tell it had that *wow* factor that could draw buzz when put on display.

But it wasn't for sale. She'd think about what to do with it later on.

Simone set the easel aside for now—she'd frame the design later to protect it—and packed up her supplies, returning them to their spots in the small office she called a studio. A minimally furnished soft-teal room with sound-proofed walls and a breath-taking floor-to-ceiling glass view, the space was Simone's favorite spot in the apartment, and she'd often spend hours at a time here when the inspiration hit.

She got up, left the room, and soon returned with a can of ginger ale in hand, settling herself on the lounge chair in the far left corner of the studio to enjoy the gorgeous view of the changing colors of sunset.

The idea for the design had come after she'd met with Jax earlier today, and Simone had hurried back to put the inspiration on paper. She'd placed her phone in silent mode and ignored all calls, so she was sure he who shall not be named was furious by now. But she needed just a few more minutes of peace before she'd face the storm she was certain was already brewing.

Her immediate connection with Jax had been unexpected. Simone had felt so relaxed in his presence she'd been herself the whole time they'd been together instead of being guarded like she usually was. He'd been sincere with no airs, unlike that brat Oswald, and his being easy on the eyes had only helped. Her two encounters today with both men had been like night and day, and Simone preferred day.

She took a gulp of her drink and closed her eyes. Something about Jax drew her in. She couldn't tell if it was because he was from a different social circle than she was or if it was something else, and she was curious to know why.

But she had to be careful to shield her heart—Ethan had seemed nice too, yet here she was with a broken heart through no fault of hers.

She frowned. Maybe she wasn't so great at being a good judge of character, like she'd thought. She'd also just come off a relationship, and now wasn't the time for another.

Thankfully, it'd been only lunch with Jax and not a date. There were no expectations between them, and she could cut off the budding friendship if she felt uncomfortable with it at any time.

However, what was most interesting was Simone hadn't thought of Ethan for even one second since she'd had lunch with Jax. Even now, it seemed like a distant memory instead of the all-consuming thought it'd been only a few hours ago. Maybe she was getting over him. If so, then she had Jax to thank for that, if for nothing else.

She finished her drink and rose. Enough dawdling. It was time to face the music she'd avoided all afternoon.

Simone strode to the cubicle where she'd dropped her phone, checked the screen, and grimaced. There were ten missed calls from her father alone. She took a deep breath, dialed his number, and waited for it to connect.

"Where have you been?" her father barked from the other end of the line.

"I've been busy," Simone replied.

"Too busy to take my calls?"

"Sorry about that." She moved over to the lounge and sat down.

"What the hell happened with Oswald? How could you just walk out on him like that? I had to smooth things over with his father."

"He came very late for the date with no notification at all. That's something even you wouldn't abide." Simone knew she had him there. Her father was well-known for detesting tardiness enough to fire people for it.

Her father sighed. "He said he apologized."

"If you can call that an apology. Accepting his behavior would have been a mark against the Addison name. I had your reputation to think about." Simone hadn't really cared about that, but she had to make her father back off.

"Okay. But make sure you don't do the same for the other dates. I don't want rumors springing up that our family is difficult to work with."

Simone didn't care about the family's reputation for something like this. She'd even *prefer* it, but of course she didn't tell her father that. "As long as they show up on time."

"It shouldn't be a problem. I've already notified the others about it."

There goes her excuse to leave the dates early. She'd have to think of other ideas now. "We'll see."

"Simone, you better do your best," he said with a clear warning in his tone.

Simone exhaled a deep sigh. He had her, and she knew it. There was only one reason she was going along with his request, and it wasn't disappearing soon.

"I need to go," Simone said. She was tired of this conversation.

"Next week's date better be good." As if it was her fault that the date with Oswald had been a disaster. "Make sure you behave." The line went dead.

Simone dropped her phone beside her and leaned back on the lounge. She'd wondered many times over the years if Sebastian Addison was her real father, and she thought the same today. Why did he have to treat her so cold and as if she was property he could trade with for the family name and business? He didn't seem to care about her happiness and her future, but only how many connections and how much business her marriage would bring. It was sad and disappointing at the same time.

But this was not the time to worry about that or

the other upcoming boring dates as she recalled the soft grey eyes that had twinkled and smiled at her that afternoon.

Getting to know Jax Dexin sounded way more interesting.

CHAPTER 10

Simone let out a sigh of relief and inhaled the fresh afternoon air as she exited the restaurant. It had taken everything within her to endure the last date on the list. Carlton's domineering behavior reminded her so much of her father there was only so much she could take of it. Thankfully, the meal had ended, and she was finally free of him, and of all the dates.

She hurried to her car as if pursued by hornets, the thought of her next appointment putting a smile on her face. Meeting Jax for lunch had become the highlight of her week. He was smart, funny, and easy to talk to. He also had more depth than she'd expected, a strong love for God, and he adored his family, no matter how annoying he'd claimed they could be. Simone envied him for this and wished she had that type of relationship with hers.

Soon she got to her car and unlocked it. As she reached for the door handle to open it, a hand seized her arm.

Simone reacted on instinct by shoving at the sweaty paw, but the ironclad grip held. She looked up to see who it was.

Carlton loomed over her, his nose flared and his eyes hard and cold. Simone hadn't heard him approach. It seemed he wasn't ready to leave like she'd thought. "How dare you walk away from me?" he said through gritted teeth.

Simone's eyes narrowed. Who did he think he was? "Let go," she said coolly. As much as she'd love to challenge him, this was a popular spot for folks in her social circle—she could already see a few eyes darting in their direction as they made their way into the restaurant—and Simone had no plans to make her family topic of the week on the gossip blogs.

But the bull-headed Carlton refused to get the message. Instead, he tightened his hold, causing Simone to wince. At this rate, she was going to end up with a nasty bruise. "I'm not sure you understand what's going on here," he spat out as he stepped closer, shrinking the distance between them and forcing Simone to inhale the nasty stench of garlic and alcohol in his breath. "Your father wants to expand his business, and you're the prize for sale. He needs us and not us him. So if I were you, I'd be the obedient daughter and play my role well."

"But you're not." Since he didn't plan to let go, it was time to kick this guy in the nuts, rumors and consequences be damned.

"Let go of the lady," a familiar voice stated in a hard, steel tone. Simone couldn't help the relief that washed over her at Jax's voice.

Carlton whirled around. "What the... Ow! That hurts!" he cried out in a now whiny tone as his hand fell away from Simone's arm. Simone rubbed the spot on her arm even as she watched their exchange.

Jax invaded Carlton's personal space, his face next to his and his lips drawn in a tight smile that didn't reach his eyes. "Beat it," he commanded in a controlled tone. "Before I call the cops."

Carlton took an involuntary step back, then turned to Simone and jabbed a finger in her direction. "It's not over. You wait and see." Then he stumbled away.

"Are you alright?" Jax asked her in a softer voice.

Even though she could have handled Carlton just

fine, she was glad he'd been her hero. "I'll be okay," she said, smiling up at him.

"Can I see?" he asked, reaching for her arm.

Simone let him, and he stroked the spot as if to wipe Carlton's imprint away, sending tendrils of electricity down her arm and causing her body to relax. She could have let him continue this all day, but they were in a public place. "Thank you," she said and withdrew her arm. "How did you know to come here?"

Jax leaned against her door and crossed his arms even as he faced her. "I got to Boston early, and I wanted to surprise you. Thank God I did, even though I could tell from the look on your face that you were ready to crush the guy."

"His nuts were about to take a beating," Simone said matter-of-factly.

"Ouch. I can't even imagine how much that would hurt."

"But it would have served him right."

"That I agree on. No man has a right to hurt a woman. I'm guessing he was your date."

"Hmmm. The last one, fortunately." She smiled at him. "Thanks for your help."

He smiled back. "You're welcome. So, are you still up for lunch?"

But Simone had lost her appetite, and she needed to take care of her arm as soon as possible. As much as she hated to disappoint him, she just needed to be in her own space for now. "If you don't mind, I'd rather go home."

Jax nodded like he understood. "Would it be okay with you if I followed you there in my car?"

Strangely, Simone preferred it. "I'd like that."

"Okay, just lead the way."

Simone pulled up into one of two side-by-side parking spots assigned to her BackBay penthouse in the building's private lot and motioned to Jax to park in the other. Then she got out of her car, locked it, and waited for him to do the same.

"Welcome to my home," she said when he'd walked over to where she stood.

"Nice entrance," he said, motioning to the Gothic-like entryway of the historic brick-and-sandstone building.

"I know, right?" The doorway was Simone's private ingress into the building, and with its own twenty-four-hour concierge and direct elevator access, it was another reason she'd bought the place. "Thanks for accompanying me home."

"My pleasure."

"I'm sorry we couldn't have the date." It was just as well too, since she could feel the beginnings of a headache.

Jax gave her a warm smile. "No worries. I'm just glad you're alright."

There was a moment of uncomfortable silence between them. Should she leave, or stay and chat some more? Simone wasn't sure what to do next, especially since she wasn't certain when next she'd see him, and she *wanted* to see him again. Finally, she motioned awkwardly to her entrance. "I have to go."

"Okay."

But why wasn't *he* saying anything? The dates were over, which meant they had no more excuse to get together for lunch. Didn't he want to spend time with her again? With a sinking heart, Simone turned to leave.

"Simone?"

Her heart leaped with hope as she turned back to face him. "Yes?"

"I'd like to see you again. If that's okay with you."

She'd wondered during the week what she'd say if he ever asked her out, but no matter how much she'd thought about it, she'd come to no conclusion. It'd seemed too soon after her last relationship, and she had no idea how one with a country cowboy would work out.

Yet she wanted to be able to see him again, and again. For some reason, it felt like she'd regret it if she didn't. But did Simone really know him as much as she thought? She couldn't afford another Ethan in her life.

"I'd like to date you, Simone," Jax said quietly. "Not just as a friend. With your residency starting in a few weeks, I know this is an important time in your life as a doctor and your life will be super busy, but I'll do my best to make sure the relationship doesn't interfere with it. So, Simone Addison, would you be my girlfriend?"

A moment of silence reigned between them.

Jax removed his hat and ran his hand through his blond hair. "Shoot! This wasn't exactly how I'd planned to do this," he muttered. He looked so cute, Simone couldn't help laughing. "I'm glad you find this funny."

Simone bit down a smile. "I'm sorry. You just looked too cute."

"Now that's a word I haven't heard being used to describe me."

"Well, you're manly and cute."

Jax stroked his chin for a moment. "Coming from you, I'll take it," he said. He took a step forward. "So what do you say, Simone?"

Logically, it didn't seem like the best time to start a new relationship. She'd just left one, and residency was about to start soon. She'd even heard horror stories of how marriages, not to mention dating relationships, broke up during the course of it. Why set herself up for heartache when it was the last thing she needed in her life?

"Simone?"

She looked up at him, into his beautiful grey eyes that called to the very depth of her soul, just as the way he'd spoken her name sent a delicious tickle down her insides, and all her reasons fell away. It was like nothing else mattered in that moment. How could she even resist? "Okay."

He drew closer to her. "You'll be my girlfriend?"

Yep, even though she couldn't believe she'd actually agreed. But hearing him say it didn't sound as strange as she'd thought it'd be. "Yes," she replied.

Jax pulled her into a hug. He smelled of cedarwood and masculine leather, a pleasing combination she wished she could inhale all day. "Thank you," he said, the words rippling against the skin of her neck.

Simone nuzzled deeper into his arms, enjoying the warmth for as long as she could before she pulled back. "On one condition," she said to him.

Jax's eyes met hers. "What? Tell me," he said.

"We don't talk about our backgrounds for now, and I'd prefer our dating is private." Simone couldn't afford the same mistake she'd made with Ethan. Not that she didn't trust Jax—she just needed to be careful with her heart, and she needed time.

Jax went quiet, and Simone could see the confusion written on his face. Was he going to ask her why? It wasn't a question she was prepared to answer. "That's fine with me," he finally said.

Her shoulders relaxed. She'd been worried he'd resist the idea. "Thanks."

"It's nothing," he replied.

But Simone knew it was a big deal. Jax seemed like the type that thrived on openness and honesty, and her words had just placed a restriction on that. Now she wondered if she'd already thrown a wrench in the relationship when it'd only just begun.

Jax released her. "It's fine," he reassured her as if he'd read her thoughts and tucked a few errant strands of hair that had escaped her bun behind her ear. "Does your arm still hurt?"

She'd almost forgotten about it, and she touched it now. "Not really."

His warm gaze caressed her face. "Put some ice on it, okay?"

"I will."

"Go on. I'll call you later tonight," he promised.

Simone nodded. She was also tired for some reason and needed to lie down. She gave him a quick smile. "Bye, Jax."

He returned her smile. "Bye, Simone."

Simone's heart fluttered. This sexy voice of his and the way he said her name would melt her into a puddle one day soon if she wasn't careful.

Yet as much as she hated to separate from him, Simone turned and headed into her building. Once she reached the double doors, she paused and gave him a quick wave. Jax, her new boyfriend. It had a nice ring to it, but only time would tell if she'd made the right decision.

Jax smiled and waved right back.

Then Simone turned and disappeared inside the building.

CHAPTER 11

Jax watched as Simone entered her building. She looked tired, and he hoped she'd be able to get some much-needed rest after the ordeal in the restaurant's parking lot.

A muscle in his jaw tightened and his blood boiled as he recalled what had happened. How dare that pompous fool touch her! Jax had held back this time, but if this had happened back in Dexin, he'd have taught the Carlton fellow a lesson the cowboy way about laying a finger on Simone. On his woman.

His face relaxed into a smile. His woman. Jax couldn't believe she'd said yes. He'd planned to ask her out at the end of lunch, since today was the last of the dates, but he hadn't been sure if she'd think he was being too forward or stupid. After all, she'd only ended her last relationship a few weeks ago, and here he was, asking her to start all over with him.

But he'd had no choice. Simone occupied his thoughts all the time now—which was strange for him—and had even infiltrated his dreams at night. There was just something about her that was so captivating, yet vulnerable and innocent at the same time. The thought of never seeing her again had almost driven him crazy.

Yet he worried about the timing. Jax remembered how terrible his brother's schedule had been during the early years of his residency. He had confidence Simone could handle her schedule just as well, or even better, yet he wondered how the relationship would fit in, even though he'd assured her it wouldn't interfere with her work.

Jax pushed up his rolled sleeves. He'd make it work no matter what and do everything in his power to support her dreams in whatever way he could. Why? Because Simone's happiness mattered to him.

He took one last look at her apartment. Though he was reluctant to leave, it was time to make some plans.

So Jax headed back to his car, backed out of the parking lot, and drove off.

He would show Simone she'd made the right choice.

"I'm so exhausted," Paisley, Simone's new friend and fellow first-year resident, said a few weeks later as she slumped into the chair next to Simone's in the residents' on-call room. "I'd be happy if I never see another patient tonight."

Simone chuckled. "Like that would happen." She leaned back and took a break from the dermatology research paper she'd been working on. "I think it's going to be a long night." She was already bone tired, and even though her night float team had admitted over five patients into the general medicine floor alone, the Saturday night was still young.

"Ugh. That would totally suck," Paisley said. Then she took another look at Simone. "But how come you look so put together, while I look like a hot mess?" she asked, strands of her short, wavy, red-gold bob spiking in different directions.

Simone's eyebrow rose. Put together? "You, my friend, are hallucinating," she said. She was just as exhausted and certain she had dark circles under her eyes. She closed them now, the faint odor of antiseptic and unwashed human bodies filling her nostrils despite the running HVAC system.

Of course, Simone had expected an intense transitional year at one of Boston's top hospitals, but going over ninety-six hours with little sleep since she'd started a new rotation in the general medicine service was more than she'd expected. She couldn't wait for this weekend shift to end.

A light snore soon filled the air, and the corners of Simone's lips turned up—she didn't need to open her eyes to confirm Paisley had fallen asleep. Simone didn't blame her—in fact, she envied her. If the research paper she was working on hadn't been due soon, Simone would have done the same.

A soft melodious tune filled the air, and Paisley groaned.

"Sorry," Simone said as she reached for her phone. She'd forgotten to place it on vibrate, which she corrected before swiping the answer button.

"Coffee delivery for Dr. Addison," said a familiar voice that never failed to warm her heart.

Simone couldn't help the smile that filled her face, and she jumped to her feet. Just the wake-up treat she needed. "Where are you?" she asked as she hurried to the door.

"In the lobby."

"I'll be right there," she said and ended the call.

She rushed out of the room, doing her best to smooth down any errant strands of her messy bun as she strode toward the elevators in her blue scrubs and slip-resistant clogs. She wished she'd had time to clean up more, but there was no guarantee her patients wouldn't need her any minute from now, so she had to make the most of this free time. Soon, she arrived on the ground floor and spotted Jax leaning against the information desk in the center of the lobby.

A sight for sore eyes, she thought, as she drank in the beautiful view in front of her. Tall, lean, and handsome, in a white dress shirt with the sleeves all rolled up and blue jeans—the sexy cowboy hat on his head, the icing on an already delicious cake—Simone would have stared at him all day if she could. Sometimes, she couldn't believe he was all hers. "Hey, you," she said with a smile as she reached him. She'd missed him, even though it'd been only a few days.

It appeared the feeling was mutual because Jax pulled her into a hug, his cedarwood and coconut scent enveloping her like a warm blanket. "I've missed you," he said.

She basked in the warmth of his attention but then remembered all the patients she'd seen and tried to extricate herself from his arms. "I'm not exactly in the best state," she said. "It's been a long day."

But Jax pulled her further into his embrace. "I don't care. You smell awesome to me." He sniffed her hair. "Well, except for the hair."

She slapped his shoulder. "Hey!"

Jax chuckled. "Just joking. You know I adore your hair," he said as he caressed the soft tresses as if it was precious treasure. Simone had never liked anyone touching her hair, but Jax had asked her permission to do so now and then, and she enjoyed the reverent feel of his fingers on it whenever he did.

He kissed it now, then released her to put a drink carrier in her hands. "Here you go. For you and Paisley."

"You don't know how much I really needed this. Thank you."

"My pleasure."

She placed the holder back on the counter, leaned against the station, and smiled up at him.

It seemed like it'd been months since Jax had asked her out, when it had only been a few weeks, but in that time, he'd shown her how much he cared for and supported her.

Jax had picked her up a few times after her shifts and dropped her off at home, did coffee runs like this one whenever he could, sent her a heart-warming wake-up text every morning, and only called her when he was sure she'd had enough rest. And on the weekends they'd agreed to spend together, Jax had come over to her apartment with his paperwork while she got some much-needed sleep after a long week, waking up only to eat the meals he'd prepared for her.

With how unpredictable her schedule was and the fact that he lived more than an hour away, Simone wondered how he did it all. She'd felt guilty for being a bad girlfriend and had said the same to him, but Jax had reassured her it was fine and his choice to support her this way.

"How was your day?" she asked.

Jax leaned against the counter and faced her. "It was great," he said. "One of our mares had her foal after a difficult pregnancy and delivery, and both mom and baby are doing great."

"That's wonderful! A colt or a filly?"

"You know what those are?"

She gave him a jab on the shoulder. "Hey! I'm not horse-illiterate, you know?" Simone hadn't mentioned to him yet that she owned a horse stable. It was covered under the background topics she didn't want to discuss.

"Ouch. That hurts," he said, fake-rubbing the area.

As if. It had only been a light tap. "You poor baby. Need me to make it better?"

Jax nodded. "A few kisses would do it."

Simone chuckled. "In your dreams."

"Ouch, that's mean," Jax said as he clutched at his chest. "Besides, I never said you were horse-illiterate. Do you ride?"

"Used to. Not a lot now."

"Maybe we'll have a horse-riding date on one of your free days. Whenever you get one."

"I'll make a note on my schedule," she teased. At his raised eyebrow, "Just kidding." Simone didn't have a "schedule"—no one did during their early years of residency, despite the mapped-out rotation *schedule*. "So colt or filly?"

"A filly. A beauty just like her ma."

"Have you named her?"

"Not yet. Would you like the honors?"

"Are you sure? Won't your brothers be annoyed?" Jax had told her he had three brothers, Max, Dex, and Rex.

Jax waved her concern away. "I'm sure they'll be fine. So, what would you like to call her?"

Simone thought for a moment. "Bella, which means beautiful," she said.

"Bella... that's a nice name. It fits her perfectly. So Bella it is."

Her pager chose that moment to go off.

Ugh. "One minute please," she said and checked the message. Some urgent labs and studies she'd been waiting on for an acute pancreatitis patient were now available. But why did it have to be ready this *very* minute?

"I have to go," she said instead with a rueful smile. "I'm sorry."

"It's okay," Jax said. "Do you want me to pick you up in the morning when your shift ends?"

Simone shook her head. "It'd be too much driving for you, since you'll then need to make it back to Dexin in time for Sunday church service. I'll be fine."

"Alright." He pulled her into a quick hug and then released her. "Go on."

Simone rose to her tiptoes and kissed him on the cheek. "Thank you," she whispered. *For being the most awesome boyfriend ever*. Then she picked up the coffee carrier. "And for the coffee."

"You're welcome," Jax said. "See you later."

She gave him a quick wave, and even though she was reluctant to do so, Simone hurried off toward the elevators.

Soon, she reached the on-call room and dropped the coffee carrier in front of Paisley. "Wake up, sleepy head. Coffee for you." She grabbed hers and strode to a workstation, where she signed in and pulled up the patient's lab results.

"Thank you," Paisley replied sleepily as she straightened. "Hmmm, this tastes wonderful. This isn't from the hospital."

"Jax brought it," Simone replied, her eyes scanning the results even as she took a sip of her coffee. Perfect. Just the way she liked it, with a little milk and sugar.

"Ooh… the adorable boyfriend," Paisley teased. "Now I need me some cowboy. Does he have brothers?"

Simone laughed. "Just drink your coffee."

"But seriously, girl, this one is a keeper."

Simone said nothing. She needed to update the third-year resident she was working with tonight on the results. Simone had suspected as much, but it was now clear they needed to send a consult to the oncology team to come and see the patient. So she finished the rest of her coffee and rose to her feet. "I'm off."

"Where are you going?"

"Cardiac floor." It was where she'd find the third-year resident, who had access to the office of an attending, whom, if rumors were to be believed, she was dating.

"Alright. Hmmm… this coffee is so good. Definitely a keeper, that one."

As Simone closed the door behind her, she couldn't help the smile that twitched on her lips.

She thought so too.

CHAPTER 13

$\mathcal{J}$ax fought back a yawn as he locked up his car in the darkness that had descended on the ranch. There'd been no traffic on the way from the hospital, so he'd made it home in good time.

"Are you just getting back?" a deep voice said from behind him.

Jax jumped. "Son of a filly! You scared me," he said as Dex materialized at his side.

Dex's eyes narrowed. "You've been acting suspicious these days," he said. "Sneaking off and coming back at odd hours."

Jax turned and headed toward the main door to their home. "Mind your business, old man."

"Me? Old? I'm only your senior by two years."

"Who would have thought?"

"Seriously though. I'm worried about you. Is everything alright?"

Jax reached the door and pulled it open, welcoming the light from the foyer. "Everything is fine," he reassured Dex.

Dex followed him into the house. "So new girlfriend?"

This would have been a good time as any to spill the news, but his family loved to meddle and he'd promised Simone, so maybe it was better to keep it a secret a little longer. "Good night, Dex," Jax said instead. He strode toward the stairs that led to the second floor and began his ascent.

"Hey!" Dex called out from the foot of the stairs.

Jax paused and gazed down at him. "Tomorrow is church, Dex, and I need my beauty sleep."

Dex laughed. "Beauty sleep indeed." Then his face turned serious. "I'm glad you're okay. I'm just…"

Worried about you. Because of Rex, who'd up and left Jax high and dry. The same one who'd betrayed Max and cut Jax off like he'd never mattered.

A muscle twitched in Jax's jaw. He hadn't been the same since Rex left, but what other choice did he have? Life had to continue, and thankfully, he'd met Simone. The thought of her brought a smile to his face.

"What are you grinning about?" Dex asked, cutting into his reverie.

He loved Dex, but brothers could be so annoying sometimes, and Jax didn't have the energy to deal with him right now.

"Good night, Dex," Jax said. He didn't wait for his reply and took the stairs two at a time until Dex was out of view.

He'd rather have Simone fill his thoughts. Jax stopped to send her a text.

Just arrived home.

A response came back almost immediately.

Miss you already. Thanks again for the coffee.

This, right here, was the reason he never tired of making the trips to Boston and back. He loved how open she was in expressing her mind to him. Of course, there were parts of herself she held back, but she'd been upfront about those too. Jax hoped with time she'd feel comfortable enough to open up to him about them. But for now, he'd take each day as they came and enjoy getting to know more about her.

He pushed the door to his room open. It was time to take a shower, go to bed, and dream about his beautiful Simone.

Yes, his night and his life were looking up indeed.

CHAPTER 14

Simone padded across her bedroom in a T-shirt and pajama bottoms and collapsed on the bed, even as shards of morning light pierced through her curtains. *Aaah…* it felt so good to relax.

Her last shift for the month was finally over, and she couldn't be any happier. The handover to the next team had experienced some delays, since her senior resident had a last-minute emergency to take care of, but she was home now and could spend the rest of the day as she wanted.

She smiled to herself at the thought of her plans for the evening. Simone had everything ready—the dress, the shoes, the clutch, the coat, and the jewelry—and she couldn't wait to dress up.

For her date with Jax. In Dexington.

Simone had never been to the nearby city and had been intrigued when Jax had announced he'd set up their next date there. Given how much he'd reminded her about it, Simone had a feeling he'd planned something special. But no matter how much she'd probed to find out more, Jax had remained mum about his plans, adamant that it was a surprise. Now she couldn't wait to see what he had up his sleeve. It'd be fun to see the city as well. They'd agreed to meet at the Bilridge Hotel, a fancy upscale hotel in the heart of the city, and Simone couldn't wait.

It was hard to believe it'd been six months since they'd started dating. Her first year in the residency program had taken up most of her time, and though she'd learned a lot, it'd been so hectic and crazy she'd been relieved when it'd ended and she'd begun the more relaxed dermatology residency years.

The one bright spot through it all had been Jax. He'd been more wonderful and special than Simone had imagined. Ethan, her former boyfriend—now she could think about him without a flicker of emotion— didn't hold a candle to him. Who would have thought that she, Simone Addison, would have fallen for a cowboy?

Yes, Jax had stolen her heart and made it his own. He'd wormed his way in just by being himself, and now Simone couldn't imagine life without him. Of course there were big differences between them—Jax was a cowboy and would always be, and Simone hadn't yet told him details about her background and how wealthy she was. But given what she knew about Jax, she had to believe they could make it work. Besides, Jax had mentioned he didn't expect her to live on a ranch. So maybe he'd thought through it all.

She stifled a yawn as she turned and tucked one of her pillows beneath her head. Right now, she needed to catch up on some much-needed sleep.

Simone needed to be all fresh and alert for her dreamy date with Jax.

An incessant ringing sound drew Simone from the wonderful dream she'd been having about Jax and her on the beach.

Grrr! Not now, not when she was just getting to the best part of the dream. She pulled a pillow over her head. Whoever it was needed to go away so she could get to the part where she'd been about to kiss Jax.

But the doorbell sound didn't let up.

Ugh. She flung the pillow away and sat up. The person at the door had better have a good reason for disturbing her peace or else...

Simone dragged herself from the bed, wrapped her robe around her, tucking her phone into its pocket, and marched to the door, determined to give whoever it was a piece of her mind. She reached the security panel and pressed the touchscreen.

The image of her father filled the space.

Simone's heart froze. What was he doing here? Her father had never visited her apartment before—neither of her parents had shown any interest in doing so, even after she'd informed them she'd bought her own place, and that was years ago. Him being here could only mean one thing.

Bad news.

A horrible, disastrous piece of information he planned to deliver himself.

She dropped her head on the wall beside the security panel, her finger a few inches away from pressing the release button. Now, why did he have to be here today of all days? Her date with Jax was happening in a few hours, and a discussion with her father before then could ruin everything. Maybe she should just pretend she wasn't home.

"I know you're in there, Simone," her father said through the door.

Simone swore under her breath. How did he even know? Could he see through doors now?

If she didn't open up, he'd get his people to wait in the parking lot for her. She'd have to leave her apartment at some point if she wanted to make the date with Jax, and they'd probably follow her to Dexington, which was the last thing Simone needed. Now wasn't the time to let her father's people, or even her father, meet Jax.

She sighed. She was screwed either way. What was she going to do?

Simone stayed silent for a moment, then straightened her shoulders before touching the button that released the door's lock.

The door slid open, and her father stalked in. "It's about time. Never keep me waiting at the door again," he said, as if her home was his to command.

"Then you need to make an appointment," she replied as she followed him into the living room after shutting the door.

Her father stopped and glared at her. "What?"

She held his gaze. "Isn't it what you expect

everyone else to do when they want to meet with you? Then you need to do the same."

Her father looked at her as if she'd lost her mind before he headed over to the couch and made himself at home. "Sit," he said.

What is he up to? Simone wondered as she settled into an opposite chair. From the granite look on his face, it wasn't happy news. What could have stirred up her father's hornet's nest enough to bring him stomping all the way to her place?

He threw a set of pictures on the coffee table between them. "What's the meaning of this?" he barked out.

Simone picked up a few of the photos, and her eyes widened as she scanned them. They were pictures of her and Jax on all their dates!

Her eyes narrowed. "You had me followed?"

Her father's steely gaze met hers. "You may not be my heir, but I won't have my daughter going out with a hillbilly."

Of all the nerve! If it was anyone else, she would have given them a piece of her mind for calling her wonderful Jax names.

Simone's jaw set into a determined line, and she folded her arms over her chest. "Jax is a wonderful man, and you can't stop me from seeing him." She'd had enough of her father's interference in her love life.

"You'll stop seeing him right now."

Simone leaned back as she settled in for a fight. "Why? I love him, and I want to marry him." She hadn't been sure before, but she was now.

Before she knew it, her father was on his feet and now loomed over her like Goliath over David. "Love?" His nose scrunched up like she'd said a bad joke. "He's only after your money. Just like that fool, Ethan. You cannot see him again."

The reminder of Ethan cut her to the quick, but Simone refused to back down. This much she was certain of: Jax was *not* Ethan.

"I'll do nothing of the sort." Besides, Simone's money was her own, and her father had no control over it. There was nothing he could do to her.

"Oh, yes you will." Her father's eyes bored down on her. "You'll stop seeing him, or I'll destroy him." His voice turned deadly. "And his family and everyone he cares about." He leaned forward with a dangerous glint in his eyes. "You know I keep my promises."

Simone shivered at his words. She knew all too well from firsthand experience that he'd do it too. It'd been like this ever since she returned home after her grandmother passed away.

Her father had a ruthless reputation for crushing anyone that dared stand in his way; it was how he'd built his massive business empire. He'd play dirty and never blink an eye about it.

Simone was used to his attacks on her—they both knew she could take it and more. So now he was going after Jax. That was always his tactic when all else failed—he'd hurt the people around her to get whatever he wanted from her. How could she have been so foolish to forget that?

She couldn't let him ruin Jax and everything his family had ever worked for. Given how proud Jax was, he'd never take her money to rebuild if it came to that. The wily fox had boxed her in, and he knew it.

In that moment, Simone wished she'd never been born into her family. Sure, she had all the money in the world, but it certainly didn't buy her happiness.

Her heart deflated, ripped and wounded once again by the man who called himself her father. "What do you want?" she asked quietly.

Her father's eyes lit up in triumph, like he'd crushed another enemy. How he could find delight in her misery was beyond her understanding. "Your phone."

"What?"

"You'll never call, contact, or speak to him ever again."

If this was the price she had to pay, she'd do so as long as Jax was safe, no matter how much the thought of it killed her. "I'll need to end it with him," she said with resignation.

"Don't bother. I already have everything planned."

Of course he did. The old fox did nothing in half measures.

"I'm waiting," he said with his hand extended.

As much as it crushed her, as much as her heart broke at the thought that she couldn't even say good-bye, Simone handed over her phone.

Her father dropped it on the marble floor, smashed it to pieces beneath his foot, and picked up the SIM card from the debris before pocketing it. Then he rose to his feet.

"Mark my words," he said coolly. "Do not contact him under any circumstances. If I find out you did, not only will I ruin him, but I'll also destroy the other person you care about."

Her heart hitched at his words. Simone couldn't

let him do *that*. She'd promised, and she'd keep her word no matter what.

Simone stayed where she was even as her father strode out of her apartment, fighting back tears as she stared at the shattered debris on her floor.

And at the decimated remains of her heart and life.

CHAPTER 15

$\mathcal{J}$ax whistled and rubbed his hands together to warm them against the mid-day chilly January winter as he headed to the mailbox. Dex had gone out early this morning to pick up some much needed supplies for the ranch and wasn't expected back until late in the day. Maggie had opted to spend the day with her friend, Miss Prissy, and Max had shut himself off in his home office, so Jax was practically alone at home.

He didn't mind—in fact, he preferred it. His date with Simone this evening was all that occupied his thoughts, and the last thing he needed was his family's interference, which was sure to happen since Jax couldn't keep the smile off his face at the thought of seeing Simone soon and having her experience the surprise he'd planned for her.

Meeting Simone and then spending much of the last six months with her had been the best time of Jax's life and a blessing beyond his imagination. She was funny, genuine, and down-to-earth, but most of all, he could be himself with her. Simone hadn't minded he was a cowboy and hadn't treated him as a novelty either. It was as if she'd seen him for who he was and had embraced him wholeheartedly.

Sure, their lifestyles were as different as night and day, but Jax could envision a future between them. Boston wasn't that far from Dexin, and thankfully, his work as the CFO of the ranch gave him the option to work virtually as needed.

Simone's job at the hospital, on the other hand, didn't allow for much flexibility, so Jax was willing to move to where she was. Though he'd had plans to build his own property on his section of the ranch with the robust funds he'd managed to set aside through meticulous savings and investments, Jax could give that up to buy a house in whatever Boston location Simone preferred, or even live with her in her apartment if that was her choice.

But all that discussion could only take place if tonight went as planned.

Because today was the big day.

The day Jax planned to pop *the* question.

His mouth went dry just at the thought of it. Though he'd put out hints in the past few weeks about it, and Simone had seemed receptive to the idea, it wasn't the same as actually asking the question.

But Jax believed it was the right time. Sure, they hadn't met each other's families yet, but Jax didn't think it was a big deal since he'd already decided to accept her family as his own, no matter who they were or how they turned out to be. He was certain his family would love Simone too.

Of course, they wouldn't get married immediately, given Simone's residency program, but Jax wanted her to know he was serious about her and hoped to spend the rest of his life with her. But the pace of their relationship was up to Simone. Jax was happy to take things as slow or as fast as she wanted.

But now it was time to get his head out of the clouds and pick up today's mail before he froze to death.

He opened the mailbox and peered inside. There was nothing in it except for a transparent mailer nestled within.

Jax frowned as he pulled it out and noticed the

folded newspaper sealed inside. He and his brothers, Max and Dex, had never been big readers of the printed newspaper—all the information they've ever needed was now available online—so seeing the package piqued his curiosity.

He tore open the transparent mailer, pulled out the newspaper, and unfolded it.

Jax had expected some mundane political headlines, but his heart took a nosedive at what stared back at him.

Billionaire Heiress engaged to Oil Tycoon.

It wasn't the headline that had arrested his attention and made his heart and body feel like it'd been stuck in an Antarctic glacier.

What drew his scrutiny was the picture of the lady on the right, the so-called fiancée.

A picture that looked exactly like Simone.

Jax's breath left him as he stared at the front page. This couldn't be right. There was no way it was Simone. Maybe it was a family relative she bore a close resemblance to.

But the jewel-encrusted locket around the neck of the woman in the picture said otherwise. It'd been a custom-made gift from Simone's late grandmother, and Jax had never seen her remove it.

Jax gripped the mailbox. It couldn't be true. That

Simone was a billionaire heiress, and that she was getting engaged. The former mattered little to him—Jax had always had more than enough to meet his needs, but the latter was a vicious punch to the gut. So what had he been? A fresh towel she'd discarded once used?

He thought they'd loved each other. Jax had opened his heart to Simone, and he'd believed she'd done the same. It'd seemed like a whirlwind romance from the first time they'd met, yet there'd been something real about it. Simone had been beautiful both inside and outside, wonderful and honest, and Jax believed they'd been building a relationship that would last forever.

But now the picture that stared back at him from the newspaper was telling him everything had been a lie, a house of cards that had crashed at the first nudge. It said she'd fooled him and thoroughly too. How could he have been so wrong? And this wasn't a dream, since the ache in his heart was only too real.

Jax took a deep breath and forced himself to straighten. *No, it had to be a lie*. He couldn't stand here and just believe whatever this newspaper was saying. It wouldn't be the first time the media had spread false news.

He pulled out his phone and dialed Simone's

number. A robotic *this line is no longer in service* greeted him instead of the familiar ring tone.

No way. It had to be a mistake. Jax dialed the number again, yet he got the same message.

He forced himself to exhale. There was no need to rush to any conclusions. There had to be an explanation for all this. Maybe something had happened to her phone, which left him with only one option.

Jax rushed into the house and, after a few minutes, returned with his car keys in hand. He entered his truck and soon exited the driveway.

It was best to meet Simone and hear the truth from her.

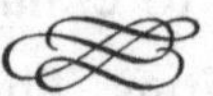

CHAPTER 16

An hour later, Jax stepped out of the truck he'd parked in Simone's private lot and stared up at the building entrance in front of him. Men in black suits and large overcoats he'd never seen before stood on either side of the doorway like sentries guarding a big treasure.

What was going on here? Were they in place to block him from seeing her? If so, they were in for a shock, because no one was going to stop him from meeting Simone today. They'd probably never met a stubborn cowboy like him.

Jax strode toward the entrance with his hands in his sherpa-lined denim coat and his boots crunching down on the concrete pavers. As he'd expected, one of the guards, a heavyset man with tree-trunk-like legs and nostrils releasing tendrils of smoke-like vapor, blocked his way. "I'm sorry, sir, you can't go in," the man said in a heavy Chicagoan accent. He appeared to be the one in charge, his eyes encased in dark sunglasses.

"I'm here to meet Dr. Simone Addison," Jax said.

"Do you have an appointment?" the man asked.

"No, but she's expecting me," Jax said. This wasn't a lie, because she had to be—she'd expect him to have seen the newspaper headlines by now.

"I'm sorry, sir, but only those with prior appointments can see her."

One of the other men came over and whispered something in the leader's ear. The leader's face stiffened, and he glared at Jax. "You have to leave the property now," he said, his tone no longer deferential.

It appeared they'd recognized who Jax was.

"I need to see her," Jax said, holding his ground. The security detail would have to report the ruckus to Simone, which would bring her down and give him the chance to see her.

"You need to leave now," the team leader reiterated, taking one step forward into Jax's personal space.

"Mr. Dexin, Mr. Dexin," a harried voice called out from inside the foyer and soon the concierge, a middle-aged man with a receding hairline, appeared, waving a white envelope in his hand. Jax had chatted with him on many occasions and found him a warm, family-friendly man. He gave Jax a pitying smile. "This is for you, sir."

Jax accepted the envelope. It was plain in front, but when he turned it over, he found it sealed on the reverse side with the familiar red wax seal design he'd created with Simone.

His heart raced. This note was from her. She must have known he'd recognize the seal.

Jax broke the seal and pulled out the card nestled within the envelope. Two words jumped out at him.

I'm sorry, written in Simone's familiar cursive.

Jax's heart cracked. He'd hoped that everything was a lie, that it was simply a mistake of some sort. But those two words now forced him to face the truth.

He, Jax Dexin, had been blind all along.

Was this supposed to be a game rich people liked to play? Go out with some unsuspecting fool, lead him on, and then dump him when they'd had enough fun? Jax had thought himself a good judge of character, but it seemed he'd been wrong, very wrong. Worst of all, Simone didn't even have the guts to break up with him face to face but had instead hidden away like some coward, a note her only response to him.

Jax crushed the paper in his hand even as his heart shattered into pieces.

Simone had made her choice.

It was truly over between them.

And as much as he hated it, Jax would respect it. He'd never force a relationship on anyone.

Jax gritted his teeth and turned away. *Keep it together,* he said to himself. He was a cowboy, able to handle any problems that came his way through the grit and determination that coursed through his vein.

He would not let them see the devastation in his heart.

So Jax squared his shoulders and headed back to his truck.

Jax didn't know how he made it back home without getting into an accident, considering how distraught he was. Darkness had fallen early with the single entryway light barely making a dent in the shadowed fog that encircled their home.

He could hear the soft laughter emanating from

within and guessed the family had gathered for dinner, yet he sat in his truck without getting out.

Jax wasn't ready to face his family.

They'd know something was wrong, no matter how much he tried to hide it, and Jax didn't think he had it in him to even pretend.

There was only one place to go.

Jax exited his truck, leaving his cowboy hat on the passenger seat, and locked it as quietly as he could. Then he headed down a paved pathway on the left until he reached a large rustic-looking timber-framed building. He entered the horse barn and strode down the wide open-concept space lined on either side with horse stalls and overshadowed above with a second-floor hay loft until he reached the stall he had in mind.

Bella, the foal that Simone had helped him name, must have heard his approach because she already had her head out of the stall and nuzzled his shirt. She'd been weaned a few months ago and now had her own stall.

"How're you doing, little one?" Jax asked even as he rested his head against her neck, breathing in her scent of leather and hay. There was just something about horses that centered him, and being here with

Bella seemed to help in calming his turbulent thoughts.

Bella nudged his shirt pocket in reply.

"Sorry, no treats there," Jax replied. The corners of his lips quirked upward as he ran a hand down her side. "But I'll get you some soon," he promised.

Bella appeared satisfied with his answer, since she placed her nose on his shoulder, tendrils of her breath fanning the side of his neck.

They stayed that way for a few minutes, horse and man alone in the world, everything else fading away in the distance. It was just what he needed and in those few moments, Jax forgot about Simone's betrayal.

After a while, Jax took a deep breath and then released Bella. "I'll be right back," he said. He headed over to the tack room at the back of the barn, retrieved some diced baby carrots and celery from a small cooler they kept on hand, and offered them to Bella.

Soon, the sound of Bella's chewing filled the air. Jax waited until she was done before grabbing a fork to muck out her stall.

The barn door opened, and Jax looked out in its direction. It was Dex. Jax turned back to what he'd been doing even as Dex approached.

"I've been looking all over for you," Dex said. "Guessed you'd be here, since your truck's parked outside and you weren't in the house. It's time for dinner."

"I'm not hungry," Jax said flatly, with his back to Dex.

"Are you sure? Maggie made peach cobbler for dessert. It's one of your favorites."

Jax straightened. "Not interested."

A warm hand rested on his shoulder. "Is everything okay?" Dex asked quietly.

Tears stung at the back of Jax's eyes. A part of him wished he could spill everything to Dex—they were that close. But how could he tell him he'd been a fool for loving and trusting the wrong woman? Some wounds were best nursed alone.

"I'm fine," Jax said instead.

Dex patted his shoulder. "I'll be here for you whenever you want to talk. Don't worry about dinner—I'll make some excuses for you with Maggie."

"Thanks."

"No worries. I'll always be here for you, little bro." Dex ruffled Jax's hair, like he'd done so many times before in Jax's younger years whenever he was scared or upset. Then Dex turned and headed the way he'd come, the sounds of his footsteps fading to nothing as he left the barn.

Jax finished cleaning out the stall, refilled the water bucket with fresh water, and then checked on the other horses. By the time he exited and locked up the horse barn, the outside temperature had dropped. But the cold air that whipped his face had nothing against the cold in his heart.

As Jax lumbered back toward the main house with his shoulders slumped as if carrying the weight of the world, he made a sudden resolve.

When he'd started today, Jax had never imagined it'd be the worst day of his life. But this would be the last time he'd ever open his heart long enough for anyone else to hurt him this badly—first it'd been his brother, and now Simone.

In Simone's case, if he had to be precise, money and wealth had defeated him.

His jaw tightened. Jax wasn't yet sure how, but he'd get through today, no matter what it took. And he'd do the same thing the next day, and the one after that. It was what cowboys did and would always do.

But more than that, he, Jax, would show them he could be as successful as they come.

He'd make sure no one would ever use money as a weapon against him in this life.

CHAPTER 17

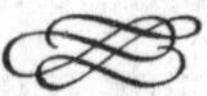

PRESENT DAY

Simone examined the skin on the left calf of the nine-year-old girl lying on the examination table. Ruby had presented at her afternoon clinic a few months ago with a large port-wine stain on her leg. The young girl who'd avoided wearing skirts or dresses over the years had wanted the large birthmark gone. So far, Ruby had received a series of laser treatments, and today was the follow-up visit for the last one done six weeks ago.

Simone straightened. "Your skin looks great," she said.

"Really?" the young girl asked enthusiastically.

Simone nodded. "It's all gone," she said with a smile as she helped the girl back to a seating position.

"Thank you, Dr. Addison," Ruby said, her smile matching Simone's.

Simone's heart warmed. This was the reason she'd specialized in pediatric dermatology—to use her skills to put smiles on the faces of children. "You're welcome." She helped Ruby down from the examination table and then gave her some privacy to dress back up.

"So she doesn't have to come here again?" Ruby's grandmother, Miss Prissy, who sat close by, asked.

Simone made her way back to her desk before replying. "No, she doesn't have to see me again."

"Thank you, Lord. You're a miracle worker, Dr. Addison. Thank you for everything."

"I'm happy we could help her. Ruby did all the hard work. We don't need to see her again, but feel free to give us a call if you have any concerns."

"Will do."

Ruby stepped out from behind the privacy screen.

"So, Ruby, any fun plans to celebrate this?" Simone asked.

Ruby beamed. "Grandma promised to buy me a new dress."

"That's wonderful!"

"We'll shop here in Boston," Miss Prissy said. "Someone recommended the Copley Place."

"They have nice shops there," Simone concurred. "I'm sure you'll find a good dress."

"That's wonderful to know. We're not very familiar with the Boston area."

"You're from Dexin, right?" Simone remembered they'd mentioned this on their first visit, and it'd caught her attention.

"Yes, it's a lovely town," Miss Prissy said. "Have you ever been there?"

Simone shook her head. "No." Which had been a mistake on her part.

"You should come visit. It's God's own paradise on earth," Miss Prissy said. "In fact, come this weekend. I'm hosting an evening singles' mixer." She opened her purse and pulled out a flier, which she handed to Simone.

Simone looked at the paper. "I'm not sure—"

"A beautiful doctor like you shouldn't be single," Miss Prissy said.

"How did you—?"

"I heard something about it."

Most likely from the nurses. Maybe it was time Simone had a chat with them about what they should or shouldn't discuss with patients nearby.

"You should meet people," Miss Prissy powered on. "I'm sure you'll find someone you'll like there."

The one person Simone would ever want to meet was likely married.

"I don't know—"

"Say you'll come. Consider it a day's vacation." Miss Prissy leaned forward. "And maybe you might meet the *one*."

"Just say yes, Dr. Addison," Ruby said. "Grandma won't give up until you promise. She's the town's matchmaker."

Simone looked from Ruby to Miss Prissy. This was a crazy idea, traveling out of town just for a singles' event.

But what if she actually met *him* there?

It seemed like a slim chance, given Dexin couldn't be that small of a place, but she'd never know if she didn't try. Besides, she had no special plans for the weekend.

"Okay, I'll think about it," Simone promised.

"I'll see you then," Miss Prissy said as she stood to her feet. "I run a bed-and-breakfast, so you can spend the night at my place if it gets late. We'll take real good care of you."

Ruby nodded in agreement. "Grandma loves to cook lots of yummy food."

"We'll see," Simone said noncommittally.

"See you soon, doc," Miss Prissy said with a twinkle in her eye. "I'm sure you won't disappoint this old lady." Miss Prissy didn't look her age one bit, even with her silvery, short bob.

"Bye, Dr. Addison," Ruby said cheerfully.

"Bye, Ruby. Ma'am." Simone watched as they left her examination room.

She leaned back in her chair, all thoughts on the invitation she'd just received.

An opportunity to head down to Dexin, and if she admitted it to herself, a chance—though a slim one—to meet Jax again.

It was only after he'd been gone that Simone had realized the depth of what Jax had meant to her. She'd been so devastated by the loss, she'd cut herself off from everyone, including her family, and only the thought of the years she'd already spent in medical training had kept her from collapsing. Instead, Simone had poured herself into her work so much so that the rest of her transitional year had been a blur.

She'd spent the next years on her dermatology residency, eventually becoming board-certified in pediatric dermatology. After working under her mentor, Dr. Guzman, for an additional two years,

Simone was ready to branch out and open her own clinic.

But no matter how much she was in demand as a dermatologist in Boston, even with a six-month wait-list, Simone wanted to get away from the city. She was tired of the demands of her family, the Boston social life, and the reminders of what she'd had and lost and needed a place where she could make a fresh start. After drawing up a list of nearby cities and towns, Dexington and Dexin had both made the cut.

Dexington had an established medical community, and Simone's practice would do well there.

But then she couldn't stop thinking about Dexin. It was a smaller town, less known, but there'd been stories and rumors of a large medical facility being opened there that was drawing the attention of the Boston medical community. Given dermatologists were a scarce commodity, she was certain they'd be willing to partner with her clinic, but would her practice thrive in such a location?

Yet the idea hadn't let go of her. And Simone knew why.

Because of Jax. It was his hometown, after all.

What if she met Jax there again? With chances that he was married and now had his own family, how would she be able to face him if she had to see him regularly in town? It would be like poking a hot iron in an open wound.

Yet... what if he was still single? Simone knew herself well. She'd pursue him in a heartbeat if that was the case.

So with all that uncertainty, Simone had wavered back and forth on her decision. What would it be: Dexington or Dexin?

Now she had this chance to check out Dexin, and in a singles' event, no less.

It really was a *crazy* idea to go down to Dexin for the mixer.

But maybe it was time in her life for one.

Simone looked out her window with interest as she drove past the "Welcome to Dexin Valley" sign in a nondescript black SUV she'd rented for the trip. She wasn't sure what she'd hoped to see, but flowering meadows that sparkled like jewels and stretched out as far as her eyes could see on either side of the road against a backdrop of towering majestic mountains and the golden hue of sunset was the last thing she'd expected.

Dexin Valley was beautiful.

Simone had been a city girl all her life, so she hadn't expected nature and country to appeal to her soul the way it did now. Why hadn't she come to Dexin all these years?

But she was here now, and that was all that mattered.

Her phone rang. Simone picked up her earbud from the console, popped it into her ear, and then pressed the answer button.

"This is Simone," she said.

"Hey, girlfriend, where are you?" a familiar voice flooded her ear. "I'm at your door."

Shoot. She'd forgotten she'd promised to go shopping with Paisley to help her find a dress for her upcoming blind date. "Sorry, dear. I'm not at home." Her GPS motioned a turn on the left and Simone drove down a winding, well-maintained road until she passed what looked like Dexin's Main Street, quaint yet with a rustic, Western feel. Her destination appeared to be a few miles away.

"Okay." Simone could hear the disappointment in her voice. "It was a long shot, anyway. I know you hate shopping."

True. Simone could do without it, but she'd given her word to help. "I'll make it up to you, I promise. How about tomorrow evening?"

"I'll hold you to it." Paisley's voice perked up with its usual enthusiasm. "But where are you?"

"You won't believe me if I tell you."

"Try me."

"I'm on my way to a singles' mixer."

"A what?" Paisley said in disbelief.

"A singles' mixer. Like where singles meet and mingle."

"You're kidding! Wait, are you my friend, Simone, hater of all blind dates, or someone else in her body?"

Simone shook her head. It was just like Paisley to be dramatic. "It's me alright."

"Unbelievable. And where exactly is this mixer taking place? And why don't I know about it? Who convinced you to go?" Paisley prided herself on always being current on the singles' social calendar in Boston.

Simone chuckled. "One question at a time. Which one do you want me to answer?"

"Okay. Where is this mixer happening?"

There was a moment of silence. "Dexin." Simone cringed as a loud scream filled the other end of the line. "Hey! Don't burst my eardrum."

"You're going to see him!" Paisley said excitedly. "Finally!"

The corners of Simone's lips turned up. "I don't know what you're talking about." Of course, she knew, but she couldn't admit it.

"Jax, Jax, Jax! It's about time."

"I never said I was going to see him. Besides, he might be married by now."

"You don't know that for sure, do you? He might be waiting like you've been waiting."

"Who said I've been waiting?"

"Then why haven't you gone on a single date since you guys broke up?"

"I've been busy. You know how work can be."

"Yeah, right. Yet most of our colleagues are married."

"But you aren't married, just like me."

"Not for lack of trying. I just haven't met the one."

"Same here."

"Mm-mm. Not the same. You, my friend, haven't moved on from *the one*."

"But I'm trying now. Like I said, it's a singles' mixer. I'll mix with other singles."

Paisley scoffed in response. "You can deceive anyone, but you can't fool me. I'm fully on the Simone-Jax train. I can't wait for you guys to marry and make little cute babies."

Simone let out a sigh. "I don't know. He probably hates me."

"That's because he doesn't know the truth. It's about time you told him. I don't even know how you held out for this long."

Simone let out an exhale. "I'm scared. What if I don't get another chance with him?"

"You can do this, my courageous friend. I'm rooting for you."

"Thanks for the vote of confidence, Paisley."

"You're welcome. Now go conquer Jax's world!"

Simone chuckled. Trust Paisley to put her at ease. She spotted what looked like the barn Miss Prissy had described to her, a beautiful standalone building with dark blue barn doors. It had a large parking space both in front and next to it, and lots of cars, more than Simone had expected, were parked in various spots. The event in question must be super popular, she mused. "I've arrived. I'll talk to you later."

"Go slay them. Ciao!"

Simone chuckled in amusement as she ended the call. Who couldn't help but love Paisley? Her upbeat personality was part of what had helped Simone survive all these years.

She searched for a parking spot until she found

one a few feet away from the building's entrance and rolled her car in and parked.

Simone let out an exhale as she scanned the view in front of her.

She was here now. At long last.

The barn doors were open, and young men in checkered shirts, jeans and cowboy hats and ladies in short dresses or blouses and jeans with cowboy boots trickled into the building.

Simone looked down at what she was wearing. A cream blouse with a royal blue collar on blue jeans paired with black Christian Louboutin pumps. She didn't think she looked too out of place, did she? Well, it didn't matter now, since there was nothing she could do about it.

It was time to face the music she'd avoided for so long.

Time to dust her rusty social skills and socialize once more.

Time to possibly meet Jax again.

Simone hopped out of the SUV and locked her vehicle. The breezy evening fall air teased her nostrils, and Simone inhaled deeply.

She could do this. She could take this step.

Even if it meant her world as she knew it would

change. Even if the truth about Jax's current status ripped her heart apart.

It was time.

Simone took another deep breath, straightened her shoulders, and made her way to the building.

CHAPTER 18

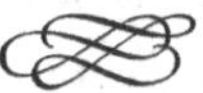

$\mathcal{J}$ax couldn't believe his eyes as he stared across the large, open, high-ceiling space teeming with young people, the air scented with a mix of fresh air, nature, and cologne.

She, Simone Addison, was actually here.

Stunning as always, with her luscious wavy black hair pulled into a braided bun with a few tendrils resting at the nape. Jax had learned a lot of hair terminology from Simone during their time together, when he'd played with and even braided her hair, and he remembered the feel as his fingers had run through it. The same fingers now curled into his palms at the thought.

But all that beauty didn't matter. He'd be stoned

if he let her wreck yet another unsuspecting young man's life.

Jax strode through the crowd, keeping Simone in his sights. The large hall, with its support beams and LED lighting hanging from its rafters, was jam-packed with cowboys and cowgirls all dressed in their finest attire—Jax couldn't remember when last he'd seen a young crowd as large as this in his town.

News about the event must have spread like wildfire—Miss Prissy had certainly milked the announcement of Dex's engagement, and the role she'd played in it as much as she could. It seemed folks had also come from the surrounding areas, and Miss Prissy must be pleased as punch about the attendance.

But Jax had no plans for a relationship, thank you. Said lady he was pursuing now had burned him once, and he had no plans to sacrifice his heart on the altar of love again.

A hand grabbed his arm, and Jax turned in annoyance to see who it was.

Nellie. Jax had known her since forever. They'd gone to the same elementary through high schools and their mothers had been close friends, so for a while their families had spent Sunday dinners together. Nellie had never hidden how much she liked Jax.

"Hey, Jax. It's nice to see you here. I wasn't sure you'd make it," Nellie said, looking as lovely as ever in a flower-patterned dress and cowboy boots. She was a wonderful lady, but Jax treated her like a sister and had never been interested in pursuing her and never would.

"Hey, Nellie," Jax said as he extricated his arm from her hold.

"Could I talk to you now?"

"I'm sorry, but this isn't a good time. I have to go."

Her face fell, crestfallen at his words. As much as it pained him to hurt her, it wasn't his fault. He'd made it clear to her a few years ago he wasn't interested in her in that way. And he really had to go.

But then Nellie tripped, and Jax reached out and caught her.

"Thank you," Nellie said in a flustered tone.

"Are you okay?" Jax asked.

She nodded, and Jax released her.

Then he looked to where Simone had been. She was gone!

"Jax—"

Jax didn't wait to hear what Nellie had to say. He hastened across the room, his eyes searching for Simone and his heart pounding in his chest. Finally, he glimpsed the royal blue collar of the blouse she'd been wearing exiting the room.

No! He couldn't let her leave. "Simone," he called out.

She glanced back at him and their eyes connected. Her eyes were full of fear, as if she couldn't wait to get away. Then she hurried out.

Jax sprinted toward the double barn doors and on reaching them, stepped out into the cool evening air.

But she was no longer there.

Simone was nowhere to be seen.

CHAPTER 19

Simone's world crashed to a standstill like they'd transported her to another planet where no human existed except her and the man whose beautiful grey eyes had just collided with hers.

Jax. More matured, but still gorgeous enough to steal her breath away.

She'd hoped against hope he'd be there, though it'd been mostly wishful thinking on her part. Jax was an attractive, healthy young man, so him being single five years after? Almost impossible. But that hadn't stopped her from wishing for it.

It seemed God had answered her prayers.

But the flash of surprise, then pain, and finally reproach in those eyes as Jax stared back at her had sliced through her heart like a knife through butter. It was as if all the hurt she'd inflicted on him replayed in those few moments.

Simone gasped as the enormity of what had happened between them, of what she'd done to him, dawned again on her.

All the courage she'd mustered to come here, all the hope she'd nursed in a tiny corner of her heart came crashing down at seeing Jax face to face, and witnessing, for the first time, the effect of what she'd done to him.

She had to leave. Simone had no right to be here, to believe she could get another chance after everything.

After she'd crushed his heart.

"Excuse me, I have to go," Simone said to the young man who'd been trying to hold her attention and turned and fled without waiting for his response.

She'd been a fool to come here. What had she been thinking? There was no way Jax would want to have anything to do with her after what she'd done. She'd only deluded herself.

She stumbled through the crowd, muttering quick apologies to the folks she bumped into on her way out until she reached the wide barn doors.

"Simone!"

Simone jolted at the sound of her name on his lips. She whirled to see Jax, head above others, striding through the crowd like a hunter after prey.

Simone's heart pounded.

She couldn't meet him.

This had been a bad idea.

But she would soon have no choice if she didn't hurry.

She rushed past the doors toward where she'd parked. Thankfully, she'd rented an SUV that didn't stand out in the sea of cars that were parked out front. Soon, she reached it and flung herself inside, only letting out a sigh of relief once she'd entered the driver's seat. Fortunately, her car was hidden from open view by the branches of what looked like a hundred-year-old oak tree.

She flattened herself across the front seats so as not to be seen and waited. After a few moments, she lifted her head to peek out, only to see Jax's silhouette had filled the barn's doorway, his eyes roaming the parking lot, searching.

Simone's breath caught in her throat and she ducked. *Please go back in*, she pleaded in her heart.

Several minutes passed before she lifted her head again. This time, Jax was nowhere to be seen. Only a few stragglers hung outside.

Simone exhaled a sigh of relief and placed her head against the steering wheel. She'd known deep down—no, hoped, if she was honest with herself—that she'd see Jax tonight.

Even though she had no right to search for him.

She thought back to what she'd seen. The news about her must have destroyed him. Hurting him had been like stabbing a dagger at her own heart, and she'd bled ever since, so it had to have been so much worse for him.

Simone had never forgotten him, even for one minute over the last five-and-a half years, a part of her hoping for another chance for them.

But she'd seen Jax hug that pretty young lady. The familiarity between them had raised an ache in her heart, made worse by the look of shock and hatred in Jax's eyes when he'd spotted Simone.

The truth was now obvious.

Jax would never forgive her for what she'd done.

Simone swiped at the tears that ran unbidden down her cheeks. No matter how much it hurt, it was time to let go.

Time to forget Jax and let him live life with the love he deserved.

Taking a deep breath, Simone turned the ignition and backed out of the parking space.

She'd never see Jax again.

Even if it meant she'd never get the chance to tell him the truth of what had really happened that day many years ago.

It was time to give up for good.

CHAPTER 20

*J*ax stood at the entrance to the barn, his eyes searching for Simone.

Where had she disappeared to?

He looked to see if he'd find the familiar dark blue Tesla she'd loved to drive, but there weren't any in the graveled parking lot. Maybe she'd brought another car, yet none stood out to him.

"Is everything alright?" Nellie asked from beside him.

Jax's skin pricked with mild irritation. He needed to find Simone and didn't appreciate the interruption. "I'm fine," he said in a brisk tone.

"Miss Prissy is looking for you," Nellie said. "It's time for the one-on-one speed dating session, and she needs your help."

"Okay, tell her I'll be there soon," Jax said. It was all Rex's fault Maggie had roped Jax into this. Why did he have to get engaged and marry suddenly, leaving Jax holding the "Help-Miss-Prissy-at-the-singles'-event" bag? Yet he had to keep his word, since he'd already promised Maggie he'd help.

Jax let out a sigh. He'd lost Simone. Standing here or even checking all the cars in the parking lot one by one wouldn't help him find her if she didn't want to be found.

Maybe it was best she'd left. The past was over and done with, and he didn't need any new entanglements with her—it could only spell bad news with the way things had gone between them. He couldn't let her ruin his life a second time.

Jax cast one last look across the parking lot, then turned back into the barn in search of Miss Prissy.

CHAPTER 21

Simone collapsed onto her couch and let out a heavy sigh. She was now back at home in Boston, but even the scenic beauty of the late evening Boston skyline, with its changing foliage in hues of red, orange, and yellow, peeking through the floor-to-ceiling windows, was not enough to calm her heart.

What a day it'd been, and she needed to talk to someone. She pulled her phone from her purse and dialed Paisley's number.

"Hey, girlfriend," Paisley said from the other end of the line. "Didn't expect to hear from you so soon."

"I'm back."

"Already?"

"Are you up for a sleepover?"

"I'll be right there," Paisley said and hung up.

Thank God for good friends. Paisley had been with her through thick and thin, and Simone considered her closer than a sister. She leaned against the couch as she waited.

Thirty minutes later, her doorbell rang. Simone had left a standing order with the concierge to let Paisley up the elevators whenever she showed up. She now checked the security camera and then opened the door.

"So what happened?" Paisley asked without preamble as she stepped into the apartment in a sunny dress, her carry-on and rose fragrance trailing behind her.

Simone led her to the main couch in the living room and waited until Paisley had relaxed on it before plopping down beside her. "I saw him."

Paisley sat up. "You saw Jax at the event? Jax, the cowboy hunk?"

The corners of Simone's lips quirked. Trust Paisley to describe him this way. "Yes."

"Is he still as hot as ever? Is he single? Did he see you?"

Ah, Paisley and her twenty questions. "I don't think he's married, but I don't think he's single either."

Paisley's face scrunched up in confusion. "Wait, what does that even mean?"

"He was at the event, so I guess that means he's single," Simone said. "But..."

"But what?"

"He had someone in his arms. A lady. A pretty lady."

"It could mean anything. Maybe he was just helping her up or something."

Simone thought back to that moment. It hadn't seemed that way. "She had the look."

"What look?"

Simone let out a sigh. "The look of someone in love."

Paisley placed a hand on Simone's arm. "I'm so sorry."

"Don't be. Maybe it wasn't meant to be." Simone had held out hope, but she'd been too late, and it was all her fault. But even knowing that and accepting it didn't mean her heart didn't hurt.

"Hold on," Paisley said with an excited look on her face.

"What?"

"He was at a singles' event, right?"

"Yes."

"I thought they exempted engaged folks from

such events, since they already have a partner. The whole point of the event is to give people a chance to find someone, right? So, wouldn't that be deception?"

Simone hadn't thought of that. "But he could have been one of the organizers. They don't have to be single."

"Did you see him helping out?"

Simone thought back to the event. "Not really."

"That means he's most likely single. You, my friend, have a chance."

Hope blossomed within Simone. Could it be possible? If Jax was single... "But I'm sure he hates me."

"Because he doesn't know the actual truth," Paisley said softly. "That you never betrayed him."

Simone dropped her head in her hands. "I don't know. You didn't see the look on his face."

Paisley placed her hands on Simone's shoulders. "I still think you shouldn't give up." A sly look came over her face. "But he may get engaged soon with Miss Pretty Lady from the event if you don't move fast, and it'll be all your fault you lost him." Paisley leaned forward. "So, what are you going to do about it?"

"I don't know, Paisley. He seemed furious, and I

don't want to hurt him any more than he already is. He deserves better."

Paisley gave Simone a shake. "You can't give up now. Get it together, sista! This might be your only chance."

She had a point. Simone couldn't afford to give up now, even if it meant getting ridiculed and rejected by him, but… "I have to think about it. Maybe I need a sign from heaven."

"Okay, you can think all you want," Paisley said. "But don't wait too long." She released Simone and relaxed back onto the couch. "Now, what are we having for dinner?"

CHAPTER 22

"You're back," Maggie, a buxom woman with short silvery hair, said from the living room as Jax stepped through the foyer of the main house back at the ranch. Becca, his brother Max's wife, sat beside her with piles of boxes everywhere and what looked like a mountain of baby clothes.

"Yes," Jax said. He'd keep the mandatory debrief short and make his getaway as soon as possible.

"Jax, could you help me move those boxes to the nursery?" Becca pointed to some large flat boxes lined a few feet away against the wall. "Those are for the crib, and even though Max said he'd take care of it after his walk with Chloe and Peter, I'd rather get it out of the way now before Chloe comes back and gets into everything."

"Not a problem," Jax said and spent the next few minutes moving them to the half-decorated nursery Becca and Max were putting together. Once he was done, he returned to the living room.

"So how was the event?" Maggie asked after Jax had settled into one of the smaller couches. "Did you meet any ladies?" She gave him a quizzical look. "And why are you back so early?"

"Miss Prissy didn't need my help anymore, and she had other volunteers that showed up."

"But you could have stayed and mingled," Maggie said. "Wasn't that the whole point of going to the event in the first place?"

"I met enough." The encounter with Simone alone had been more than sufficient in knocking him off-kilter, and he hadn't recovered.

"Jax, are you even listening?" Maggie said.

"Sorry, what?"

"Maggie was talking to you," Becca said.

"You've got something on your mind?" Maggie asked, the corners of her eyes crinkling with concern.

"I'm fine," Jax said.

Maggie and Becca exchanged worried looks but said nothing else.

Maggie's phone beeped, and she checked the screen. "It's Rex. He's on his way home."

It was the signal Jax needed to disappear. "Do you still need my help here?" he asked. "I'd like to head home if that's okay. I'll pass on dinner."

"Go on," Maggie said in a resigned tone.

Maggie was certainly disappointed, but Jax couldn't help himself.

He didn't want to run into his twin brother. The mere thought of meeting him made Jax's head hurt, and seeing him was enough to make him run the other way, so he'd been avoiding the main house and the stables as much as possible.

He sighed. Jax hadn't known so much resentment against Rex had built up in his heart, and now he had no idea how to clear it.

How had Rex been okay with surviving without him all these years? He'd thought their bond was strong before Rex had left, but it seemed only Jax had felt that way. And even after he'd returned, Rex had sure taken his sweet time in mending their broken relationship by getting engaged first, which made it all too clear Jax wasn't important to him like he'd thought.

He stepped outside. Jax could take his truck, but he left it in the parking lot and took a circuitous route back to his own home on the ranch, hoping the cool evening air and the vibrant scent of wildflowers would clear all the thoughts churning in his head.

As he reached the front of his home, he spotted Rex's place in the distance, but with the way things were between them, one would think the Great Wall of China existed between their homes.

However, the biggest wall of all was between him and Simone. Why had she shown up in his town? It'd been over five years, for goodness' sake, even though she'd looked as beautiful as ever, and his traitorous heart had skipped a beat.

Jax thought back to how the evening had gone. What was she hoping to achieve, showing up before him? Her appearance here couldn't have been a coincidence.

But no matter her agenda, regardless of if she was single, engaged, married, or divorced, Jax wanted nothing to do with her.

Not now and not ever.

A week had passed since Simone had gone down to Dexin, yet it seemed like the encounter had occurred only yesterday. Thankfully, Simone's mentor, Dr. Guzman, had travelled out of the country for a speaking engagement at a conference so she'd covered his patients as well as hers, which had made for a very busy week and less time to think about Jax.

She stifled a yawn, even though it was only late Friday afternoon, as she finished updating the electronic medical records of the last patient she'd just seen in the clinic. Eight-year-old Lydia, whose mother had passed away, had been referred to their clinic for second-degree cigarette burns inflicted on her by her stepfather. The cops had arrested the man, and her maternal aunt, who was now her legal guardian, had brought her in.

Simone had been seeing her for a few weeks now, and the burns were healing well with minimal scarring, which Simone hoped would fade away with time. But the same couldn't be said for the emotional scars, and thankfully, Lydia was seeing a therapist for those. Simone sent up a quick prayer for the soft-spoken little girl.

"Is there anything else you need, Dr. Addison?"

Simone looked up to see her nurse, Blair. The petite, blue-haired nurse was standing by the doorway. Blair was a favorite with the kids—she had a way of putting them at ease that made Simone's consultations with them much easier.

"I'm good," Simone said.

"Any plans for the weekend?"

"Just the usual. Sleep and get some work done."

Blair shook her head at Simone's words. "You need to get out more, you know. Meet other young people."

"I'll be fine. What about you? What are your plans?"

"Tim and I are going up to a ski resort in Vermont." Tim was Blair's boyfriend.

Simone lifted a skeptical brow. "In fall?"

"Not for snow skiing. There's a ton of other fun stuff like zipline tours, trampoline swings, space biking—"

"Did you say space biking? What's that?"

"We wondered too at first and looked it up," Blair said. "It's some sort of contraption that's like a Ferris wheel, only smaller and with fewer spokes, and you're strapped into a bike instead of a seat. The space bike looks cool, and we can't wait to try it out."

It sounded interesting, but Simone wasn't big on thrill park rides. Except when on a horse, she liked her two feet on the ground. "Have fun," she said instead.

"We will. Enjoy your weekend."

"Will do. See you on Monday." Blair gave her a quick wave and left.

Simone leaned back and inhaled the antiseptic-tinged fresh air. Her weekend suddenly sounded boring after hearing Blair's planned adventures. Maybe she'd go horse riding. It'd been a while, and she'd missed her horses.

The buzz of her phone interrupted her thoughts. Simone picked it up, glanced at the screen, and then answered. "Aren't you supposed to be enjoying the Paris nightlife by now?" she said.

Dr. Guzman laughed from the other end of the

line. "I'm getting too old for that. The presentations and small talk got me all exhausted, and right now, I'm on the balcony of my hotel room enjoying the view with a wine glass in my hand."

"Thanks for the interesting imagery."

Dr. Guzman chuckled. "You're welcome." Then his voice turned serious. "Listen, I called because there's someone I think you need to meet. I know you've been thinking about moving away from Boston. Dexin Valley is some distance from Boston, yet it's close enough for you to come by anytime you want, and not too far for your existing patients to come looking for you. Dr. Max Dexin is a well-known ER doctor and a good friend of mine, and he's recently established a new hospital facility in Dexin. I'm sure you've heard about it."

Simone sat up. A doctor who had the same last name as Jax. Could they be related? If she remembered correctly, Jax had an older brother who was a doctor. Could it be him? A tingle of excitement buzzed in her stomach. "Yes, I have. It's been all the news in the Boston medical community."

"Well, he's looking to establish partnerships with some specialists and he reached out to me regarding dermatology. I figured your interests were aligned, and a conversation with him might be in order. But he'd need a fast decision from you. So, what do you think?"

"I'm happy to chat with him, but I haven't decided one way or the other about the clinic's location."

"That's fine. Would this weekend work for you to see him? I know his schedule has been crazy, and I expect it to get worse over the next few months, but he has some free time tomorrow afternoon. Do you think you can head down to Dexin and see him? He's tied down with some personal commitments, so right now, he can only meet you at his home office. But he's a good guy and one of the few men I trust, so you have nothing to worry about. Does that work for you?"

Well, she'd had nothing concrete planned for tomorrow. "It does."

"Great! I'll let him know you'll be coming and will forward his address once I receive it, along with his phone number."

"Sounds good."

"Alright. I need to go. The view is calling my name."

Simone chuckled. "Have fun."

"Have a good evening, Dr. Addison." The call disconnected.

Simone rose to her feet and paced her office.

Unbelievable. It had to be the same Max Dexin. Simone didn't think the last name was *that* common, but she could be wrong. But either way, this was happening in Dexin.

She'd told Paisley that only a sign from heaven would make her take a chance, and maybe this was it. If not, how could she explain this?

Simone's face grew warm. She was going to Dexin.

And maybe, just maybe, she'd see Jax again.

CHAPTER 24

Jax ran a hand through his hair as he paced Max's home office late Saturday morning. "Can you guys get off my case?" he said both to his brother Max, who leaned against his desk, and Maggie, who sat on the adjacent black sofa in the office.

"We're only worried about you," Maggie said. "You haven't been yourself lately."

Jax stopped pacing and faced her. "I just have a lot of work on my plate right now. Besides, I don't recall any of you being pressured like this. For goodness' sake, Maggie, you were single for a long time and only just got married."

"Don't be a brat. You're not me," Maggie replied curtly.

"Sorry," Jax said in a contrite tone. He ran his hands through his hair again. "It's just... I don't understand what the fuss is all about."

"Come here," Maggie said, and patted the seat at her side. Jax complied and settled beside her, her familiar scent of cinnamon and spice enveloping and warming him. "I know you got burned before—"

Jax's eyes widened in surprise. "How did you know?"

"A mother's instincts," Maggie said, a hint of her Bostonian accent slipping out. "We figured you wanted to process it all by yourself, so we left you alone. But then you come back yesterday with that look on your face, the same one you had years ago. That's why we're concerned. We can't just stand by and watch you go back into that dark place again." She placed a hand over his. "Did something happen? We just need you to be okay. Besides, Miss Prissy said you didn't socialize with anyone yesterday, even though most of the eligible ladies in our town and the environs had shown up."

Jax placed his other hand over hers, the weathered hands that had lovingly taken care of him and his brothers after their Ma passed away. "Maggie, I'm fine," he reassured her.

Maggie didn't seem convinced by the look on her

face. "Then why aren't you even going on dates? It's been five years, and I haven't seen you with anyone."

Five years, six months, and eight days, to be exact, but he couldn't tell her that. Jax had flirted with the idea on and off, but somehow he hadn't been able to make himself go on one. "There's no reason to—"

The blare of the home security alarm interrupted his speech. Jax watched as Max strode to the security panel and checked the screen. "There's a car at the gate," Max said. "Must be the doctor I have an appointment with."

"Regarding the hospital?" Maggie asked.

"Yes."

"Okay. I'll let Becca know so she can meet him or her at the door." She rose to her feet.

"Thanks," Max replied, and pressed the button to release the gates.

Maggie headed to the door, but turned just as she reached it. "This conversation is not over," she said to Jax.

Jax watched as the door closed behind her, and then his shoulders slumped. "This is madness."

Max moved over to his desk and shuffled through some papers. "I don't think you can get out of this one," he said. "Maggie is really worried about you."

"But this is my private business," Jax protested.

"There's nothing like that where a mother is concerned. I never understood it until after Chloe came into my life. Besides, you have to admit you've been acting strange since Rex came back."

"I don't want to talk about that."

Max straightened and faced Jax. "How long are you going to let this thing between you two continue? You guys are brothers. At some point, you have to hash it out with him."

Of course, Jax couldn't avoid Rex forever. But he just wasn't ready to deal with it right now. Even more so with the added complication of Simone suddenly showing up in his town. There had to be a reason for it. He shot to his feet. "I have to go."

"I'll walk with you." Max stacked the papers he'd pulled out at the center of his desk. "It's time to meet my appointment, anyway."

Jax waited until Max had come around before heading toward the door. As they reached it, he pulled it open for Max to step out first.

His eyes widened, and his heart thundered at the sight before him.

This couldn't be happening.

Standing on the other side of the door was the last person he'd expected to see.

CHAPTER 25

Simone rolled down her car window and stared up at the massive black gates in front of her as the Saturday morning's fall breeze fanned her face and the scent of honeysuckle filled her nostrils. It'd been easier than she'd expected finding this place. She didn't know what she'd been thinking, but she hadn't expected it to be a ranch!

Could this be where Jax lived? Jax hadn't shared anything about the ranch he'd grown up on, because of her condition on the relationship. Yet the thought that this might be his home sent warm thrills down her spine.

Don't get your hopes up, she cautioned herself. It was possible Jax and Dr. Dexin weren't related.

Moreover, she needed to focus on the business at hand.

But how was she going to get in?

Before she could pick up her phone to call Dr. Dexin and let him know she was here, the gates swung open as if on command. Simone peered closer and noticed an embedded security camera in the top section of the wrought-iron arch that overshadowed the gates.

Nice. Maybe she'd put one like this at her horse stable. She made a mental note to speak to the stable manager about it.

Simone drove through the gates and down a long paved-turned-cobblestone driveway that ended in an impressive log-and-stone house surrounded by an extensive, well-manicured lawn.

The place looked like something out of a storybook, rustic yet magnificent, with the clear blue sky and mountains in the background. Very much like a place Jax would enjoy living in.

Get a hold of yourself, Simone thought. This wasn't the time to be thinking about Jax. She was here for a business meeting, after all.

Simone found a spot to park in and got out of her rented vehicle. She smoothed down her light blue blouse tucked into grey slacks, picked up her satchel from the front seat, and locked her SUV. Then she made her way to what she assumed to be the main entrance to the house.

The door swung open, and a stunning brunette dressed in a loose floral blouse and skinny jeans, looking like someone who'd stepped out of a magazine, stood in the doorway.

"You must be Dr. Addison," she said with a warm smile. "I'm Becca Dexin, Dr. Max's wife. Welcome to our home. I hope it wasn't too hard to find."

Simone smiled in return. "Nice to meet you, Mrs. Dexin," Simone said to the woman, who looked vaguely familiar. Had she met her before? "It wasn't a problem getting here."

"You can call me Becca. Please come in," Becca said as she led the way into the house.

Simone's eyes widened in appreciation at the intricate interior design of the living space, built of log and stone, yet maintaining a warm and inviting vibe. "You have a lovely home," she said.

"It is, isn't it? Max's parents built it," Becca said, her green eyes sparkling. "This way. Max is expecting you in his office." She led Simone past double French doors and down a hallway that seemed more modern than the living room area, with its dark hardwood floors and recessed lighting. Soon, they reached a large walnut door on the left.

"Here we are," Becca said. As she reached for its handle, the door swung inward and two men stepped into view: a bespectacled gentleman that looked to be in his forties with a younger version of him by his side.

One who was very familiar.

It seemed the face-to-face meeting that had been a long time coming was finally here.

Simone's heart dropped as she stared back.

Jax couldn't believe his eyes. Simone was standing right in front of him in his family home! How was that even possible?

"What are you doing here?" he asked in a voice as cold as ice as he recovered himself in time.

Becca looked from Simone to Jax. "You know each other?"

"Hello, Jax," Simone said quietly, her face expressionless.

Jax's eyes narrowed, and he took a step forward. How dare she come here? Was this some screwed-up idea to get back into his life? What was she thinking? He had to find out. "We need to talk," he said, his eyes focused on Simone.

"Hold on," Max said from beside him. "What's going on here?"

Simone extended a hand to Max. "Dr. Dexin, it's nice to meet you. I'm Dr. Addison. Dr. Guzman made the referral?"

Max returned her handshake. "I'm glad you made it, Dr. Addison."

She had an appointment with Max? There was no way she wouldn't have guessed he was related to Jax, just from their surnames and being from the same small town. He didn't know her plan, but he had to stop her from becoming entangled with his family!

Jax grabbed her arm. "We need to talk now," he hissed in her ear.

"Dr. Dexin, could you give me a minute?" Simone said to Max. "I'll be right back."

"Sure," he said. But Jax could tell the turn of events confused him.

"Come on," Jax said and led her away from Max's office and back down the hallway.

CHAPTER 27

Simone let Jax pull her away down the hallway until they were a safe distance from where Max and Becca stood. She hadn't gotten over the shock that he was right here in front of her. But she had to keep her cool, no matter what. She was here for business, or so she told herself.

"Why are you here?" Jax asked, cutting to the chase.

Simone pulled her arm from his and lifted her chin. "To discuss business with Dr. Dexin," she replied.

"Did you know—"

"He was your brother? I didn't know, though I wondered at the last name."

"Really? So it's a pure coincidence that you're here meeting with a doctor who just so happens to live in the same town and has the same last name as I do."

"It is," Simone said as she held his gaze and fought the urge to smooth out his furrowed brow.

"I want you out of here."

Sure, they had an unpleasant history between them, but this was about her work and career. One she'd worked far too hard for. "Or what, Jax?"

Jax stepped closer. "Don't push me, Simone."

His familiar scent of cedarwood and masculine leather wrapped around her like a warm caress, threatening to buckle her knees.

Simone couldn't let him get to her and drive her away. After all, she had her work reputation to protect, even if she felt remorse at the pain her presence brought him. "Dr. Dexin was the one who invited me here, not you," she whispered, as if to soften the blow of her words. "So I'm going to go back in there and have my discussion with him first. Don't tell me you plan to mess with your brother's work for personal reasons."

A muscle ticked in Jax's jaw. "This conversation isn't over."

"I'll talk to you later, Jax. I'll see you in about an hour," she said, before side-stepping him and heading back to Max's office.

CHAPTER 28

Jax followed her back to Max's home office. Simone had to be dreaming if she thought things would go the way she wanted.

"I'm sorry for keeping you waiting," he heard her say to Max as he reached where they stood.

"It's not a problem," Max said. He looked from her to Jax. "But I need to ask: how do you know my brother?"

Simone's eyes shifted to Jax's, as if she expected him to answer the question.

Jax's nostrils flared. How dare she look to him to clean up this mess she'd created! What gave her the right to think she could just invade his life and mess with it like she wanted? Did Simone really believe he was weak for letting her break his heart with no repercussions? Maybe it was time for her to learn a very important lesson about hurting others.

An idea dropped into Jax's mind, one so insane he'd have kicked someone else if they'd suggested it. But somehow it seemed perfect for the moment—she'd pay for daring to disrupt his life again and get a taste of her own medicine. Besides, it would help get Maggie and his family off his back, a reprieve he sorely needed.

"She's my fiancée," Jax said without preamble.

The silence that followed was deafening, so quiet one could hear a pin drop on the floor.

Jax kept his attention on Simone, watching for her reaction to his news.

Simone's face paled, and a barely audible gasp escaped from her at his words.

Jax couldn't help the wintry smile that crossed his lips as he watched her fight to regain control. *Good.* This would teach her to be careful around him. He, Jax, was not a pushover. He ignored the questioning look in her eyes and instead dared her to refute his claim.

Becca was the first to recover herself. "Jax, I didn't know you were in a relationship!" she said.

Well, he wasn't until this very moment, but she

didn't need to know that. "It wasn't public news, was it, babe?" Jax said, giving Simone a saccharine smile.

It was now or never. She could go along with the farce or rat him out to be a liar. He could practically hear the gears of her mind working overtime at the sudden turn of events.

"It wasn't," Simone said finally, her eyes locked with his, a certain openness he hadn't expected mirrored in them.

A tingle of uncertainty crawled down Jax's spine. Why wasn't she fighting back? What was she thinking?

Before he could decipher the meaning behind her behavior, Simone had turned back to Max. "I hope it's not a problem."

"It's not," Max said. "I'm just surprised this is the first I'm hearing of it."

"Jax didn't know I was coming here today," Simone said. "Dr. Guzman reached out to me suddenly, so I haven't discussed it with him. I figured it'd be a pleasant surprise, and besides, I didn't want our relationship to color the discussion."

"So that's why Jax seemed shocked to see you!" Becca said. "Anyway, welcome, Simone," she said, offering her a smile. "It's great to meet you."

"Same here," Simone replied with a warm smile.

"Dr. Dexin, if it's okay with you, could we begin the meeting?"

"Sounds good to me," Max said.

Simone placed a hand on Jax's arm as if it belonged there, sending tingles down his arm, and her familiar fresh floral scent wrapping around him like a cloak. "I'll talk to you later, babe," she said softly to him.

Wow, he had to give it to her. She'd recovered quickly. Well, two could play that game.

"Just call me once you're done, darling," Jax replied with a Western drawl as he covered her hand with his.

He sensed her breath quickening as he'd hoped and couldn't help the pleasure that coursed through him at knowing his accent and the brush of his skin against hers still affected her.

"This way, Dr. Addison," Max motioned toward his office.

Simone released Jax's arm, the absence of her touch leaving a bereft sensation behind, and followed Max in. Soon, all that stood between Jax and Simone was a closed office door.

Jax rubbed the spot where her hand had rested as he stared at the door. She seemed to have taken everything in stride. Had he underestimated her, only to let a fox into the hen house? He had to keep his guard up, no matter what.

A hand on his arm drew his attention back to the present.

"Come with me," Becca said, looping her arm with his. "You, my friend, have some major explaining to do."

Jax allowed Becca to drag him to the living room. This was a conversation he couldn't evade, so he might as well get it over and done with.

Becca settled on the long couch and patted the space beside her. "Sit."

Jax obliged her and sat down. "What's up?"

Becca wriggled a finger in his direction. "Don't pretend as if you don't know what we need to talk about."

Well, he wouldn't make it easy for her, so Jax feigned innocence instead. "What do you mean?"

"Jax!"

"Okay, okay. You mean Simone?" Becca nodded and waited. "She's really my fiancée." Simone had backed him up earlier, so Jax was now committed to his story, no matter what.

"Who's what?" a familiar authoritative voice said.

Jax's heart sank as he turned his head to see Maggie step out of the kitchen, the smell of freshly baked bread following her. He didn't know she was still in the main house. Jax had assumed she'd left and returned to the home she shared with Peter, her husband, on the ranch.

"Jax has a fiancée," Becca said. "She's meeting with Max now."

Steely eyes met his as Maggie focused her attention on him. "Really?"

A bead of perspiration broke out on Jax's forehead. He could tell Maggie didn't believe him—she had to wonder why he hadn't mentioned it earlier. He'd be in big trouble if she started digging and caught him out on the lie, especially since he and Simone hadn't matched their stories. Jax had to make his escape, and fast.

He jumped to his feet. "I need to make an urgent business call," he said. He truly had one of those, but he'd planned to do so in the afternoon. Yet making the call now was as good an excuse as any.

Becca's eyes widened in surprise. "Jax—"

"I'll see you both later." Jax didn't wait for their response and instead raced out of the house like a cat with its tail on fire. He only let out a sigh of relief once he was out the main door and into the warm sunshine.

That was close. Scary Maggie was not someone to trifle with, if he wanted to keep his head on his shoulders. He needed to get the story right with Simone before he met Maggie again, which meant staying away from the main house until Simone was done with her meeting.

Jax hurried down the driveway and headed toward his home.

It was best to hide there and wait for Simone's call.

CHAPTER 29

Simone followed Max into his office, a large room with floor-to-ceiling windows on one side that let in a lot of natural light and extensive bookshelves on the other walls.

"Please sit," Max said as he motioned to a tufted visitors' chair that faced his large desk, while moving behind it to settle into his swivel chair.

"Thank you," Simone said as she sat down.

"Is there anything I can offer you?" Max asked.

"I'm good, thank you."

"Thanks for coming at such short notice."

"My pleasure."

"I didn't think I'd find a dermatologist interested in moving into the area." Warm blue eyes stared at her with interest.

Simone adjusted her hands on her lap. "I'd been considering leaving the Boston scene, so Dr. Guzman's call was timely."

"If you don't mind, can I ask why? Because of Jax?"

"One of many reasons." She wasn't really engaged to Jax, but he was definitely an influence on her decision. But getting away from her family and carving out a more private life for herself was the primary reason.

Max studied her for a moment. "Okay," he finally said. "Let's get down to business, shall we?"

Simone straightened. "Works for me."

Max leaned back in his chair. "I'm not sure how much Dr. Guzman told you about the Dexin Medical Center."

"Not much," Simone replied. "Only that it's a new hospital facility in the area, and you're looking to establish partnership with specialists, including a dermatologist."

"Right. Dexin Valley and its surrounding towns have grown over the years to become a thriving little community. However, we need to head into Dexington city for most of our medical needs, which isn't ideal since it's about an hour or two away from here, depending on traffic, especially when we have emergencies. So my family and I decided to open an ER center here, staffed with the best doctors and state-of-the-art equipment.

"So far, we've hired enough experienced medical staff in Emergency Medicine, ICU, General Surgery, Pediatrics, Ob-Gyn, and Radiology. Dr. Peter Taylor, a well-known New York general surgeon and Maggie's husband, and I, an ER attending, will be in charge of the center. We want to grow this facility to become a model center with deeper specialization and research in each Emergency Medicine subspecialty than the typical trauma center, while remaining nimble and flexible in our approach."

"Sounds very interesting."

"It is. Yet, even with all these, we realize other non-ER medical services are just as important, so we want to establish partnerships with specialists in these areas so we can refer our patients to them, ensuring continuity of care without deviating from our core focus." Max inclined forward as he steepled his hands together. "That's where you'll come in."

Simone nodded in agreement. This she understood.

"We've noticed an increasing demand for dermatology-related services in this area," Max continued, "which may be due to the influx of new families settling into the community. Not only have we seen demand for general dermatology services, but for cosmetic dermatology, surgical dermatology, and aesthetic services as well. But I know, given the strong demand for dermatologists nationwide, that you have long waitlists, so we're open to working out an arrangement that would be mutually beneficial to both of us."

"I didn't know there was such a demand for our services in this area."

"I was surprised too when we noticed the trend, given we are primarily a ranch community. But it appears cowboys and cowgirls love to take care of their skin just like everyone else. Dr. Guzman mentioned you might be looking to open a clinic here."

Simone nodded. "I haven't decided yet, but it's definitely under consideration."

"What if I sweeten the deal by offering you a free lot of prime land right on Main Street?"

Simone perked up. "That's a very generous offer," she said. Getting land on Main Street in Dexin Valley had seemed impossible from her call with the real estate broker just this morning. Could it be Max was the owner of the only empty lot of land right on Main Street the real estate broker had mentioned?

It'd be awesome if it was even available, though Simone preferred to pay for it instead.

"We like our doctors to be happy," Max replied. "Besides, you're practically family."

That right there was another reason she had to pay for the land. What if the truth about her fake relationship with Jax got exposed? Then it would seem like she'd scammed Max out of the land. "I'll only take you up on the offer if I pay the fair price for the land," Simone said, determined not to take no for an answer. Of course, Max had no way of knowing she was a billionaire.

"Okay, if you insist." Max said, the corners of his lips tilted up in a smile, one that was very much a replica of Jax's. It was amazing how much they resembled each other. "Does this mean you'll be joining us?"

Simone chuckled. "I'm definitely interested in the partnership, whether my clinic is located here or elsewhere. But we'll need to hash out the terms."

"No problem. Let me know what you have in mind, and I'm happy to meet them as much as I can."

"I'll have my lawyer put together a draft. How about I get back to you in a week? It would also give me enough time to make a decision about my clinic location and let you know one way or the other about the land."

"Sounds good to me. It's a deal." Max extended his hand for a gentleman's handshake. Simone shook it in return. "Welcome onboard, Dr. Addison."

Max had no idea how much this deal meant to her. "Thank you."

A knock sounded, and the door swung open. Becca came through bearing a tray filled with drinks and delectable desserts steaming with enough fresh bakery smell to set Simone's mouth watering.

"I hope I'm not disturbing anything," Becca said with a smile.

"You came at the right time," Max replied, his eyes filled with tender love as he gazed at his wife.

Simone's heart twisted in sadness. This was what she'd lost—a chance at this kind of relationship with Jax. Would he ever forgive her?

"Oh good," Becca said as she placed the tray in front of Simone. "Feel free to grab whatever you like," she said. "They're fresh out of the oven."

"Thank you," Simone said.

"Would you like to join us?" Max asked.

"Can I?" Becca asked.

Max nodded. "Our business discussion is done."

"Great." Becca pulled up the other visitor's chair

closer to where Max sat and settled in. But it meant two pairs of eyes were now turned in Simone's direction.

Why did it seem like an inquisition was about to start?

Simone picked up a warm brownie and bit into it, then popped the rest into her mouth. Where was Jax when she needed him? "This is delicious," she said, her mouth full of brownie, even as her hands scrambled to pull out her phone onto her lap. Thankfully, his number had been imprinted on her mind all these years.

"Thank you," Becca replied.

Simone kept a smile on her face even as she sent an urgent text to Jax.

Help.

CHAPTER 30

Jax checked the spreadsheet in front of him once more, but the numbers didn't change. The cost of feed and hay had gone up, much more than he'd forecast for the month.

He removed his glasses and rubbed the bridge of his nose. He'd have to chat with Dex and Fred, the ranch manager, to understand what was going on there. Hopefully, it was just because of inflation and not because of any hidden costs. As the ranch's CFO, Jax had to make sure its finances had no leakages of any kind.

His phone pinged with the sound of an incoming text, and Jax reached for it even as he scanned his spreadsheet one more time before glancing at the phone's screen.

He froze at the word on the screen and then jumped to his feet. It had to be from Simone, though it was an unknown number. This could only mean one thing, since Simone was supposed to call him once she was done with her meeting: his family had descended on her like a cat about to devour its favorite fish.

Jax shut off his computer and raced out of his home office and then his home. He had to get to her before their story fell apart. Simone could hold her own, but his family was anything if not tenacious.

Soon, Jax arrived at the main house. They weren't in the living room, which meant Simone was likely in Max's office. He hurried through the French doors and entered Max's office without knocking.

"What is—"

"Sorry, Max, for barging in," Jax said, ignoring the scent of cupcakes and brownies that filled the air. "Are you done with your meeting? I need to talk to Simone before she heads out."

"Jax, why do I feel you're up to something?" Becca said, with a twinkle in her eyes.

Trust Becca to have a good read on him, but Jax wasn't admitting anything. "Sorry, Becca, didn't see you there."

"How did you know Max's meeting was over?" Becca asked.

"Sixth sense?"

"Sixth sense indeed."

"Hey, you can't blame a guy for being in tune with his fiancée. So, Max, are you guys done?"

"We're finished here," Max replied. "I'll wait for your call, Dr. Addison."

"I'll get back to you soon," Simone replied with a smile, a sharp contrast to the "help" text he'd received. But Jax knew better.

He reached for Simone's hand and helped her to her feet. "I'll see you guys later," he said to Becca and Max. Then he led Simone out of the office.

Jax kept his hand linked with hers even as they made their way through the hallway, into the living room, and out the front door. He tried to ignore the feeling of rightness he felt, like her hand was where it belonged.

He released her hand once they reached her car.

"Thanks for coming to my rescue," Simone said.

"It's nothing."

"I'll understand if we pretend what just happened in there didn't happen."

"Why? Are you so quick to want nothing to do

with me that you can't even pretend to be my fiancée anymore?"

"It's not that—"

"Then what is it?

Simone took a deep breath and looked him in the eye. "I know you said it in the heat of the moment to keep your family from meddling in your affairs. But you don't have to keep up the pretense if you don't want to."

He took a step toward her. "Do you want to keep up the pretense?"

Her breath quickened. If he hadn't been looking closely, he might have missed it. "It's fine with me," she said, maintaining eye contact with him.

As he stared into those eyes, Jax knew if he wasn't careful he'd be swallowed hook, line, and sinker back into them.

He broke eye contact first. "Okay. Let's take care of some housekeeping items first. Are you married?"

"No," Simone replied.

He'd assumed that was the case, with her showing up at the singles' mixer. "Engaged?"

"No, well, except for this."

"Going on blind dates?" The question slipped out before he could help himself. Now why did he ask? It wasn't his business, anyway.

"No. The singles' mixer was the first one in five years."

Jax's breath hitched. She couldn't mean that, right? That she hadn't been with anyone since him.

"What about you?" Simone asked.

"What?"

"Are you engaged?"

"I wouldn't need this fake relationship if I was, would I?"

She shrugged. "I had to ask. Any lady of interest in your life?"

"None that matters. And how about you? Any rich young men waiting in the wings? The last thing I need is anything that would shame my family."

"None," she said quietly.

The air between them grew heavy, silent, and awkward with the memories of what had happened between them.

"Was that your number?" Jax asked after a moment. "The one you sent the text with?" He had to ask, though he was sure it was a yes.

"Yes, that's my number," she said.

So, she'd kept his number on her phone all these years. Why? The question raced through his mind like an arrow, but Jax flicked it aside. It probably meant nothing, and there was no sense in thinking otherwise. Besides, she'd been the one to end the relationship, not him.

Jax saved her new number on his phone. "So you're now a dermatologist," he said.

"A pediatric dermatologist, though I sometimes see a few adult cases."

"Congratulations."

"Thank you," Simone replied, her cheeks turning pink.

Was she blushing? Why? Hadn't she been the one to kick him to the curb? "Are you planning on working with my brother?"

"I'm not sure yet. Would that bother you?"

It could complicate things, but they'd figure it out. "It doesn't matter to me."

Her face fell at his words.

But what was she expecting him to say? He wanted nothing to do with her business, for his heart's sake, except for this fake deal between them, which was exactly what it was—fake, not real.

"You still work on the ranch as the CFO," she said.

"Mm-hmm," he said noncommittally. "Still, and will always be a cowboy."

"That's nice."

Nice? Sure, she'd said nothing against him being

one while they'd dated, but wasn't that one reason she'd ended things between them? Because he came from a world different from hers?

Simone was bringing up all these confusing thoughts in his mind, and it was time to get away from her. For now, even though his body craved to spend more time with her, and his fingers itched to tuck an errant strand of hair behind her ear.

"So let's be clear," Jax said. "Everything between us is fake. There's no relationship, and we won't need to talk or contact each other, unless there's a reason from my family's perspective to do so. Is that understood?"

"What if someone wants to make a move on me in my circles? Can I introduce you as my fiancé? In case it gets back to your family."

She had a point, though it was unlikely their families would run in the same circles. "Maybe as a boyfriend." Posing as a fiancé outside of his family would be too complicated. Folks would start expecting wedding bells, and that was a quicksand he had no plans to step into. *Keeping it uncomplicated is the best way*, he told himself.

"Alright," Simone said.

"Anything else?"

"None at the moment."

"Good. Have a pleasant trip home."

She nodded and unlocked her car.

Jax opened the door for her. His ma had raised him right, no matter what had happened between him and Simone.

"Thank you," she said and entered her SUV.

He watched as she locked in her seatbelt, gave him one last look, and then reversed out of the parking space before driving off.

"Why didn't you kiss her?" a familiar voice said from behind him.

Jax jumped. "Come on, Dex. You've got to stop springing out from behind me like this."

Dex wrinkled his nose. "I smell something fishy."

Jax kept his face impassive. "I don't know what you're talking about. Mind your business."

Dex's face turned serious, and he laid a hand on Jax's shoulder. "Just be careful, okay? I don't want you getting hurt again." Then he patted Jax's shoulder and headed into the family house.

Jax watched him leave. Hurt again? What did Dex know? Yet Jax couldn't ask him. It would lead to all sorts of questions, and knowing Dex, would eventually make their farce of a fake relationship come crashing down. So, no, he wouldn't ask.

Dex turned back to Jax as he reached the house

entrance. "Oh, and by the way, Maggie wants you to bring her for Sunday dinner." He winked and then entered the house.

Jax's heart sank. Sunday dinner. He'd forgotten about the one meal everyone in his family had to attend. It was tomorrow, and the whole family would be there. He'd been avoiding it for a while now because of Rex.

But Maggie had given a command, and he had to obey.

Jax would have to face both Rex and Simone, since he had a feeling Simone would make it, even with the last minute's notice.

He ran his hand through his hair. What was he going to do?

CHAPTER 31

Simone couldn't get over what had happened today as she settled into her couch in a black T-shirt and cream pants, her curtains open to receive the late afternoon sun rays. She'd left for Dexin this morning to meet with Max, hoping he was Jax's brother, and had returned this afternoon engaged to said Jax, even if it was a fake one.

Jax. He'd looked even hotter up close than when she'd seen him at the event. When he'd touched her, her nerve endings had gone on overdrive. But she'd sensed an angry undercurrent running through him, something that'd never been there before, and one she believed might be her fault.

Because she'd hurt him.

Simone's heart had dropped when he'd called her

out as his fiancée. If someone had hurt her as much as she'd done him, she doubted she'd ever want that person within standing distance of her, much less even holding his hand and announcing a relationship with him.

She straightened. Wait a minute. Could this be revenge for what she'd done?

Her shoulders relaxed. Well, she'd be happy to be his fake fiancée a million times over if it made him feel better.

Simone opened the jar she'd brought with her from the bedroom, scooped some of the skin cream, and rubbed it all over her hands, her nostrils inhaling its faint citrus and coconut scent, even as her thoughts continued to whirl.

But how did she truly feel about this fake relationship?

It was a blessing, for sure. Fine, it could end up in heartbreak for her when it was over, but she considered it a full push through the door of Jax's life, when all she'd been hoping for was a crack through the window.

Nothing or no one was going to make her miss this chance of a lifetime.

Her phone rang from where she'd placed it on the coffee table.

Simone leaned forward to check who was calling.

Her heart skipped a beat. It was Jax. Was she dreaming?

She scrambled to answer it. "Hello?"

"Hi, Simone," he drawled.

Butterflies rose in Simone's stomach. "Hi, Jax," she managed to say.

"Did you arrive home safely?"

"Yes, I did. Thanks for asking." It couldn't be the reason he called, could it? She didn't think he liked her that much yet to do so, though it could be his usual cowboy manners showing up.

There was a moment of silence on the line before he spoke again. "Maggie just invited you for Sunday dinner with the family. Can you make it?"

Simone sucked in a breath. Sunday dinner. With Jax's family. An invitation to the inner circle. Did this mean what she thought it meant?

Get your head out of the clouds, Simone, she chided herself. It was just a simple dinner, and she was a fake fiancée, after all. If it was anything more, Jax wouldn't have wanted her there, and he wouldn't have called to ask. "Sure," she said.

"Okay. I'll let her know you'll be coming."

"Is there anything I need to know before then?"

There was a pause on the line. "Let's stick to the

general story as much as possible," Jax then said. "We met five years ago and dated on and off until a few weeks ago when we got engaged."

"So we first met at the hospital in Vegas."

"Correct."

"And the engagement?"

"Two weeks ago. At a dinner at the Bilridge Hotel."

Simone froze. Was he referring to the one dinner that never happened because she'd ended the relationship? Why?

"So I'll see you on Sunday?" Jax's voice intruded on her thoughts.

"I'll be there," Simone promised.

"Alright." The line went dead.

The phone slipped from Simone's grasp onto the couch as her mind raced.

The dinner at the Bilridge Hotel.

She'd regretted missing it over the years, but she'd never imagined it'd never left his thoughts. If Jax had selected it as their fake engagement spot, then it meant it'd been something special to him.

Her head dropped into her hands as her heart ached with the knowledge.

She'd been such a fool. Jax must have been meaning to ask her to marry him then, and she'd slammed the door in his face without knowing. She truly deserved every bit of his attitude toward her right now. She'd hurt and scarred the heart of the man she loved. How was she going to make it up to him?

Simone raised her head. There was one thing she could do. She'd be the best fake fiancée ever, no matter what it cost her. She had to help his heart heal and be whole again, even if their fake relationship eventually ended and he married someone else. Yes, she would do this for him.

But first Simone had a dinner date to plan for.

It was time to call in reinforcements.

CHAPTER 32

"**Y**ou did what?" Paisley screamed from the love seat across Simone as her short, wavy, red-gold bob swayed with her. Simone had invited her over and updated her on all that had transpired earlier today.

"Relax, Paisley," Simone said. "It's just a fake relationship."

"With your heart on the line," Paisley pointed out. "You think I don't know you?"

"I miss him," Simone said quietly. "I didn't realize how much until I saw him again."

Paisley rose and then settled beside her. "I know, babe. But this is risky." She took Simone's hand in hers. "Do you recall how devastating it was for you when he left the last time? You were like a zombie for over a year, and I worried if my friend would ever come back. I don't want you going through that again."

"It won't be the same this time around," Simone reassured her as she placed her other hand over Paisley's. "Of course, it'll hurt if it doesn't work out, but it'll be a closure of some sorts. Besides, I owe him this much."

"Only because he doesn't know the whole truth. Will you ever tell him?"

"I don't know, but I can't think about that for now. I need to make sure he's okay first."

"Don't you think him knowing would help him too?"

"I'm not sure." It wouldn't change what had happened between them and could make things worse. It was best to deal with this at Jax's pace. "Anyway, I don't believe now is the right time to tell him the truth."

Paisley patted her other hand on Simone's. "If you say so." Then she released Simone's hands. "What's next?"

Simone leaned back. "I have to find an outfit for the Sunday dinner. I don't know what to wear."

"Did you say Sunday? What about the standing dinner with *your* family?"

Simone had forgotten about it, and she'd even promised her mother she'd be there when she'd called earlier in the week to confirm.

But she couldn't blow this opportunity with Jax, so there was only one choice.

Simone picked up her phone and dialed. "Hello, Mother," she said when the line connected.

"Simone. To what do I owe the honor of this call?" her mother asked pleasantly.

"I won't be able to make tomorrow's dinner," Simone said.

"But you already promised." Her mother seemed disappointed.

"I'm sorry, Mother, but something came up."

"Is everything alright?" Her mother had shown more concern than usual toward Simone in recent times, and Simone was unused to it.

"Everything's fine. Just something I need to take care of."

"Are you sure? What happened?"

"It's nothing. Just something that came up I need to handle."

"With work? Okay. I'd hoped to see you tomorrow, but it is what it is. Oh well, next time."

Simone didn't bother correcting her assumption. The last thing she needed was her mother letting anything slip to her father, and a work excuse would typically not raise his suspicions. "Thanks, Mother. I'll talk to you later."

"Okay."

"Bye." Simone ended the call.

"I take it your mother wasn't happy about it," Paisley said.

Simone nodded. "But it's fine." She'd hoped for a chance with Jax, and she wouldn't let anything mess it up now. "What were we talking about before?"

"What to wear for the dinner."

"Yes, that. I'm thinking we either check my wardrobe for a suitable outfit or go shopping."

Paisley's eyes sparkled. "I'm sure you know what my vote's for."

Simone jumped to her feet. "Shopping it is then."

"That's my girl." Paisley rose as well and looped her arm over Simone's shoulders. "Don't worry, I'll help you pick the best outfit ever. Jax won't know what hit him when he sees you."

Simone turned to her. "Do you know you're the best girlfriend ever?"

Paisley grinned. "I aim to please. Let's go!"

CHAPTER 33

Simone had messaged Jax when she'd stopped to buy gas after she'd entered Dexin, so by the time she arrived at the ranch's main house that cool Sunday evening, she found him waiting for her outside, leaning against the wall like a photo model ready for his shot to be taken. How could he look more dashing than ever in a light blue shirt tucked into jeans, his familiar cowboy hat on his head? Simone wished she could capture this moment forever.

Jax straightened and reached her side by the time she'd parked in an available spot. He opened the door for her, and Simone got out onto the cobblestoned pavers. Fresh breezy air tinged with a familiar scent of cedarwood and masculine leather hit her nostrils, and she resisted the urge to inhale deeply.

"Hello," Simone said instead.

He acknowledged her greeting with a nod. Simone waited, hoping Jax would comment on the lovely green dress she'd bought for the occasion, but he said nothing else.

Her heart sank. Maybe he no longer liked her or found her attractive like he used to. But there was nothing she could do about it—you couldn't force someone to love you if they didn't. Yet she couldn't help the disappointment that coursed through her. *Chin up*, she told herself. She was here now for a dinner with Jax's family, and that had to be her focus.

"Is there anything else I need to know before we go in?" Simone asked.

"Not really," Jax replied. "My family ain't complicated."

His response chafed at her, a reminder her own family was anything but. "What about our story? Anything new you've thought of I need to keep in mind?"

Jax shook his head. "Everything remains the same. We stick to what we agreed on. We met five years ago and got engaged two weeks back."

Simone wished it were true, but having Jax in her

life even this way was better than all the years she'd missed him. "Who's at the dinner?" she asked as she locked her SUV.

"My foster mom, Maggie, and her husband, Peter. He's a surgeon, by the way. Used to be famous in New York."

"Wow! I didn't know she'd married." A memory of Jax with Maggie had slipped out once while they'd dated in the past, and Simone hadn't forgotten. "How do you feel about it?"

"He's a wonderful man and good for her. Fits right in. Then there's Max and his wife, Becca, who you've met."

"She's stunning."

"Used to be a celebrity."

Little wonder Simone thought she'd looked familiar, like someone she'd seen in one of those celebrity magazines Paisley loved.

"Max has a five-year-old daughter, Chloe, but she's already in bed," Jax continued. "So you won't get to meet her yet. Then there's Dex and his fiancée, Zoey, who's also a doctor."

"It seems you have a lot of MDs in the family." Simone would have fit right in if their relationship was real.

Jax shrugged. "It turned out that way. Finally, we

have Rex and his fiancée, Tara, and their teenage daughter."

Simone's eyes widened in shock. "Rex? He's back?" She'd learned briefly about his twin brother when they'd dated, and any mention of Rex had been a sore point for Jax.

"Hmm. Just a few weeks ago."

Simone laid a hand on Jax's arm. "How're you doing?"

A fluttering feeling arose in her belly when Jax didn't shrug her hand off. "I'm okay," Jax replied in a tight voice.

"I'm sorry."

Jax stayed silent, but Simone felt his muscles relax a little at her words.

Simone's heart went out to him. It seemed things were still rough between the brothers. Rex's disappearance, maybe just as much as her own betrayal, had deeply hurt Jax. He didn't deserve what they'd both done to him.

Then Jax stiffened and brushed away her hand as if he'd remembered how things truly were between them. Simone's hand felt empty, cold, as if it'd lost something, a place where it'd fitted.

He cleared his throat. "Anyway, that's who we have at the table today. Shall we go inside?"

Simone nodded.

Jax placed a hand at the small of her back, and electric tendrils fired up and down her spine at his touch. "Oh, I forgot to mention we'll also have to pretend to be affectionate when necessary," he said, his voice a gravelly whisper against her ear. "Hope it's okay with you."

"It's fine," Simone responded. It was more than *fine*. She'd missed his touch, and it appeared her traitorous body did too, because now it craved for more.

"Alright." Jax led her up the driveway until they reached the door. "Smile," he said quietly. "I can see a pair of eyes already peeking through the curtains. Just pretend you're in love with me."

If only he knew that wasn't hard to do, because she was and had always been a goner for him.

"Ready?" he asked as they reached the door.

"As ready as can be," Simone replied.

"Okay. Here we go."

Jax turned the knob and opened the door, letting her in. "Come in, sweetheart," he said in a loud voice with a Western drawl, like he'd flipped a switch as he pulled her to his side. "Welcome to the Dexin family and my family home."

A flurry of footsteps hurried in their direction, and

soon some of the familiar faces she'd met yesterday appeared.

"You're welcome!" Maggie said with the brightest smile Simone had ever seen as she pulled Simone into her arms. She smelled of cinnamon, roses, and home, and Simone basked in her warmth. "It's great to see you again."

"My pleasure too, ma'am," Simone said with a smile.

"Oh, just call me Maggie, like the rest of them," Maggie said as she released her. Then she turned to her side and gestured to a distinguished-looking gentleman. "This is my husband, Peter."

"Welcome to the family, Dr. Addison," Peter said as he shook her hand.

"You can call me Simone," she replied.

"Simone it is," he said with a smile.

"Welcome, Simone," Max said next, his hand extended as he shook hers in a warm grip. "I had no idea when I first reached out about work that you were also my sister-in-law-to-be."

"It wasn't your fault," Simone said. "I didn't know you were the same Max Jax always talked about."

"He talked about me?" Max said with a side glance at Jax. "Hope they were all good things."

"The best," Simone reassured him.

"Now why do I find that hard to believe?" Max said. "Simone, feel free to reach out to me any time you want naughty stories about Jax."

"You won't dare," Jax warned, taking a step in Max's direction.

"Boys, stop," Maggie ordered.

"Don't mind them," Becca said with a laugh. "They're always like this. Hello, Simone!" Becca looked beautiful as ever in a pair of jeans and a stylish baby doll dress that barely hid her baby bump. Simone wished she could look as good as Becca did if she ever got pregnant.

"Hi, Becca! You look stunning."

"Why, thank you!" Becca's cheeks flushed with pleasure at her words. She smacked Max's arm where he stood by her side. "See? I told you this outfit looked good."

Max chuckled, an endearing look in his eyes as he gazed down at his wife. "You look beautiful as always, my love."

"Now you say," Becca muttered under her breath.

"I'm Dex," said a younger version of Max, who could have passed for his twin. "And this is my fiancée, Zoey."

A beautiful brunette with a warm smile shook

Simone's hand. "Nice to meet you, Simone. Welcome to the family."

"Thank you," Simone said. "I heard you're an MD, too. "

Zoey nodded. "Emergency Medicine. And you?"

"Pediatric dermatology."

"Wow! That's a hard residency to place into. You must be in demand."

"It can be busy. Do you work in Dexin?"

"Just started. Got an offer from Max I couldn't resist."

"Can we shelf the shop talk for now, people?" Jax interjected. "I'm hungry."

"I'm Rex," a face that looked the same yet different from Jax said to her.

So this was the elusive Rex. "Nice to meet you," Simone said with a warm smile. "Welcome back."

"Thank you," Rex said, his smile matching hers. "And this is my wife, Tara Rose."

"The wife/fiancée," Tara said with a twinkle in her eye. "That's a story for another day."

"And this is our beautiful daughter, Hailey," Rex said, pulling forward a slim, teenage girl, who was the mirror image of Tara. Simone wondered what the story was, given Tara looked to be in her early thirties.

"Hello, Ms. Simone," Hailey said.

"Nice to meet you, Hailey. Just call me, Simone."

"Thanks, Aunt Simone."

Simone hid a chuckle. This was a girl who knew her mind and stuck to it, like a lot of teenagers did these days. She'd seen enough of them in her clinic to know.

"Alright, everyone. It's time to eat," Maggie said. "Jax, Simone, we'll wait for you while you go wash your hands."

"Yes, ma'am," Jax said. "This way, Simone."

Jax led Simone down a hallway on the left to what looked like a mud room, with a log bench against one wall, rows of boots on the low shelves, jackets and raincoats hanging on higher racks, a few closets set on the opposite wall, and an open door she assumed led to a bathroom. Simone had one at her horse stable, but they'd built this one to match the architecture of the home, and it was lovely.

"You can wash up first," Jax said. "I'll wait outside." He moved toward the door.

"Hold on," Simone said, halting Jax in his tracks. "I only need a second to wash my hands." She moved toward the bathroom without waiting for his reply and stepped in.

It was clear they'd spared no expenses in the bathroom's design with its brick walls set in subtle shades of warm brown that matched its beige marble floor tiles, a large oval distressed mirror above the sink, and antique-brass fixtures for both the sink and shower areas.

Simone could feel the full gaze of Jax on her as she reached the sink and washed her hands. She wasn't sure why she'd asked him to stay—maybe she was a masochist at heart and just loved to be tortured by his aloof presence.

Once she'd finished, she reached for a towel to wipe her hands, but there was none on the towel holder and plenty of used ones in the towel basket a few feet away. *It must be because of the number of people in the house tonight*, she thought to herself. She turned to the left to see fresh towels stacked on the upper racks of the towel shelf—the lower racks were empty.

Simone stood on tiptoes and reached for a towel, but her fingers barely brushed any of them.

Suddenly, a figure loomed over her from behind, the powerful scent of cedarwood, masculine leather, and hints of coconut filling her nostrils and wrapping her like a warm coat on a frosty night. Jax reached over and lifted a few towels from the racks.

"You could have asked for help," he said, not moving away nor handing the towels to her.

Simone's breath caught in her throat. Her heart raced from his nearness, and she fought the urge to reach out and touch him, to pull him down for a kiss on those sumptuous lips, the taste of which she'd never forgotten.

After what seemed like forever but was probably only a few seconds, Simone bit her lower lip to come to her senses. She wasn't sure what she'd do next if they stayed in this position any longer. "Thank you," she said.

"You're welcome." Jax stepped back and handed her a towel, placed another on the towel holder, and the rest on the lower racks where they'd be more accessible.

Simone wiped her hands slowly, giving herself a moment to calm her racing heart. She was sure her face was flushed, and she hoped others at the dinner table wouldn't notice.

"I'm done," she finally said as she tossed the used towel into the towel basket.

"Give me a minute, and I'll be right out," Jax said.

Simone stepped out of the mud room. She needed that extra moment too to recover herself. By the time

Jax came out, Simone was back to her calm self. Soon they rejoined the others, who still waited in the foyer.

Maggie led the group through the living room and into what Simone guessed was the dining area. A massive farmhouse dining table like she'd never seen sat in the center of the room, piled high with a sumptuous array of food, with its tantalizing aroma wafting through the air. Simone's mouth watered and her stomach growled in anticipation just from looking at all the food.

"We had to get an extension to accommodate everyone," Jax whispered from beside her.

"Grab a chair where you can," Maggie ordered.

Everyone got seated, and Simone found herself sandwiched between Jax and Rex. *This would make for an interesting dinner*, Simone mused.

"Max, would you lead us in prayer?" Maggie asked.

"We thank you, God, for this wonderful family and for all the delicious food we're about to eat. Bless the hands that prepared it. Thank you for bringing Simone into our lives. In Jesus' name, we pray."

There was a chorus of *Amen* all around.

Then they all dug in. The food was delicious, and

Simone couldn't get enough of the roasted barbecued chicken served over hash browns and topped with bacon shavings and smoked Gouda cheese sauce. *I'll work out tomorrow*, she promised herself as she took another spoonful.

The sound of laughter and conversation filled the room with the atmosphere, warm and inviting. Simone found herself smiling or making small conversation in between bites. If this was how family dinners were meant to be, she wanted more of them in her life. Soon, all that was left was dessert. Simone's favorite was the fruit and cake kabob, with toasted cake, grilled apples, and strawberries on a stick. She even added a small dollop of ice-cream on top to go with it. *Delicious*, she thought as she practically inhaled the last piece.

"I'm glad to see you're enjoying the meal," Becca said from across her.

"It's delicious," Simone said.

"Thank you. It's actually the work of Dex and Maggie."

Simone's eyebrow rose. "Dex?"

"Yes," Dex chimed in. "I'm a fantastic cook, if I say so myself. Unlike someone I know sitting beside you."

Was he referring to Jax or Rex? Simone wondered as she took a sip of water.

"Hey, I can cook," Jax protested. So he'd meant Jax. "I'm just not crazy about it like you." He gave Max a curious look. "Why are you staring at me like that?"

Max dropped his utensils on the plate and leaned back. "I'm wondering why you attended the singles' mixer if you were already engaged to Simone."

"Can you say no to Miss Prissy?"

"Ok. I take back my question."

Simone chuckled. She knew first-hand how forceful Miss Prissy could be.

"What's funny?" Dex asked Simone. "Have you heard about Miss Prissy?"

"I've met her a few times at my clinic, and she invited me to the mixer as well. I was there too."

Surprised glances turned in her direction. "Why did you attend?" Becca asked.

"Miss Prissy didn't know I was engaged, since Jax and I had kept the engagement private." *Please God, forgive me for the lie.* "Besides, I needed to keep the other ladies off Jax." She could say this one was true.

Maggie cast a scolding look at Jax. "You could

have just told me you were in a relationship, and I would have let you off the hook," she chided.

"I'm sorry, Maggie," Jax said with a sheepish smile. "I just wanted to keep our relationship under wraps a little longer."

"Why? We're on your side here."

Peter placed a hand on Maggie's. "Sometimes young men need to take their time on some things."

"But I didn't raise him to be deceitful," Maggie said.

"I'm sorry, Maggie." Jax got up, came around to where she sat, and gave her a hug from behind. "Things were a little complicated."

"Don't do that again."

"I'll try."

Maggie swatted his hand away. "Try? You better not do that again, or my skillet may visit your behind!"

Jax chuckled. "I'm too old for that, Maggie, but I get the message. Straight and narrow it is."

Maggie smiled. "You better."

Simone watched the scene playing out in front of her. So this was what it meant to have a mother who cared for her child, and Maggie wasn't even Jax's biological mother. Suddenly, Simone wished she was truly a part of this family, and not some fake fiancée that would eventually leave.

"I hope the family isn't too much for you," Rex said from the other side of her.

Simone turned to face him. "Your family is wonderful. I'm having a great time," she replied.

"Good. I know we can sometimes be too much, especially for folks who don't know us."

"I love it. The camaraderie and banter I mean. And it's obvious you guys care for each other."

"Thanks for saying that," Rex replied with obvious pride in his voice.

Simone felt a familiar arm snake its way around her shoulder and pull her away. It seemed Jax didn't like her talking to Rex. She turned to see him back beside her, an inscrutable look on his face. "It's getting late," he said.

This was her cue to leave, so she rose to her feet. Jax got up as well. "Maggie, thank you so much for inviting me to dinner," Simone said. "I had a wonderful time, and the food was absolutely divine. But it's time for me to leave. I need to get back to Boston tonight."

"You could stay at Jax's place," Maggie said. "I'm sure he can behave himself for one night."

Maggie had no idea Simone was more afraid of

what *she'd* do if she stayed with Jax. It would be like detonating a primed bomb. "It's fine," Simone said. "I'll need to head into work early tomorrow."

"I'll make sure she gets home safely," Jax promised Maggie.

"You don't have to follow me back to Boston," Simone said. "It's no problem."

But the frown on Maggie's face said she thought otherwise.

"Really, it's fine," Simone reassured Maggie. "It's not that long a drive. I'll have Jax let you know once I get home."

Maggie studied her for a moment and then nodded. "Okay."

"I'll see her off," Jax said.

Maggie came around and gave Simone a hug. "It was great seeing you. Don't be a stranger. Our home is open to you twenty-four-seven."

"Thank you," Simone said as she returned the hug and then released her.

"You should totally come for the slumber party," Zoey said.

Simone turned in her direction. "Slumber party?"

"Yes," Tara replied. "It's a post-wedding slumber party for our female doctor friends from Dexington. Becca, Zoey, and I will be there. Since Becca is pregnant, we've decided to host it in Dexin instead of Dexington. It'll be lots of fun, and it's next Friday evening at six. Say you'll come."

Simone couldn't remember ever attending a slumber party, even as a child, but she'd heard it was a load of fun.

She glanced at Jax. Attending the party might bond her more with his family, and she didn't think that was something he'd want. Her eyes widened when Jax gave her a tiny nod.

Simone turned back to Tara and Zoey. "I'll be there," she said.

"Awesome," Zoey said. "We'll have matching PJs available in your size, so you don't have to worry about what to wear."

"Thanks again for the invitation. Have a good night, everyone."

"You too," they all chorused.

Simone gave them a last wave before heading out, with Jax by her side. They exited the house and soon reached her SUV.

She unlocked her vehicle and then faced him. "I hope dinner went well by your standards."

"It was okay," he said noncommittally.

"I'm surprised you said yes to the slumber party."

"It would have been weird to say no."

Simone's heart fell. So this was his rationale for giving the go-ahead. For a minute, she'd hoped for a different reason, like maybe wanting her to get to know more about his family. But beggars couldn't be choosers.

"Okay. Thanks for dinner." She turned back to her car and opened the door.

"Simone…" Her skin tingled where his hand touched her arm.

She looked back at Jax. "What?" she breathed. Her heart pounded as she waited to see what he'd do.

His hand dropped. "Nothing."

Simone studied him for a moment and then entered her vehicle.

"Let me know when you get home," Jax said.

"Will do."

She shut her door, started her engine, and backed out of the parking lot. Soon all she could see in the rearview mirror was Jax standing in the distance as she drove out of the ranch.

Simone would never know what he'd been about to say or do, but she still had a chance to reach his heart.

Thank goodness for slumber parties.

CHAPTER 34

Jax left the cool, breezy night behind and entered his home, a single-level house made of stone and log just like his brothers' places, but with one exception—his had an attached workroom. The interior, from the large open-concept living and dining area to the gourmet kitchen with its massive granite countertop and kitchen stools, boasted various shades of blue and grey decor, with the occasional bold zigzag or multi-color stripe pattern to give it some pizazz.

He hung his car key on its hook near the door, headed to his master bedroom, which was bathed in soft shades of blue—Jax had painted each bedroom a different color—and changed into his work clothes of long-sleeved Henley and pants before heading to the workroom.

Jax punched in a complicated set of codes on the keypad and then entered the cavernous space, the smell of honey and coconut tickling his nose.

His shoulders relaxed. This was his happy place, and he loved to work here each night before heading to bed.

Jax had picked up the candle-making hobby after the breakup with Simone. Unlike Dex and Rex, who'd loved leatherworking and tinkering with vintage cars respectively since forever, Jax had no hobbies growing up, despite enjoying various activities over the years. He'd fallen in love with the craft after he'd discovered it during another session of endless browsing on the internet to avoid thinking about Simone.

Jax had then turned the space into his workshop and installed a separate ventilation system. The blended scent of beeswax and coconut wax and the few scented oils he liked to use calmed him and helped him sleep better. From what had started out as a hobby, Jax now supplied some local and out-of-state shops with his creations, and the resulting sales funded a few local charities.

He grabbed and donned his apron, work gloves,

and high-top work boots from the rack by the door and headed to the curing area of his workshop to check out the batch of chess piece candles he'd made more than a week ago as a special order from an upscale boutique gift shop in Dexington. Jax examined each piece and nodded appreciatively. The candles were curing nicely, and in just a few more days, would be ready for shipping.

Jax then moved to his experimentation area, where he tried out new designs and new molds that caught his fancy. He'd been focusing on marbling lately, and the resulting colors and designs he'd come up with were interesting, yet not up to his personal standard. Jax settled in on his work stool and soon lost track of time, fine-tuning some of the promising designs and checking to see if they were replicable. By the time he checked the industrial clock on the wall, it was almost midnight.

He pulled off his gloves with a sigh. As much as he'd love to spend the night here, he had to be up early tomorrow morning to help with the horses.

Jax cleaned up the work area, returned everything back to its designated spot, and then closed the workroom door behind him. After a quick shower and a glass of warm milk with some cookies Dex had given him yesterday, Jax settled into bed. The thoughts he'd kept at bay while working came rushing back.

An image of Simone in her green dress filled his mind. She'd looked stunning, and it'd taken everything in him to keep his hands off her. But more than that, it had impressed him how she'd seemed at home with his family, like she'd always belonged there.

Jax frowned. He had to be careful here. He'd only gone along with Maggie's invitation just to show Simone what she'd missed by cutting him out of her life—his wonderful family, the camaraderie amongst them, and the comfort of knowing they always had your back no matter what.

But he had no plans to give her a second chance or a place in his life. Since she'd burned him once without looking back, what would stop her from hurting his family next? That was a risk he'd never take.

He'd only hoped for revenge when he'd declared her his fake fiancée, but he had to admit having her around was more difficult than he'd imagined it'd be. She'd gotten his thoughts and feelings all mixed up, and right before she'd left, Jax had almost pulled her in for a goodnight kiss, a ritual they'd had when they'd dated. That would have ruined everything and complicated matters.

Worst of all, seeing her chat with Rex had annoyed him. It was already bad enough the whole family had accepted Rex so quickly, but he didn't need Simone to do the same. She had to be on his side, not Rex's.

Jax couldn't deny he avoided interacting with Rex whenever he could. His feelings got all twisted up whenever he sighted Rex, and Jax wasn't ready to address the issues between them.

Yet it surprised him how he felt. If anyone had told him he'd react this way with Rex back in town, he wouldn't have believed it. What was he avoiding? But it scared Jax to dig deep into himself to understand why, so it was easier to just run away. He chose to ignore the issue, even though he sensed things would come to a head between them sooner rather than later.

Because dealing with Simone was already hard enough without adding Rex into the mix.

Jax sighed and tucked his pillow in snugly around his head as he felt himself drifting off to sleep.

One thing was for sure.

He had to be careful around Simone if he wanted this farce to continue.

CHAPTER 35

Simone's phone rang as soon as she stepped into her home. The roads had been clear tonight, so she'd made it back to Boston sooner than she'd expected.

She pulled the phone from her pocket and stared at the caller ID, tempted to toss the phone under a couch cushion and ignore it until she'd taken a much-needed shower. But experience had taught her it was better to rip off the band-aid now than later.

"Hello, Father," she said.

"Where were you tonight?" her father demanded in a no-nonsense tone. "Your mother said you had work commitments, but we both know dermatologists don't work weekends."

"Seeing patients in the hospital or clinic isn't the

only work we do. I had prior commitments," Simone said as she dropped her handbag on the couch.

"Don't play smart with me."

"It's been a long day, Father." She let out a sigh. "What do you want me to say instead? That I didn't feel like engaging in any verbal spars with you tonight?" Which was partly true.

The line went silent. He mustn't have expected her to say that. "Make sure you don't cancel on your mother next time," he said after a moment. "It's important to her."

"Noted," Simone said. "Good night, Father."

"Good night," her father responded. Then the line went dead.

Simone collapsed back onto her couch. Thankfully, she'd dodged that bullet. But maybe she shouldn't have been so snippy with him on the call. The last thing she needed right now was her father poking his nose into her business.

Her phone rang again.

Simone stifled a groan. Who could it be this time? Her face relaxed after she checked the screen, then knocked off her heels as she answered. "Hey, girlfriend."

"I've been waiting for your call like forever," Paisley said.

The corners of Simone's lips turned up into a smile. Trust Paisley to exaggerate as usual. "I just got in."

"So how did the dinner go?"

"It was nice."

"That's all you're going to say? I need deets!"

"Seriously, it was nice. Like how a family dinner should be. You know that warm and fuzzy feeling like you're where you're meant to be and with people who genuinely care about you and see you? That's how it was to me."

Paisley squealed. "I'm so happy for you. You needed it."

"I really did. My heart felt light and happy."

"So how was Prince Charming? And his brothers?"

Simone thought for a moment. "He was cold, not that I blame him. But his brothers were very welcoming."

"Tell me more. About the brothers, I mean."

Simone chuckled. "They're hunks just like Jax. The total package, if you ask me. Unfortunately, they're taken. I met their significant others as well."

"That sucks. I wouldn't have minded a cowboy for myself and becoming your sister-in-law would have been an extra perk."

Simone laughed. "Sorry to burst your bubble."

"It's okay. These are the first days yet. Maybe we'll find one the next time you go, say a cousin or a close friend. You're going there again, right?"

Simone relaxed on the couch. Trust Paisley to remain optimistic, as usual. "Hmm. His sister-in-law, Becca, invited me to a slumber party next week."

"Wow. You must have impressed her!"

"I don't think so. They're just really nice people."

"Slumber parties are so much fun. What did Jax say about it?"

"He didn't react negatively to the idea, so I'll assume he's okay with it. Speaking of which, I need to let him know I'm home."

"You're ditching me now?"

"You know I'll never do that. Best friends forever."

"It's fine, it's fine. Gotta keep Mr. Lover Boy happy." Then Paisley's tone turned serious. "I'm happy for you, my friend."

"I'm glad. I wasn't sure they'd like me, but it turned out I shouldn't have worried."

"I hope things work out between you two."

"I hope so too."

"Well, I'll let you go before Lover Boy wonders what happened to you."

"Talk to you later, girlfriend."

"Bye, darling," Paisley said cheerfully.

Simone chuckled and ended the call.

She considered calling Jax but ended up texting him instead.

> Just got home. Thanks for inviting me to dinner.

A response came almost immediately. Had he been waiting for her call?

> You're welcome.

> Please send my regards to Maggie and your family. I had a great time meeting them.

> I'll let them know.

It appeared he wanted to keep his responses short and to the point. Well, Simone didn't want to come across as too clingy in hers. Maybe it was best to end the conversation here.

> Good night.

> Good night.

Simone dropped her phone beside her. Jax could

be as cold as he liked, but it didn't matter. She'd be patient and would wait, regardless of how long it took to break down his walls.

Thank you, God, for the opportunity to see him again next week, Simone prayed, as she rose and made her way to the bedroom.

Now she had a slumber party to look forward to.

Simone parked in front of the Dexin home and stepped out with her overnight bag. Jax had called earlier to ask if he could pick her up, but she'd declined. It'd been a busy day at work, and she hadn't been sure when she'd be done. Thankfully, her last patient had cancelled, so she'd made it home, showered, and left Boston on time.

"Did you have a good week?" a familiar voice asked from beside her.

Simone's heart did a flip as she turned. Where had he appeared from? Jax looked hot as ever in a black T-shirt paired with jeans and cowboy boots, the warm colors of the clear sky serving as an effective backdrop. It seemed he was a T-shirt man these days instead of the rolled-up sleeves he'd always preferred.

But she didn't mind.

Not at all. Not when she could view his corded biceps whenever she liked.

"I did," she said. They hadn't spoken at all during the week, and Simone had been hesitant to call him, since the relationship was fake after all. "You look good."

"Thanks. You don't look so bad yourself." Simone was in a simple white blouse and skinny jeans paired with boots to match the country vibe. "Let me take that." He reached for her overnight bag.

"Thank you," she said and handed it over to him.

"Becca is waiting for you inside, and the other ladies are already here."

"Okay." Simone was looking forward to meeting the ladies from Dexington, since they were doctors as well.

They stepped into the home and met Dex in the living area.

"Hello, Simone," Dex said cheerfully.

Simone gave him a warm smile. It never ceased to amaze her how alike Jax and his brothers were. "Hi, Dex. Nice to see you again."

"Same here."

Jax dropped the overnight bag at the foot of the main couch. "Becca should be here soon. She's putting the finishing touches to the slumber party venue."

The timing worked for Simone. She'd agreed to meet Max anyway before heading into the slumber party.

"Would you like anything to drink?" Jax asked.

"A glass of water would be fine."

"Okay." Jax headed into the kitchen.

"Why don't you sit?" Dex said.

Simone perched on the edge of a loveseat. "Thank you."

Dex grabbed a seat as well. "So what do you think of Dexin Valley?" he asked.

"Other than it bears the same name as your last name?"

Dex chuckled. "Yes, other than that."

"I think it's cute."

He laughed. "That's a word I've never heard used for this town."

"It's true. I love its cozy vibe, and life seems to be much slower here."

Dex's eyes twinkled, and he leaned forward. "Could you see yourself living here?"

"Dex, leave my girl alone," Jax interrupted as he returned with a tray sporting a glass and a bottle of water.

"Hey, I'm just making conversation," Dex said.

"Yeah, right." Jax placed the tray on a side table beside the loveseat. "Here you go," he said to Simone. Then he settled in beside her.

"Thank you." She opened the bottle and poured a generous amount of water before gulping it all down. "Sorry. I was thirsty."

"No worries."

Dex stared at them suspiciously. "Are you sure you guys are engaged?"

"What do you mean?" Jax said.

"How come you guys never kiss?"

Simone's ears warmed. His brother just had to be nosy.

"Says who?" Jax fired back.

"I don't believe you," Dex said.

"Why do you care?"

"Prove it. It shouldn't be hard to give her a kiss." Dex turned to Simone. "Don't you think so, Simone?"

Of course, Simone wouldn't mind a kiss from Jax, but what he wanted was what mattered.

"Dex, leave my girl alone," Jax warned.

Dex leaned back and grinned like a cat who'd eaten a canary. "You guys are really not dating. Hmmm… maybe Maggie needs to know."

If looks could kill, Dex would have died on the spot from the glare Jax gave him.

Simone touched Jax's arm to calm him. The last thing she needed today was an altercation between brothers.

Jax turned to her, and his eyes searched her face. "I'm sorry," he breathed. Then he pulled her in and kissed her.

Simone's heart took off like a race car set loose on the tracks. What started off as a mild kiss that sent sparks down her spine turned into a punishing one that crushed her lips yet lit a fire in her. This wasn't the Jax she'd known—this was a man marking and claiming his territory, letting her know her lips belonged to him despite what she'd done. But Simone wasn't some meek lamb, though she'd hurt and now owed him, so she pushed back, pouring all her love and desire for Jax into that kiss. She had to let him know he'd always mattered to her, and that had never changed over the years.

"Woah! Totally didn't expect that," a child's voice said.

They broke apart like naughty kids caught with

their hands in the cookie jar. Simone had forgotten they had an audience, and that audience had increased in the time they'd been kissing to include Max, Becca, and a beautiful girl with startling blue eyes and short red hair who had to be their daughter, Chloe.

Simone's face warmed, and she wished she could crawl into a hole and hide.

But then Jax pulled her into a hug, into that chest she was so familiar with. This was the Jax she knew, the one that always protected her from awkward situations in the past. "Chloe, you know you should close your eyes when adults are kissing," Jax said.

Chloe shrugged. "It was entertaining, watching you almost eat her up like that." She turned to Max. "Daddy, kiss Mommy like that, too. I'm sure she'll like it like Aunt Simone did."

"Chloe!" Max and Becca chorused, their faces flushed with embarrassment.

"Sorry," Chloe, the five-year-old going on fourteen years, said with a contrite look on her face. "I'll go to my room now. Nice meeting you, Aunt Simone. Mommy already told me about you." She turned and headed to the wing she shared with her parents. But then she looked back and gave Jax and Simone a thumbs up and a smirk before running down the rest of the hallway.

Simone's lips twitched into a smile. Chloe was sure special. Such a beautiful child. She wished she'd have one like her in the future, though she wasn't sure when that would be, with the way things were with her and Jax. Would the pretend relationship always be pretend?

In the meantime, she sent a silent thanks to Dex for making the kiss happen. It was everything she'd dreamed of and so much more, and now she even had Jax's arms around her. What more could she want?

"Simone, it's nice to see you again," Max said. "Why don't we head over to my office for a quick chat before I hand you over to Becca?"

"Sounds good to me," Simone said, though she would have loved to spend the rest of the day in Jax's arms, even if it meant missing the slumber party.

Jax released her. "Don't worry, I'll take care of the overnight bag," he said quietly. "I'll see you tomorrow morning."

Simone nodded and rose to her feet. "After you," she said to Max.

Soon, they sat on the couch in Max's office.

"I'm sorry about Chloe," Max said. "She meant no harm."

"Don't be. She's adorable," Simone said.

"She is, isn't she?" Max said with a beam of pride on his face. "Well, I'm glad things are going well with you and Jax."

Simone's face and ears felt impossibly hot at his words. She'd really made a fool of herself. "Thanks," she mumbled.

"Okay, let's get down to business," Max said as he straightened. "I received a physical copy of your signed version of the agreement a few hours ago. Thank you for that."

Their legal teams had met a few times and revised the agreement to the final version Simone and her lawyers had signed yesterday. "I prefer physical paperwork over an electronic signature," Simone replied. "Hope that works for you."

"That was perfect. My lawyers and I have already signed it, and it should be on its way back to yours."

"Awesome." They'd concluded the land transaction as well.

Max rose to his feet and extended a hand to her. "Welcome to Dexin Medical Center, Dr. Addison."

"My pleasure, Dr. Dexin. I look forward to working with you once the clinic is all set up."

"Let me know if you need the info for my contractors. They did a fantastic job for the hospital and kept to the timeline. I also have a building team who oversaw the hospital project, and I'm more than happy to outsource them to you for however long you need them."

"Really? That would be wonderful." It would make life easier for Simone to have a local team on the ground.

"Great. Let me make some calls and set things up for you."

"I need a favor, though."

"What?" Max asked.

"Would it be okay if I broke the news about this to Jax myself?"

"Sure. This is business. I won't breathe a word about it unless you do."

"Thank you once again, Max."

A knock sounded on the door, and Becca poked her head in. "Are you guys done?" she asked. "I need Simone."

"She's all yours," Max said, and winked at his wife.

Becca's ears turned red, and her face lit up with a smile.

"Have a wonderful evening," Simone said to Max as she stood.

"You too, Simone. Enjoy the slumber party," he replied.

"I will."

"Let's go, Simone," Becca said, looping her arm with Simone's. "Why don't we head over to *my* office?"

CHAPTER 37

Simone had never been to Becca's office before, but Becca had transformed the space into a pink and gold slumber party wonderland. Soft pink teepees covered twin size pink-covered air mattresses filled with throw pillows in matching colors and each with its own mini-nightstand.

She'd then arranged them in a semi-circle to face a wall with a large, flatscreen TV. Plush cream and gold rugs covered the floor with pink and gold decorations and dimmed lights hanging from the ceiling.

A section of the space boasted an array of finger foods with tantalizing smells—shrimp cocktail, mini cucumber sandwiches, cheese-stuffed cherry tomatoes, sandwich rolls, crispy stuffed mushrooms, cilantro tomato bruschetta, shrimp salad appetizers, buffalo wings, asparagus wraps, cauliflower bites, salad kabobs, veggie-stuffed jalapenos—and desserts. Simone's stomach growled at the sight of all the food. She'd eaten nothing since she'd left work and couldn't wait to dive in.

"Wow. I can't believe this used to be an office," she said.

"I know, right?" Becca handed her a set of soft pink pajamas with gold lining. "Here are your PJs. Hopefully, they're the right size."

"Thank you," Simone said as she accepted them.

"The bathroom is this way." Becca pointed out a door Simone had missed. "Your overnight bag is already there."

The corners of Simone's lips turned up. Jax had kept his word.

A few minutes later, Simone was back in the office after changing into the pajamas. They were softer and comfier than she'd expected, and fit her just right. She'd even found a pair of house slippers nestled in the pack she'd received.

By this time, Tara and Zoey were now in the room, as well as three other ladies Simone didn't recognize, all dressed in the same pajamas as her.

"Hello, you must be Simone," said one of them, a

gorgeous redhead of average height. "I'm Jasmine Banks. It's a pleasure to meet you."

"Me too. I'm Simone Addison," Simone said.

Jasmine's eyebrow rose. "Addison of Boston?"

Had she heard of Simone's family? "Yes."

"I've heard of your father," said the second tall lady with a model physique and lovely dark hair. "My father-in-law, Phillip Dexington, might have mentioned him before."

It wouldn't have been good news then. Her father was well-known as a ruthless businessman. "You mean Dexington of Dexington city?"

"The same," the lady replied. "I'm Alicia Dexington."

"Nice to meet you," Simone said.

"And I'm Dana Roman," said the third petite lady with a sun-kissed blonde pixie cut.

"It's a pleasure to meet you," Simone replied.

"I'm glad you came," Tara said with a smile.

"Thanks for inviting me."

"Well, ladies, we can get started," Becca said as she breezed into the room. She had on the same outfit, but they'd customized it to accommodate her baby bump. Yet she glowed like she was ready to pose for the paparazzi. "How about pictures to commemorate the event?"

"Sure," Jasmine said. "I have a selfie stick that would work."

They gathered around and took several poses, including silly ones. Simone couldn't remember when she'd laughed so much. The evening was already starting off better than she'd expected. Soon everyone grabbed some hors d'oeuvres and desserts and settled on the air mattresses.

Simone bit into the crispy mushrooms stuffed with creamy crab, artichoke, and spinach filling. "This tastes so good," she said with a full mouth.

"Maggie made them," Becca said. "She's the best cook ever."

Zoey nodded in agreement. "I think I might have gained a few pounds since I got engaged to Dex."

"How do you do it, Aunt Becca?" Jasmine said. "You've maintained your figure." That was when Simone noticed the resemblance between them and the matching green eyes.

"I ride every day," Becca said, "but not since I got pregnant. Now I take long walks around the ranch."

"How far along are you?" Simone asked.

"Almost five months," Becca said. "I have some time to go."

"You don't look it."

"Thanks. But I can't wait for it to be over. I'm

tired most of the time and feel sleepy at random times."

"A boy or a girl?" Simone asked.

"A boy," Becca said. "All the guys, especially Max, are so happy about it. I hear they've been planning all the things they'll teach him around the ranch."

"Dex said they've also signed up for babysitting and diaper duty," Zoey said.

"Max already made a roster," Becca said with a smile.

Alicia and Dana burst out laughing while Jasmine shook her head. "Guys. Always planning," she said. "But that's a fantastic idea. We should totally get our guys in Dexington to do the same once one of us gets pregnant."

"I agree," Alicia said. "I'll bring up the idea with Blake. That's my husband," she said to Simone.

"Wait! Are you preggs?" Dana said.

"Not yet. But who knows? It's better to be ready with these things."

"I agree," Tara said. "You've got to warm them up to the idea."

They continued chatting as they ate until they were done. Then they cleared the plates and left them on a kitchen trolley cart outside the room where Max would take care of them.

"This feels so good," Tara said as she stretched out on her air mattress.

"I know," Becca said. "Max had them custom ordered. Said he wanted me and the baby to be comfortable."

"I can just lie here and do nothing else," Alicia said. "It's been a long day at the hospital."

"What's your specialty?" Simone asked.

"Internal medicine," Alicia replied. "Jasmine is an ob-gyn, and Dana is a pediatric surgeon. How about you?"

"I'm a pediatric dermatologist in Boston, though I sometimes have adults patients."

"Nice," Jasmine said.

"I'm an ER doc, and Tara is a radiologist," Zoey said.

"That's like a whole hospital right here," Becca said. "You ladies can just open up your own facility. I'll be your CEO."

"That's not a bad idea," Dana said. "But location would be a problem. We have Dexington, Dexin, and then Boston."

"True. Also, Max would have a heart attack since

he just opened Dexin Medical Center," Becca said. "But it's a nice dream."

"So, do we want to watch a movie now?" Alicia asked.

"Can we first talk about the elephant in the room?" Jasmine said.

The other ladies all nodded with knowing smiles.

Simone's forehead furrowed. What elephant? She'd noticed no topic they'd needed to address.

"That kiss was so hot, Simone," Tara admitted. "He sure wanted to gobble you all up."

Simone's face grew warm, and she hid her face in her hands. This was so embarrassing.

"Hmmm… I've got to give Josh some pointers. I need a kiss like that," Dana said.

"True," Alicia said.

"You guys, stop," Simone said as her ears heated.

"Okay, okay, we'll stop," Becca said. "But for the record, that was a hot kiss," she said as she fanned herself. "I didn't know Jax had it in him."

"It's always the quiet ones," Dana said.

"I wouldn't call Jax quiet," Zoey said. "Now, Rex, he's the quiet one. With that bad boy look, I'm sure those are his types of kisses." She winked at Tara.

"Hey, stop talking about my man!" Tara protested. "I love his kisses just fine, thank you."

"Oh, we know. He's always sneaking in a kiss whenever he gets a chance. We see you guys," Becca said.

"You ladies are all bad. Bad, bad girls that love kissing," Tara said.

The girls laughed. "Nothing wrong with kissing your man," Jasmine said. "Just wait until you get married. Then you get the total package. It's heaven, I tell you," she finished with a smirk.

"That's so unfair to us unmarried ones," Zoey said. "You're evil!"

"Sorry," Jasmine said. But the look on her face said she wasn't sorry at all.

Simone watched the exchange and camaraderie in wonder. Who'd think a bunch of lady doctors could be at ease and banter with each other like this? Paisley would love it here.

"What are you thinking?" Dana asked quietly from beside her.

"My friend Paisley would fit right in here with you guys," Simone said.

"Then invite her next time."

"Really," Jasmine said from across her. "A friend

of Simone's is a friend of ours, and the more the merrier. She's a doctor too, right?"

"Yes, she's a neurologist."

"You should totally bring her," Alicia said. The rest of the room nodded in agreement.

Simone's heart warmed. They hadn't met Paisley, yet they'd already accepted her into the fold just because of her. This was what she'd been missing all these years. Her eyes misted at the thought.

"Don't cry," Becca said. "You'll get us all bawling too." She was already wiping at her eyes.

"I'm sorry," Simone said. "It's just surreal, you know, all this warmth and acceptance."

"Especially from ladies who understand all the years of training and suffering we had to undergo," Dana said.

"Besides all the extra baggage we've had to carry all our lives," Jasmine said. Alicia put a hand on Jasmine's like she understood what she meant.

Simone nodded in agreement. They got it. They really did.

"Simone," Becca began. "I know something is going on between you and Jax, something you guys can't talk about." Tara and Zoey nodded. "But I want you to know it'll be okay. Everything will work out just fine, I promise," she said, her voice like a soft blanket that enveloped Simone.

Simone didn't know when the waterworks began, the tears pouring down her face like a river that had just broken through a barrier.

Jasmine scooted up and wrapped her in a hug, the others surrounding them, murmuring words of encouragement and hope to her. They stayed that way for a while, all the despair, self-hate, and guilt pouring out of Simone, replaced by all the love and warmth she was receiving.

After some time, the tears dried up and someone handed her some tissues, everyone else giving her some room to breathe. Simone dried her eyes and blew her nose. "Sorry for being a mess," Simone said.

"We'll take messy any day," Alicia said. "We've all had those days and come out just fine."

"Absolutely true," Jasmine said.

"I can't have kids of my own," Dana said.

"I had one that I gave up because of postpartum depression, and I couldn't tell her I was her mommy," Alicia said.

"I had a sister and stepmom who hated me," Zoey said.

"I had the breast cancer gene and had a double mastectomy," Jasmine said.

"I was raped and gave up the child from it for adoption," Tara said. "Thankfully, I have her back in my life."

Wow. These ladies had been through some really tough patches, yet here they were, happy and with the loves of their lives. Simone hoped this would be her one of these days.

"Max's stalker drugged me, and we ended up married without knowing it," Becca said. Jasmine burst out in laughter.

"Hey!" Becca said.

"Sorry, Aunt Becca," Jasmine said between chuckles. "I can't help it. This story gets to me every time. And guess what?" she said to Simone. "They got separated for five years and didn't know they were still married! Only found out when they reconciled and tried to get married again."

The rest of the group broke out in laughter.

"I'm glad I'm your source of entertainment this merry evening," Becca said, the corners of her lips turned up in a smile.

"You're welcome," Dana said, which elicited more laughter from the group.

"I'm so sorry for slobbering at your slumber party," Simone said to Alicia, Jasmine, and Dana.

"Don't worry about it," Alicia said. "What's a slumber party without some slobbering?"

Dana nodded. "It's true. Jasmine did the slobbering at the last one."

"Hey, I wasn't the only one!"

"Well, you were the lead singer, and we were the backups on that one," Alicia said.

"You ladies are so funny," Tara said. "Are you always like this?"

"Sometimes worse," Becca said. "Okay, now that all slobbering has ended, can we visit the main agenda for this slumber party?"

Jasmine gave her a quizzical look. "We have an agenda?"

"Of course," Becca replied. "We want to hear all the details about newly married life from you guys."

"Really?"

"What do you ladies think?" Becca asked Zoey and Tara.

"Yes!" they chorused.

"See?"

"Okay. I'll start," Dana said. She leaned forward. "What is it with guys and throwing their socks on the floor when there's a perfectly good laundry basket a few feet away?"

"Girl, you married a mama's boy," Becca said.

Dana's eyes widened. "How did you know? He says his mom picked up after him at home, and it didn't matter at his place, since the housekeeper took care of it when she came to clean and cook in the morning."

"So what did you do?" Zoey asked with interest.

"Well, I have this godmother who's like a second mom to me. She's single and always ends up on interesting dates. Met one guy who was an inventor, and he'd invented this robot that you could tell what to say and what action would trigger those words. I remember he'd given her a model, so I asked her for it."

Everyone, including Simone, leaned forward to hear where this story was going.

"Once I got home, I set it up to speak as soon as the bedroom door opened and waited on the bed for Josh to return from the hospital," Dana continued. "Josh got back, opened the bedroom door, and this robot blasted out, 'Josh Roman, put your dirty socks in the basket!'" Everyone burst out laughing. "Josh was so startled he obeyed the command before it could say another word!"

"Oh my goodness," Tara said as she wiped tears from her eyes.

"So what happened next?" Zoey asked.

"The robot now speaks any time he enters the bedroom. It does the same for me, but I ignore it. Josh has begged me to remove it, promising he'll never drop his socks on the floor again. But I told him I'll take it away only after he's proven to me for ninety days that he can drop the socks in the basket before the robot speaks."

"Why ninety days?" Becca asked with interest.

"Because that's more than enough time for it to become a habit!"

"That's sneaky of you," Alicia said with a laugh.

Dana shrugged. "It's that or pick up socks after him for the rest of my life, and that ain't happening."

"I agree," Becca said. "Better to train him early."

"But he's still the best husband in the world, dirty socks saga and all," Dana finished.

As they chattered away, Simone felt her heart grow light. This group, this acceptance, was what she'd needed all her life.

And it had all happened because of Jax.

CHAPTER 38

Jax heard their laughter as he crossed the foyer to grab a snack from the kitchen. The ladies seemed to be having a great time, something he was sure Simone would enjoy.

But what had he been thinking when he'd given her that kiss? Was he so starved of her touch he'd almost made a fool of himself? And right in front of his family, too! His brothers must think he'd become a maniac.

Jax had holed up in his home office right after the incident. He'd avoided going to the horse barn, since Dex and Rex would have gone there to make sure the horses were down for the night. Dex, for sure, would have said something—his brotherly concern for Jax could be overwhelming sometimes. But the rumbling of his stomach and the thought of a nighttime snack had drawn Jax out to the main house despite the late hour.

"What's up, bro?" a voice said from beside him.

Jax nearly jumped out of his skin as he turned to face Dex. "You scared me!"

"Do you have something to be afraid of?" Dex said as he reached for the coffeepot on the kitchen countertop. The deep-roasted aroma of freshly brewed coffee emanated from it as Dex poured some for himself.

"Nothing."

"So, why did you almost maul Simone over there today?"

Trust Dex to just go there. But had Jax been that hard on her? He'd only meant to kiss her because everyone had been expecting it, but didn't know why he'd gone overboard. But this wasn't a conversation he wanted to have with Dex. "Don't know what you're talking about," he said.

Dex leaned against the countertop and looked Jax in the eye. "I don't know what's going on between you two, but don't you think it's time you man up and talk about it with her?"

"It's none of your business, Dex."

"It is, when you're acting crazy, yet you obviously love her."

"Love her?" Dex surely had it all wrong.

"Yes, you fool," Dex continued. "You have the hots for her, and your eyes track her every movement, even when you think we don't notice. But, Jax, a relationship is not all roses. Sometimes you have to work out the hard stuff, no matter how difficult it is to tackle. It's the only way you can get past it. And Simone seems like a good person."

If only Dex knew. But Jax would never throw Simone under the bus in front of anyone, no matter how much he hated her now. It was best to just pretend this conversation with Dex never happened. "I have to go," Jax said.

But it seemed Dex wasn't done. "Remember how Ornie used to attack that muddy spot beside the horse barn over and over again?" Ornie was the resident goat and Chloe's pet. "Don't be like him."

"What's that supposed to mean? Am I now a goat?"

"You can be stubborn like one sometimes." Dex took the mug of coffee he'd poured for himself and left the kitchen.

Jax slumped against the rustic cabinets. Maybe he was being stubborn, but he didn't know how to be anything else around Simone. She was turning him upside down and inside out, making him feel all out of sorts, and he had to protect his heart from getting hurt again.

He let out a sigh. Maybe it was time to end this fake engagement.

The next morning, Jax stood on his porch as he drank his coffee and stared out at the magnificent view of the distant mountains before him. He loved spending a few minutes here each morning, but this time, the view didn't calm his tumultuous thoughts.

Jax rubbed his forehead with his free hand. He'd turned and tossed all night and now had a mild headache to go with it.

The thought of breaking up with Simone had him in twists, despite the fakeness of the situation. Maybe he'd gotten too used to having her by his side, a habit and nothing else. It couldn't be he was falling in love with her again.

No, it couldn't be that. Hadn't he learned his lesson the first time? Maybe this whole fake relationship had been a mistake, though it sure didn't feel like one. Her nearness thrilled him, her laughter, when he could hear it, warmed his soul, and his eyes couldn't get enough of her, so much so that he felt a part of him was missing when he couldn't see her.

Jax ran a hand through his hair. How could he be this way after their history together?

But no matter how he felt, no matter how much he wanted to keep her in his arms and never let go, Jax wasn't sure he trusted her enough to stay true to him. And that was the fundamental problem. She behaved like she'd always liked him, yet she'd been the one to end the relationship, and now she was back. Why? He'd waited to see what she'd do, yet she hadn't bothered to give him any explanation for her actions.

Trust was important to Jax in any relationship. How else would they be able to weather the storms of life together as a couple if it didn't exist between them? Because storms would surely come, no matter how rich or poor they were. Jax had to trust she wouldn't just up and leave him one day, and with Simone, there wasn't that guarantee. He couldn't afford to let himself sink any deeper than he already was, and he wasn't sure he'd survive another heartbreak from her.

Jax let out a long exhale, his decision made. His family, who meant the world to him, would be disappointed in him when they found out, but it had to be done.

He'd end their relationship today after he'd made sure she got home safely, no matter how much it'd cost his heart.

CHAPTER 39

The ladies woke up late on Saturday and spent the rest of the morning and afternoon exploring Dexin together, so Jax and Simone didn't leave Dexin until evening. By the time they arrived in their separate vehicles in front of her home, the sun had already set.

Jax stepped out and waited for Simone to exit her SUV. It was time to let her know about his decision.

Simone got out, and Jax couldn't help noticing how radiant she looked in the graphic tee she wore over blue jeans. He'd miss her, but he had to do what was right for his heart.

"Thanks for following me back," Simone said.

"You're welcome," Jax said.

They both fell silent, and the air between them

grew awkward.

"I have something to say," they both said at the same time.

"Okay, you go first," Simone said.

"You first," Jax said.

"I insist. Please."

Alright. He'd do as she'd asked. "Simone... I don't think this fake relationship thing is working, and I think it's time we end it."

Simone stilled, and her face fell. "Why?"

Well, that was a question he wasn't expecting. "The reason doesn't matter, since it was never real."

"I need to know."

Did he have to give her a reason? "Why? Like you told me the truth when you broke up with me?" Jax took a step forward. "Since we need reasons now, tell me, Simone, why did you break up with me? You wanted another man, and then you got him. Fine, let's go with that."

By now, Jax's emotions were getting all worked up, but he kept a tight control over them. It was time he got answers. He moved closer. "So why are you back now, Simone? And don't give me that cock and bull story about work." Jax shifted until he'd backed her up against her vehicle with no room to run away. "Why are you back in my life, Simone?" His voice had dropped an octave lower. "To stab me in the back again?"

"I never wanted to hurt you!" Simone cried out. "I had no choice!" She put her hands over her face.

Jax took an involuntary step back. "What do you mean, you had no choice? I need the truth." She fell silent. "Now!"

Simone's shoulders fell. "My father vowed to ruin you and your family if I didn't break up with you," she said in a tone so heavy, like she had the weight of the world on her shoulders. "He's my father, but he's scary when he needs to be, and he never breaks his promises. Ever."

Her knees collapsed under her as if her words had deflated her, and she crouched. Jax moved back some more to give her room. "I couldn't let him ruin you," she continued in a broken voice. "You were the best thing that ever happened to me, the rain that quenched my thirsty heart and the sunshine that made it alive again, and I couldn't let him destroy you. So I had to agree to his terms. To cut you off in the manner he wanted and get into an engagement that would net him millions of dollars."

Jax couldn't believe what he was hearing. This couldn't be true.

"But I didn't realize how much you'd eroded my

heart, and it broke me," Simone continued in a dejected voice. "I lost myself after you left, and I didn't care about anything anymore. Days passed, and I didn't even know what time of the week it was. I could only pour everything into work, since it was the only thing that helped me get through each day without you. My father had no choice but to break the so-called engagement to save face." She looked up at Jax. "Living without you all these years has been hell."

Jax froze like a robot, all thoughts deserting him. Simone loved him. She'd always loved him.

He collapsed against her car and ran his hand through his hair. He'd been a fool—he should have pushed harder when she'd cut him off. Instead, he'd given up. "I didn't know…"

Simone rose to her feet and edged closer to him. "I'm sorry, Jax." She placed a hand against his chest, and her touch ignited his skin there. "I'm sorry for breaking your heart."

Their eyes met, and Jax saw the truth reflected in them. Yet something held him back. But why now? Why hadn't she come all these years to look for him?

Simone let her hand fall away and rested her back against her vehicle as she stared out into the quiet street. "It took me a while to recover from what had happened between us," she said, as if she'd read his mind. "I also needed to be strong enough to stand up against my father, and I couldn't take the risk during residency. My father is very influential and could have made it impossible for me to finish."

She'd mentioned her father twice now. They'd never talked about their family while they'd dated, and now Jax had to know. "Who's your father, Simone?"

Simone turned and looked him in the eye. "Sebastian Addison."

Jax became motionless. The famous corporate raider who was a terror to any company he'd set his eyes on? *The* Sebastian Addison? Jax had first heard about him in business school and on the financial news ever since. Word on the financial street was he wasn't a man to cross. No wonder Simone had broken up with him. Sebastian Addison would have kept his promise.

He ran a hand through his hair. Jax had been wrong about Simone. All wrong. He'd made a mistake and had given up. Jax had failed to protect both her and what they had together from her father. "I'm sorry, Simone."

"It's not your fault, Jax. You didn't know." She wrapped her arms around herself. "I should have discussed it with you, instead of facing it all alone. I'm the one who's sorry."

They'd lost so much. Themselves, their love, and their future together, all because of a man with an insatiable appetite for money and business.

Jax straightened. But it wasn't too late now. They could rebuild what they'd lost and plan a new future together. Because, like Dex had said, Jax still loved her and Simone felt the same way, too. No matter how ferocious her father was, Jax would face him if needed. He was a Dexin, and Dexins were fighters. He wasn't afraid of the man. Jax loved Simone so much he'd protect her with every fiber of his being.

"Jax..."

He turned and pulled her into his arms where she'd always belonged, even as her familiar rose and jasmine scent mixed with the fresh evening air encircled them both. She was back, truly back in his life. "I love you, Simone. I always have."

She broke down and sobbed, like his words were what she'd waited a whole lifetime to hear.

Jax pulled her in closer. She'd been wounded as much as he had, and he was sorry he hadn't seen that. He held her, stroking her back until her sobs subsided. He hadn't been there for her before, but he'd be here now.

"It was all my fault," she said.

"You did what you could. I've heard of your father, so I understand why. But know this…," he tilted her chin up and wiped away her tears until she could look him in the eyes, "I'll never let you go again."

"I always want to be with you," she whispered.

Jax stroked her cheek. "Me too." He'd keep his promise no matter what it took.

"About my father—"

"I won't let him hurt us again, and you don't have to worry about my family," Jax said. "We ain't that brittle," he finished with a deep Western drawl.

Simone's face lit up, and she laughed, the sound warming his heart and his insides. She was back. His Simone was back. Jax decided in that moment to find more reasons to make her laugh.

Then her laughter died, and her face turned serious. "There's one more thing I need to tell you," she said.

Another secret? Nothing could surprise him anymore after what she'd revealed so far. "What is it, my love?"

Simone took a deep inhale and let it out.

This had to be serious, Jax thought.

CHAPTER 40

Simone looked Jax in the eye. "I'm a billionaire." There. She'd said it.

Her insides twisted in anticipation as she waited for his response. Would Jax be disappointed in her for hiding such a truth from him?

The corners of Jax's lips twitched up. "Well, get in line and settle in," he said.

"Huh?"

"I thought the ladies told you at the slumber party."

"I'm not sure I follow," Simone said.

"Jasmine is an heiress, and she, Dana, and Alicia are all married to billionaires. Oh, and Becca too."

"You mean…"

"Yes, Max is a billionaire, and Rex is almost there

himself. It's nothing new in my family. So, like I said, get in line."

Simone couldn't help the laughter that escaped her. She'd been worried for nothing. "I didn't know."

"How could you? We'd promised not to talk about our families when we'd first dated. So don't worry. You'll fit right in. Besides, I'm not doing so badly myself."

Simone's eyebrow rose. "Really?"

"Really. Let's just say I have more than enough to take care of my family."

"That's good enough for me." She didn't mind sharing all she had with Jax.

"So, is there any other thing I need to know while we're doing this whole baring-our-hearts exercise?"

Simone thought for a moment. Maybe it was from Jax's nearness, but nothing came to mind. She chuckled. "I think that's it for now. What about you? Any secrets?"

"Hmmm… I have three brothers who drive me bonkers but who I'd fight to the death for and vice versa. I come from a town that's as gossipy as they come, but they're also super loyal, and I have an extended family that practically owns the city of Dexington."

Simone straightened. This was news. "You mean you're related to the Dexingtons? To Alicia?"

Jax nodded. "Alicia's husband, Blake, is a distant cousin of ours. That's why you have the Dexington, Dexin names."

"Ah, I see."

"I only mentioned it to let you know that my family can stand up to your father if need be. You have nothing to fear."

It felt good to know they'd be fine no matter what tricks her father pulled. Simone looked him in the eye. "So, do I get another chance?" She had to hear him say it.

Jax chuckled. "What do you think?"

"I don't know…"

The crush of his lips on hers didn't give her the chance to finish what she'd wanted to say. Jax kissed her like he was a drowning man, and only her lips kept him alive. Yet, there was the underlying tenderness beneath it all that had always been a signature of his kisses and one she'd always enjoyed, though she could get used to the new take-charge element his kisses now brought.

Simone gave back as much as she received and allowed the kiss to engulf her from the inside out. She lost track of time, space, and her bearing, her whole being focused on receiving the love Jax poured out to her. She lost any sense of where she began and where Jax ended.

"Get your hands off her!" a harsh, familiar voice barked out, jolting Simone back to reality.

Simone jumped back and stared at the last man she'd expected here.

The last man she wanted to see.

CHAPTER 41

Her father's presence loomed over the space as he marched toward them with Derek, his main assistant, at his side. "How dare you?" he boomed out.

Simone's emotions spun in a panic. She'd expected they'd meet her father eventually, but not now, and certainly not like this.

Then she felt Jax thread his fingers through hers, and the warmth from his touch calmed her. He pulled her to his side while extending his other hand to her father. "Good evening, sir. I'm Jax Dexin, Simone's boyfriend. It's a pleasure to finally meet you."

The storm reflected in her father's eyes warned how angry he was. "I know who you are. Now step away from my daughter," he commanded.

Jax released her hand, but then wrapped an arm around her shoulders instead. "I'm sorry you got to find out like this, but I love your daughter, and I plan to marry her."

Her father scoffed. "You'll do no such thing. Security, get this man out of here."

Simone now noticed the bodyguards that had flanked her father, only a few feet away from where their convoy vehicles waited. These guys were part of his personal security detail, made up of retired Marines and Navy Seals, and were more than capable of getting the job done.

She adjusted her feet into a fighting stance on the concrete pavers, letting Jax's arm fall away and pushing her shoulders back. After losing Jax, Simone had trained with a famous Boston mixed-martial arts instructor over the years for a moment like this, though she'd never imagined it'd come. No body-guard, trained or not, was going to stand between her and her man. "You won't have your way this time around, Father."

"You think you can stop me?" Her father bellowed out an amused laugh. "Have you forgotten what I'm capable of?"

Simone fought the familiar panic that usually arose at her father's words and pushed it down way deep until it turned into a steely resolve. She, no, they, could do this. "I'll do whatever it takes," she said. She glanced at Jax, and he nodded his agreement. Maybe it was time for her father to see cowboys had those corded muscles for a reason.

Her father chuckled, and then his eyes turned to slits. "You can't stop me," he said.

"But I can," said the last voice Simone expected to hear.

Simone's eyes swung in its direction, her mouth dropping open as a figure stepped into view.

"Annabella, what are you doing here?" Simone's father asked. His face held a quizzical look as Simone's mother approached in black Christian Louboutin heels, beautiful as always in a grey belted dress with pearls gracing her neck, every strand of her wavy kinky hair sculptured in place.

"Stopping you from doing something foolish," her mother said as she reached them.

"How did you get here?" His eyes searching the direction she'd emerged from. Her mother hated driving for reasons best known to her.

"I took a cab." At her father's astonished look, "I can get one of those, you know. Now, be a dear and get in the car," she said in a soft tone, but one that brokered no argument.

Her father obeyed, his bodyguards entering the car behind him.

Simone's eyes widened. In all the years she'd known her mother, she'd never seen her speak to her father this way, but it was more surprising to see his obedient reaction.

"Jax Dexin, is it?" her mother said to Jax.

"Yes, ma'am," Jax replied and looped his hand once again with Simone's.

Her mother noticed, and the corners of her lips twitched. "It's nice to finally meet you," she said with a warm smile.

Wait a minute. Was this her mother, or had someone replaced her? Her mother showing interest in her affairs and even knowing Jax's name? Simone pinched herself to be sure she wasn't dreaming.

"Me too," Jax said. "I'm sorry we had to meet under these circumstances."

"Then you can make it up by having dinner with us soon," her mother said.

"It'd be my pleasure, ma'am."

"Great. Once I set a date, Simone will get back to you with all the details, won't you, dear?"

Her mother inviting Jax to dinner? Was there a catch somewhere, a case of attracting a butterfly with nectar and then killing it? Not that Jax was a butterfly —he'd qualify better as a tiger, beautiful but dangerous when necessary.

"Don't worry, Simone," her mother said, as if reading her mind. "I don't plan to stand between you two." She sighed. "But right now, I need to chat with your father, and I'd rather it be a private conversation." She turned back to Jax. "It was great meeting you."

"Same here, ma'am," Jax said.

Her mother nodded. "I'll see you soon." With that, Simone watched as her mother headed to her father's car, entered, and then the convoy drove away.

Simone collapsed against Jax. "That was unexpected."

"Are you okay?" Jax asked as he wrapped his arms around her.

"I think so. It's just my mother… she's different. I almost couldn't believe that was my mother!"

"I'm glad she came, though I would have stood up to your father no matter what."

Simone laid her head against Jax's chest. "You did good."

Jax chuckled. "You were feisty too."

"I was, wasn't I? I wasn't going to lose you a

second time, even if it meant fighting off those guards."

"My tigress." Jax leaned down and kissed her.

This time the kiss was soft, warm and enveloped them into a world where it was only her and Jax, and nothing else existed.

Jax broke off the kiss a few minutes later. "Simone, this has to be for real this time. I'm not sure I can survive a second heartbreak from you."

"Don't worry, this is it for me," Simone reassured him. "You can't drive me away from your side even if you wanted."

"Well, that won't happen. You're stuck with me now."

Simone burrowed further into his arms. It was like she'd come home, to the place she was always meant to be.

But then a thought occurred to her, and she stiffened.

"What's wrong?" Jax asked.

"I'm worried about my mother. My father has always threatened me with their divorce whenever I got out of line or refused to do whatever he wanted. Despite what happened tonight, I'm not sure if my mother is strong enough to survive on her own if that happens."

"Do you want to go home and check on them?"

Simone nodded. She couldn't let her mother pay the price for her actions.

"Okay. Go," Jax said.

"But what about you?"

"What would you like me to do?"

"Wait for me here, if that's okay."

"I can do that."

"Thank you. The apartment's security code is still the same."

Jax leaned forward. "Why?" he asked in a low, teasing tone. "You were hoping I'd come back?"

Simone's cheeks warmed. "I guess I held out a tiny hope."

He chuckled. "Feels more than tiny."

She tapped him on the chest. "Hey! That's not a sin."

"I never said it was." Jax's eyes zeroed in on her lips. "Now go, before my mind does what it's thinking."

CHAPTER 43

Simone stepped into her family home. The grand mansion appeared dark and silent—her mother must have sent away the house staff for the rest of the night—but she heard faint sounds coming from the second floor.

She climbed the ornate stairs and followed the voices until she reached her parents' bedroom. The door was ajar, and some of her parents' conversation filtered out.

"I won't let you do that to our daughter again," her mother said.

"You mean your daughter," her father responded.

Simone's heart caught in her throat. What was her father talking about?

"So that's what this is all about," her mother said.

"For goodness' sake, you're the only father she's ever known!"

Simone's heart pounded so loudly in her chest she feared they'd hear it from within the bedroom. This couldn't be what she thought it was, could it?

"I can't help it when she looks so much like him!" her father shouted.

Simone's thoughts reeled. Who were they talking about? No, it couldn't be... Her knees threatened to buckle, and she leaned against the wall for strength.

"Is that why you've been so harsh on her all these years?" her mother said.

There was a moment of silence. "It's because you still love him," her father then said.

Simone's hand gripped the edge of the wall. Had she been born outside wedlock?

Her mother sighed. "He's been gone for many years, Sebastian. It's you I'm married to now."

Simone found it hard to breathe as her mind spun. Her father was someone else, not Sebastian Addison. Now everything that had happened between her father and her made sense.

So this was why he'd treated her so poorly all the time.

Little wonder he'd always hated her.

They'd both lied to her all these years...

Simone's breath caught in her throat, and she struggled to breathe. She needed air. She had to get out of here. This was all too much.

She spun, crashing into the door before hurrying down the stairs.

"Simone, wait!" she heard her mother say from behind her.

But Simone couldn't talk to her right now. She needed to be alone. In a safe place away from everyone.

She needed Jax.

CHAPTER 44

*J*ax looked up as the security lock to Simone's apartment clicked and the door swung open. He'd been pacing and praying as he waited for her return. Jax hoped they'd resolved the issue amicably.

His eyes widened as Simone shuffled in, her shoulders slumped, and her eyes full of unshed tears.

Jax hurried to her. "What happened?" he asked. "Are you okay?" He wrapped his arms around her.

"No, I'm not. It's…"

"Hold on." He shut the door behind her and engaged the lock. Then he led Simone to the sofa. "Tell me everything," he said.

Simone told him. What she'd overheard and what

she'd thought about as she'd driven home. It was a miracle she'd arrived safely.

"Now I know why he treated me differently all these years," she said. "It's all because I'm not his daughter."

"I'm sorry," Jax said softly. The news must have been a terrible blow.

Simone exhaled. "Don't be. It is what it is. But this is all too much for me right now."

Jax pulled her closer. "It'll be alright. Eventually."

"He must really hate me. Said I looked like my biological father."

"Did you talk with your mother?"

Simone shook her head wearily. "I couldn't stay there another minute."

The doorbell rang. Simone and Jax looked at each other.

"Let me check who it is," Jax said. He got up and padded to the security panel in the foyer and pressed a button. Simone's mother's image filled the screen. "It's your mother."

"I don't want to speak to her right now," Simone replied.

"Do you want me to tell her to leave?"

Simone nodded. "Maybe another day. Today is too raw."

"Okay. I think it's better I call her and let her know." He returned to Simone, who'd pulled out her phone and scrolled to a number before handing it over to Jax. Jax dialed the number on his phone and waited. "Good evening, Mrs. Addison," he said as the call went through.

"Who's this?" the familiar voice said from the other end of the line.

"Jax Dexin, ma'am. I'm with Simone right now."

"How is she? Is she okay?"

"I think it might be best to chat with her tomorrow."

Her mom let out a sigh. "I hadn't wanted her to find out this way." There was a moment of silence. "Let's do that. Please take care of her."

"I will, ma'am."

"I'm glad she has you by her side. Tell her I love her."

"I will."

"I'll be back tomorrow morning, then."

"Maybe mid-day might be better."

"Okay. Please tell her it's not what she thinks."

"I will."

"Good night." Jax waited until her mother ended the call.

"What did she say?" Simone asked in a whisper.

"That she loves you, and it's not what you think it is. She'll be back tomorrow."

Simone flopped her head against the back of the couch. "I'm not sure I'll be ready to see her. I just wish they'd leave me alone."

Jax pulled her into his arms. He wished he could take all the hurt away from her. "Why don't we just forget about all this for tonight?"

"Will you stay with me? Tonight?"

He couldn't leave her all alone with her thoughts. "I'll stay."

"Thank you," she whispered.

He kissed the top of her head. "Everything is going to be okay."

CHAPTER 45

Simone woke up to the clear morning light streaming in from between the curtains in her bedroom. Her head hurt, and she pressed a hand to her temple. She looked down at herself and noticed she still wore yesterday's clothes. What had happened? Then the events of yesterday came rushing back to her, and she drew her limbs close to her body.

It'd been all a lie. All these years she'd called the wrong man her father. Simone had craved his attention and love, doing all she could to please him, but she'd only ever gotten ashes instead. What a waste it'd been. Now it made sense why she'd lived with her grandma instead of her family all those early years of her life.

She stayed quiet for a few minutes, her mind turning over everything that had happened. After a while, she straightened. The truth still hurt, and she didn't know when it'd stop.

But one thing was certain.

Simone had suffered enough at her father's—no, stepfather's—hands without knowing the truth.

But no more.

She'd move on now without him in her life, no matter how much it hurt.

Simone glanced at the nightstand. Her heart warmed as she spotted the glass of water and bottle of painkillers resting on its surface. Jax must have left it for her.

But where was he?

Then she heard the sounds coming from the living area.

Simone downed a tablet of the painkillers before chasing it down with the water and headed to the bathroom where she washed her face, brushed her teeth, and ran a quick brush through her hair. Simone changed into lounge pants and a T-shirt from her walk-in closet and headed to the living area.

Jax had his back turned to her as he worked at the stove, the smell of sausage, eggs, and toast filling the air. He turned as if he'd sensed her presence.

"Good morning," Simone said as she gave him a back hug. He smelled of leather and aftershave, a heady scent of his she loved. "I see you found the T-shirt." Simone had kept a T-shirt of his he'd left behind as a reminder of him, and Jax was wearing it now.

"Good morning," he said jovially, and gave her a kiss on the cheek. "How do you feel today?"

The sight of Jax in the white T-shirt over jeans sure made her feel better. There was nothing like waking up to a handsome man in your kitchen. Better yet if the man was yours. Simone released him and plopped down on a kitchen stool. "Much better," she replied.

"Glad to hear it," Jax said. "I made breakfast." He plated the sausage and eggs, added some toast, and placed the dish in front of her. "Coffee or orange juice?"

"I'll stick with orange juice for today."

Jax grabbed the juice from the refrigerator and poured her a glass.

"Thank you," Simone said. "Aren't you eating?"

"I will." He reached for another plate and piled on the food.

"I'm sorry I made you miss church."

"It's okay," Jax said. "I watched an online service."

"You should have woken me to join you."

"I figured you needed the rest."

"Hope your folks aren't worried, since you didn't make it back home last night," Simone said.

"I called them yesterday to let them know. I travel sometimes for work, so they're used to it." Jax placed his plate on the granite countertop and then settled on a kitchen stool beside her. "Why don't we eat?"

Jax prayed, and they ate. The food was simple, but delicious. It surprised Simone that she'd worked up an appetite. Soon they were done, and Simone picked up the empty dishes.

"You don't have to do that," Jax said. "I'll take care of it."

"No way am I letting you do the dishes after cooking breakfast," Simone replied.

"How about we do it together?"

As Jax washed the dishes and Simone dried them, their arms grazed against each other, sending shivers of familiarity and warmth down her spine. Simone couldn't help but remember all the countless times they'd done this simple chore together, and how it always felt like a small reminder of their love for each other. She'd missed this.

Once they'd wiped down the kitchen, they moved over to the couch. Simone grabbed the remote and flipped through the TV and cable channels, but nothing caught her attention.

"What's your plan for today?" Jax asked.

Simone leaned her head against his shoulder, feeling safe and content in his nearness. "Nothing much." She needed some time to just clear her head and make sense of everything.

Jax twirled her hair around his fingers.. "Your mother already called this morning to ask how you're doing."

"Okay."

"She sounded like she hadn't slept all night."

Simone said nothing in response. She was too tired to sympathize with anyone right now. After all, her mother had hidden the truth from her.

"She mentioned she'll be here around noon." He looked up at the clock on the wall. "And it's eleven a.m. already."

With a reluctant heart, Simone rose to her feet. "I guess I should go shower."

"Simone…" She turned. "I can ask her to come back another time if you'd rather not speak with her now."

"I can't delay the inevitable. Might as well get it

over and done with."

"You can do this," Jax reassured her.

Simone gave him a small smile and then headed to the bedroom. She took a shower and dressed in a simple purple and white blouse paired with a pair of jeans and her hair in a ponytail.

The doorbell rang.

Simone poked her head out and gave Jax the go-ahead to answer the door before stepping back in and applying some light makeup. As the familiar scent of jasmine wafted into her apartment, Simone knew without being told her mother had arrived.

She took a deep breath, exhaled, and then stepped out of her bedroom. "Hello, Mother."

Her mother turned to face her. Jax was right. Her mother appeared a lot less put-together than usual. "Hello, Simone."

"Would you like anything to drink, ma'am?" Jax interjected.

"A glass of water, please," her mother said as she sank gracefully into the loveseat.

Simone sat on the couch opposite her. Jax brought two glasses of water and placed them on the coffee table between them, one in front of her mother and the other in front of Simone.

"I'll be out for a while," Jax said to Simone.

She wasn't sure she could face her mother alone without him. "Please stay," Simone said.

Jax crouched and tucked an errant piece of her hair behind her ear. "I think you need this time with your mom, but I can be in the study if that helps."

"I'd like that," Simone replied.

"Okay." He gave her a kiss on the forehead. "It's gonna be alright," he whispered. Then he made a beeline for the study and shut the door behind him.

Simone was now alone with her mother.

Her mother took a sip of her water and then looked Simone in the eye. "I'm sorry I hid the truth from you," she said.

"What's the truth?" Simone asked.

"It's best I start from the beginning." Her mother leaned back on the loveseat. "Your real father, Amos Easton, and I met one night at a book-store. He was this genius artist who'd worked hard over the years and was starting to make a name for himself in the art world. I'd come to the bookstore to buy some art supplies and bumped into him. It was love at first sight. I'd never believed in it, but I fell so hard for him I couldn't imagine marrying anyone else."

Her mother's hand played with the pearls at her neck. "We started dating soon after, and after a few weeks, I brought him to meet my parents. You can imagine how that worked out."

Simone had heard about how strict her grandfather had been, so it wasn't a stretch to picture his reaction.

"My father stood against the relationship and insisted I break up with him," her mother continued. "It turned out he'd arranged an engagement to Sebastian Addison without my knowledge. But there was no way I was entering a loveless marriage when I had already met the love of my life, so I asked my parents to end the engagement. They refused."

Her mother let go of the necklace. "I couldn't change their mind, so your father and I eloped," she continued. "Those first few weeks were the best times of my life, and your father was the sweetest man ever. He was kind, hard-working, and generous, and we were happy together. But he wanted us to make peace with my parents."

She took a sip of water before continuing. "On our way to my parents' home, we got into an accident with a drunk driver. I woke up in the hospital only to learn your father had shielded me, receiving the brunt of the collision and died on the way to the hospital."

Her mother paused, her eyes distant, as if lost in the memory of that moment.

"My entire world collapsed at the news." Her eyes now glistened with unshed tears. "Then I found out I was pregnant. I'd noticed that morning I'd missed my period, and your father and I had planned to stop by the hospital after visiting my parents. But to get the actual confirmation that you'd come into our lives when he was now no longer here to meet you was too much to bear. The news felt like the final weight that broke the camel's back, making it all too real that he was gone and would never come back. I couldn't function after that, sinking into a world of depression and despair.

"Your grandparents were worried about me and feared high society wouldn't accept me back. Young, pregnant, with no husband by my side, especially since they'd annulled my marriage without my consent while I was in the hospital. Society at the time differed from the way it is now. It turned out your stepfather had always had a crush on me and so he stepped up, determined to follow through with the engagement and marry me, despite knowing I was pregnant with another man's child. I no longer cared at that point since my Amos was gone. We got married and life continued, but never has a day passed that I've forgotten my Amos."

"If my father was that important to you, then why

did you check out of my life when I'm his only living legacy?" Simone asked. "You were never there for me, and you saw how my stepfather treated me."

Her mother leaned forward as if to reach for Simone's hands, and Simone drew back. Her mother touched the glass of water instead. "I'm sorry," she said. "It was all my fault. I found it hard to get over the loss and lost interest in most things over the years. But I came to my senses when I saw how devastated you were when Jax was gone from your life. It reminded me of what happened with your father and made me realize I'd been selfish and thoughtless, and Amos would have been disappointed in me all these years. So I decided to change and do better. But I'd let your stepfather take over my life all these years, and it can be hard to take back that control."

Her mother leaned back and brushed a strand of hair away from her face. "I also wanted to make amends, but I didn't know how to approach you. How could I when I'd failed you for so many years? You have to realize we parents don't always know more than our children. We can be cowards too, afraid we'd be rejected if we tried." Her hand rubbed the ruby ring on her left middle finger. "That's when I decided to watch over you and him from afar."

"Him?" Simone asked.

Her mother gave her a small smile. "Jax Dexin. I knew you loved him, and I needed to make sure he stayed single until you guys met again. Thankfully, he poured himself into his work and never looked at another woman over the years. But when I heard about the upcoming singles' mixer, I guessed there was a chance he'd meet someone else, so I thought I'd help get you moving in the right direction."

Simone's curiosity piqued. What was her mother talking about?

"I found out the organizer of the event, a Miss Prissy, was the guardian of one of your patients. I had an idea, so I dropped by your clinic one fine early morning on the day she was supposed to come."

"How did you even know the schedule?" Simone's clinic was meticulous about patient privacy.

Her mother gave her a thoughtful look. "Let's just say your stepfather isn't the only one who has his ways. Anyway, I happened to be in the same elevator Miss Prissy was in, and mentioned quite loudly that Dr. Addison was single, wouldn't mind settling down in a smaller town, and needed to mix more with other single folks like her. Miss Prissy took care of the rest, and so here we are."

Simone shook her head. Unbelievable. She didn't

know her mother had been hard at work behind the scenes.

Her mother leaned forward. "What kind of mother would I be if I let you lose the love of your life when he feels the same way about you?"

"But he hated me at the time."

Her mother waved away her objection with a flip of her hand. "Hate. Love. It's the same thing." Then remorse filled her face. "I'm sorry, Simone. For all the pain I've ever caused you, and for not being a good mother to you. For not been there for you. Do you think you can give me a chance to make it up to you?"

This was a lot to take in. Her mother's indifference had hurt her a lot over the years. She'd watched her friends and classmates with their mothers and families and wished she'd had one like them. But it'd always been one disappointment after another.

Yet she'd never expected her mother to ask for forgiveness and even go behind her back to help her win her love back. As much as her heart resisted opening up and getting hurt again, Simone wanted to give it a chance. It would be a struggle, since breaking old habits was never easy.

Simone had emotionally detached herself when it came to her family, and undoing that conditioning could be harder than she anticipated. But she had to try. "It'll have to be baby steps," she said to her mother. "We can't just be best friends from day one."

Her mother breathed a sigh of relief, as if she'd been holding her breath waiting for Simone's response. She took one of Simone's hands in hers. "Thank you. Thank you. I won't blow this opportunity, I promise."

Simone slipped her hand from her mother's. "Like I said, baby steps." She took a sip of her own water. "So, my father. What did he look like?" How much did she take after him?

Her mother rose gracefully to her feet. "I'd like to take you someplace," she said.

"Do you need me to go with you?" Jax asked Simone as they stood outside the open car door of her mother's chauffeur-driven Bentley. She'd had no time to tell him the details of the conversation she'd had with her mother, and her mother already waited in the car.

Simone held his hand as she shook her head. These days, she couldn't help touching him, maybe to set her mind at ease that he was right here with her. "I'll be fine. I'll be back as soon as I can."

"Okay," Jax said. "I'll be here." He gave her a kiss that warmed and reassured her yet again of his love, and closed the door after her as she slipped into the car seat.

The chauffeur backed the car out of the parking lot and a few minutes later, they were on their way. The car was silent as they rode, with Simone and her mother each preoccupied with their own thoughts.

Soon they reached Beacon Hill, one of Boston's oldest neighborhoods and famous for its charming, narrow cobblestone streets, federal-style row houses, red brick sidewalks, and gas-lit street lamps. Simone could still see some tourists making their way through the streets, though it wasn't as busy and traffic-stopping as it could be during the summer months.

The car reached a charming brick row house with black and white shutters and then turned into an alley on its side to reach a private entrance which slid open to reveal an underground parking garage. The chauffeur drove in and parked in one of two available spots.

"We're here," her mother said and got out.

"I didn't expect I'd see an interior parking spot in Beacon Hill," Simone said after she'd stepped out. Resident street parking was the norm, and even then, open spots were hard to find.

"I had the row house remodeled," her mother said as she led the way to an elevator. She pressed the elevator button, and the doors opened. Simone and her mother entered. Her mother scanned a card she'd pulled from her burgundy Hermès Birkin bag against the elevator card reader and pressed the button for the first floor.

Once the elevator reached its destination, Simone and her mother stepped out into an unexpected space: a baby-blue walled open space with luxury vinyl wood tile flooring and the faint smell of watercolors in the air. Large windows on the north side boasted stunning views of the Boston Public Garden and allowed in the natural daylight.

A kitchen sat at the opposite end with custom granite countertops, Sub-Zero & Wolf kitchen appliances, and dark blue cabinets. Simone noticed the right wall was lined with large rolling work tables, shelves filled with brushes, paints, and other supplies, and a wall-mounted art drying rack. A dedicated left wall showcased an array of watercolor artworks, drawings, and sketches. There was another door at the back, and Simone guessed it led to either a bedroom or a workroom.

In the middle of the space sat a large easel with its matching stool and a small rolling cart filled with more brushes and paints by its side. A large, comfortable-looking, dark red leather couch located a few steps away from the easel completed the room's decor.

"What's this space?" Simone asked as her eyes continued to check out the room.

"My studio," her mother said. "I come here a few times a week to get away from everything."

Simone's mother had always appreciated the arts, but Simone hadn't known her mother painted as well. She knew little about watercolors, but it was obvious her mother had talent from what she saw hanging on the left wall. "I didn't know you painted."

"I'm sorry I never showed you this side of me. But that's not why I brought you here. This way." Her mother led her up a flight of stairs to the second floor. There were two doors on this level, and her mother led her to the one at the far end. She pressed a series of numbers using the keypad on the door and then pushed it open.

Rows of hanging racks of upright artworks, each one covered with UV-protective glass, filled the low-lit room. This room appeared climate controlled and the faint scent of oil paints and solvents hung in the air.

"These are your father's paintings," her mother said.

Her father's paintings. The artwork of the man

she'd never gotten the chance to meet. Simone stepped in between each row and studied them. From what she saw, from the originality and artistic expression, these pieces deserved to be on display in any top gallery in the country. "He was talented," she said.

"He sure was," her mother agreed, her face beaming with pride. "Your father had a story for each painting, and anytime I come here, especially when I miss him, I take out a painting and try to recall the story he'd told me about it."

"What about this one?" Simone pointed to a painting of a white majestic bird with beautiful, luxurious pink feathers perched on a tree against a backdrop of snow falling in the background. "What's its story?"

Her mother's face lit up as she recalled the memory. "Your father painted it on the day I bumped into him. It'd snowed that day." She pulled a white glove from her pocket, donned it, and caressed the edge of the painting. "He said I was the bird: beautiful, graceful, yet sheltered. I couldn't agree more."

Simone could see why it'd caught her attention: it had reminded her of her mother. Her father had had a true gift. "I wish I'd met him," she said softly.

"I wish you had too. He was a good man, and he

had a heart of gold. He looked forward to us having kids. In fact, I named you Simone, because that's the name he'd picked for our daughter if we ever had one."

Simone's breath caught in her throat. He'd looked forward to her. Her father had wanted her.

"Your father grew up an orphan," her mother continued. "Yet he didn't let it define him. He was the best man I'd ever met, and you can be sure I've met a lot of them."

That had to be true, from what Simone had seen of high society, especially since her mother was more extroverted than she was. Even now, she still caught the eye of every man whenever she entered a room. "Do you have a picture of him?" she asked instead.

"I have something better," her mother said and led her to a covered painting tucked in at the end of the row they were in.

Her mother carefully rolled back the covering to reveal a painting of a man with a woman in his arms, staring out as if into the face of a camera, expressions of pure joy on their faces. The image appeared so vivid and so real. Simone didn't need to be told the woman was a younger version of her mother, but it was the man that captured her attention. It was like she stared into a mirror, her facial features strongly reflected in his face.

Simone also understood something else.

Her parents had both been of mixed racial descent.

This could be why Simone's hair had a more springy vibe than her brother's. She'd always thought Michael took more of Sebastian Addison's genetic make-up than her mother's, but it turned out Simone had had two strong gene pools to pull from.

"Do you think—"

"Your stepfather treated you the way he did because of your father's racial descent?" her mother asked.

Simone nodded. It'd been her first thought as soon as she'd seen the painting.

"Sebastian doesn't care about any of that. Contrary to what you'd think, he had several black friends back in college, many of whom he keeps in touch with to this day. Besides, I'm mixed, and he still has a crush on me, even after all these years. It's more that you look a lot like the man who stole the heart of the woman he loved. He's never forgiven Amos for that."

She glanced at her mother. "Did they know each other?"

"I think they'd met once before at a college event, but that was years before I met your father."

Simone's eyes scanned the room again. She could see her mother had preserved the paintings well in this room, but her father's works deserved more. "Have you ever thought about displaying these at a gallery?" she asked.

"Sometimes," her mother said. "But then I'd drop the idea, since I selfishly want to keep them all to myself." She stared wistfully at the painting in front of her. "They're the last reminders I have of your father—well, apart from you, of course."

But her mother had cared more for these paintings than she'd done her.

"I'm sorry for everything," her mother said, as if she'd read Simone's thoughts. "I'm sorry I hurt you, and I'm going to do my best to be a proper mother to you, if you give me the chance."

Then she reached for a purple velvet pouch Simone hadn't noticed nestled behind the painting and handed it to her. "This is for you," she said. "From your father."

Her father? How? He'd been dead by the time she was born. She opened the pouch and pulled out an off-white, long, flat, rectangular box.

"He wrote you a letter," her mother said. "It's about time you have it."

Simone opened the flat box and pulled out a cream paper with yellowed embossed decorative edges. She unfolded it to see a legible cursive handwriting that hadn't faded over time and began to read:

Dear Simone,

Your mother might think otherwise, but ever since she'd told me she missed her period this morning, something inside me told me you'd be a girl.

This might sound strange, but I wanted to write you a letter immediately, the first of many letters to come, if God wills.

My darling Simone, a beautiful name that means 'God has heard,' I haven't met you yet, but I want you to know I love you.

You're a gift from God to your mom and me, and I promise to love, support, and cherish you all the days God gives me on this earth.

You are special to me, to us, and will always be.

Thank you for coming into our lives and our hearts.

My precious little girl.

Your Daddy,

Amos.

Simone's eyes misted as she stared at the words, and she didn't know when the tears fell. She wiped them away so as not to damage the letter and then took her time to reread the words over and over again.

Her father, even when he hadn't even met her, had loved her.

In those moments, Simone allowed the words to sink deep into her heart and into the very core of her being.

Then she folded the paper and tucked it back into its box and stared at the painting of her father, her mind memorizing his image and features.

As her heart settled into a peace and calm she'd never known, Simone sent up a silent thank-you.

Because now she knew the truth.

Her real father had looked forward to meeting her.

Simone had been special to him.

Her father had always loved and wanted her.

CHAPTER 47

Jax stood by the floor-to ceiling windows for a few moments. Daylight had given way to early evening, and now the city's bright lights had come on, creating a beautiful and vibrant sight that contrasted well against the darkening night sky. But it couldn't distract Jax from wondering how things were going with Simone.

He moved back to settle on the sofa, flipping through the TV channels, but then abandoned the remote to head to the kitchen. He needed to do something, anything, to keep himself busy.

Because he was worried about her.

Jax had done some work on the laptop he'd had in his truck and had even scrubbed the apartment from top to bottom, but none of that had distracted him from his thoughts about Simone.

The news about her father had been a shock to her, and he was sure she was still having a difficult time processing it. Simone may have looked all calm on the surface, but he could tell she was struggling on the inside. But who wouldn't be the same when they'd just found out the father, whose approval they've always sought but never got, was not their real father? Yet, without enough time to deal with the news, she'd had to follow her mother to another destination, to learn more news that may or may not complicate issues further.

For Jax, within the past twenty-four hours, he'd seen a new side of Simone, more layers to her than he'd known in the time they'd dated. She was more vulnerable, in a way that all Jax wanted to do was protect her, yet it made her even more human and relatable to him.

It didn't matter to him who her father was or if her family had secrets that would rather not see the light of day. Simone was still Simone, the woman he'd fallen in love with many years ago, hated for a few more to protect his heart, and who was now back in his life again.

The one who'd loved him enough to break herself and their relationship to protect him and his family.

Simone, who'd never given up hope and had mustered up the courage to come looking for him, knowing fully well he'd treat her without mercy.

She'd done it all for him.

But now it was Jax's turn. He'd make it up to her.

This time, Jax would protect her, no matter what it took.

An hour later, Jax heard the door's security beep. The door opened and then shut as Simone stepped in, her shoulders hunched as if all the cares of the entire world had fallen on them.

He took quick strides to where she stood and wrapped his arms around her. "Are you okay?" he asked as he rubbed her back.

She gave out a sigh that touched somewhere deep within him. "I'll be fine now." She burrowed further into his arms. "This is nice."

Jax pulled her in further and kissed the top of her head. "Are you tired? Do you want to lie down?"

"I think so."

Jax lifted Simone into his arms, cradling her

against his chest. She felt as light as a feather, almost as if she'd lost weight overnight. As Simone rested her head against his shoulder, the scent of coconuts from her shampoo wafted through the air, enveloping them in its tropical essence.

With each deliberate step toward the bedroom, Jax savored the feel of Simone in his arms and felt a sense of protectiveness over her, as if wanting to take over what ached her and keep her heart safe. In the bedroom, Jax gently laid her on the bed, took off her heels, placed her feet on his lap, and rubbed them to ease the aches away.

"Thank you," Simone said softly.

"Do you want to talk about it?" Maybe opening up about what had happened with her mother would help.

Simone adjusted herself until she was sitting up and then shared with him all her mother had told her about her father, what she'd observed at the studio her mother had kept in memory of him, and how she'd told her each painting's story. "Seeing how much I take after him was so surreal," she said. "But the best part was realizing he'd loved me." She closed her eyes briefly and then opened them, her eyes now shining with unshed tears. "I had a father who loved me."

During the time they'd dated, Jax hadn't understood how terrible her relationship with her stepfather had been. Simone had avoided talking about her family, yet he hadn't expected Mr. Addison's treatment of her to have been so bad she'd doubted her family's love for her.

Jax brushed an errant strand of hair away from her face. It was all his fault for not showing her how much he loved her, such that her stepfather's indifference wouldn't have mattered so much. "I'm sorry I wasn't there for you all these years."

She gave him a warm smile. "You didn't know, and it was my burden to bear. But you're here now, right?"

Jax pulled her into his arms. "I'm not going anywhere. You can't get rid of me this time, even if you tried. You're stuck with me now." He was never leaving her again.

"Hmmm. I like the sound of that." Simone snuggled deeper into his embrace. "Let's stay stuck together."

He chuckled. "Any way you want it, baby."

"Jax?"

"Yes?"

"I need…"

"What is it?" Jax said. "I'll give you anything you

want." He'd do it too, even if it meant catching the moon for her.

She rested her head against his shoulder, her soft hair caressing his skin through his shirt. "I'd like to go home," she whispered. "Please take me home, Jax."

Jax's heart warmed as the meaning of her words dawned on him. Simone Addison had just claimed his life and his home as her safe place.

"It would be my pleasure," he said.

CHAPTER 48

$\mathcal{M}$aggie wrapped Simone in a tight embrace as soon as she stepped through the door of the Dexin family home that late evening. Jax had called ahead to let Maggie know they were coming and had only hinted Simone needed some place to rest, which was fine by Simone. She wasn't ready to share the details of her family drama with anyone else.

"Welcome, dear," Maggie said.

"Thank you," Simone said as she returned the hug, even as the smell of cinnamon, spice, and fresh bread, the smell of home, enveloped her.

"I have a room all ready for you. Would you like something to eat? I can have Jax bring some food up."

Simone's stomach rumbled in response, and Jax chuckled. "I believe that's a yes," he said.

The emotional day must have made her hungry. "I'd like that, as long as it's not a bother," Simone said.

Maggie waved her concern away. "Not at all. Consider this place your home," she said. "Jax, why don't you take her upstairs and then come back and pick up the tray?"

"Okay. Thanks, Maggie."

"Always a pleasure." Then Maggie turned and headed to the kitchen.

Jax led Simone up the winding staircase until they reached the second floor and then down the hallway to a room at the end. "Here we are," he said, and opened the door to a large room decorated in pale blue and pink.

"This is beautiful," Simone said as she stepped in and looked around. Somehow, its accent furnishings of warm brown and antique-brass worked with the rest of the house's decor. "Are you hiding a sister, by any chance?"

Jax chuckled as he dropped her bags beside the large king-sized bed. "Anyone who's stayed here always thinks that. Ma always wanted a girl, so she decorated this room instead."

"It's really nice."

"Thank you. You can settle in while I grab some food for you. I'll be right back." Then Jax left the room, shutting the door behind him.

Simone removed her shoes. The floor warmed her feet, and she guessed it was heated.

She checked out the rest of the space. There was a large walk-in closet almost as big as the one she had at home, a side parlor where she could work from if she wanted, and a luxuriant bathroom with antique-brass sink fixtures and a sky view. She returned to the main bedroom and took a few minutes to hang up her clothes in the closet, put away her shoes, and freshen up.

There was a knock on the door.

"Come in," she answered, and Jax stepped through, looking as delicious as the snacks on the tray in a white polo shirt open at the collar. He placed the tray on the bedroom bench and settled right beside it on the bed.

"Thank you," Simone said and sat down on the other side. "This looks delicious, though I'll need a workout if I consume all this. You're going to have some, right?" Mashed potato pancakes, scotch eggs, sweet potato chips, mini cinnamon rolls, ham and egg biscuits, donuts, mini beef enchiladas, coffee cake, and freshly squeezed orange juice filled the tray.

Jax chuckled. "Don't worry. No one expects you to finish this. I'll help."

They dove into the food and chatted as they ate. Maybe it was something about the air at the ranch because soon enough Simone felt a lightness in her heart as Jax brought her up to speed about the happenings at the ranch and especially about Ornie, the goat. Simone had never laughed so hard as Jax regaled her with his antics.

"It's like everyone takes a detour once they see Ornie coming," Jax said. "No one wants to end up with mud on their faces or horse poop on their behinds."

Simone couldn't help the laughter that escaped her. "Oh my goodness, you guys must love him."

"We have no choice," Jax said with a smile on his face. "He's Chloe's pet, and you don't want to mess with her."

Simone could imagine that. The spunky little girl had stolen her heart, even though she'd embarrassed Jax and Simone about the kiss.

And speaking of kisses, Simone's eyes strayed to Jax's lips as he swallowed a bite of the coffee cake.

What she wouldn't do to kiss away the cake crumbs at the corner of his lips.

"What is it?" Jax said as he dabbed his lips with a paper napkin.

Simone pushed down her disappointment. There was no way she was telling him what she'd been thinking, now that the cake crumbs were gone.

Jax leaned forward until his lips were next to Simone's ear. "I know you wanted to kiss me," he whispered.

Simone's face warmed. Had she been so obvious?

Jax lifted the tray, placed it on the floor, and then pulled Simone into his lap. "You want some kisses, don't you?" he said, his face close to hers and the scent of his aftershave cologne tickling her senses.

"I…"

"You need to say it."

Why was he being such a tease? Didn't he want them too?

Jax placed a light kiss on her forehead, sending sparks of electricity down her spine. "Say it, Simone."

No. Why did she have to be the one to say it?

He kissed the top of her nose, and the sparks extended to other parts of her body. "Say it."

No way. As much as she craved more, she wasn't going to embarrass herself and vocalize it.

Then he kissed the corners of her lips, taking a moment to savor them. Butterflies rose in Simone's stomach in response. "Say it, Simone, or I'm going to stop here," Jax said in a low voice.

No! She needed more. Besides, what was the big deal about getting embarrassed if she got kisses in return? she reasoned.

"I want kisses," she breathed.

Jax devoured her lips like they were a limited edition and going out of sale soon. She'd thought the kiss Chloe had witnessed was hot, but this was like two hundred percent on the scalding scale. Jax pulled her in deeper into his arms and claimed her lips like they belonged to him and he now had command of them. Just as Simone thought she'd combust from it all, Jax ended the kiss.

"You drive me crazy," he whispered into her hair.

That makes two of us, Simone thought.

"I wish I could just marry you tomorrow," he continued.

Simone leaned back to stare into his beautiful grey eyes. "Is that a proposal?"

He pushed strands of her hair away from her face. "It's just a wish. I know this isn't the right time."

Simone agreed, though she would have said yes if he'd asked. But she wasn't telling him *that*.

"What would you like to do the rest of tonight?" Jax asked.

"Would it be okay if I skipped dinner? I'm full and can't imagine eating anything else tonight." *She was also not ready to face questions from the rest of the family.*

Jax ran his fingers through her hair, and Simone bit back a groan of pleasure. "I know you'd like some alone time, too."

This man sure knew what she needed, and her heart warmed. "Thank you for understanding."

"No worries. Let me run a bath for you, and then I'll let you be." He gave her another kiss on the forehead and then lifted her onto the bed before heading to the bathroom. A few minutes later, he was back in the room. "You're all set."

"Thanks, Jax." Simone rose to her feet and gave him a kiss.

"You're welcome. Although if you continue kissing me like this, I just may not leave."

Simone chuckled dand gave him a playful slap on the shoulder. "Be gone with you."

Jax smiled and the left dimple she was a sucker for showed up.

Ah, finally, Simone thought. She'd missed seeing it. She stood on tiptoe and kissed him there.

Jax pulled her into his arms. "Woman, you're making this hard." He kissed her forehead and then released her. "I'll see you tomorrow."

Simone nodded, though she now regretted leaving his arms and sending him away. Her eyes followed as he left the room.

She leaned against the wall by the door and listened until his footsteps faded away. Simone's heart was full and overflowing. How could she love one man so much? But choosing him had been the best decision she'd ever made. She didn't imagine she'd ever meet another man as kind, warm, and caring as Jax was. But best of all, they connected on some deep level, and he got and understood her.

Simone stifled a yawn. It was time to wash away the emotional stress of the day and get some much needed rest.

But first she had business to take care of.

She called Dr. Guzman to let him know she wouldn't be in for the next few days. He promised to notify the office manager, who'd reschedule her appointments and send an automated message out to her patients so they wouldn't make the wasted trip in.

Then Simone went for a soak in the vintage clawfoot tub. The tall sides of the tub and its spacious interior gave her a sense of privacy and coziness she hadn't expected, and Simone wondered if she could install one like this in her home.

Jax had filled the tub such that its water level was just as deep as Simone liked. The bath salts and essential oils he'd added relaxed her enough that Simone closed her eyes and breathed in deeply, letting the worries of the day fade away.

After a while, when she felt both her physical and mental muscles had relaxed, Simone stepped out of the bath, wrapped herself in a towel robe, and changed for the night. As she slipped into bed, she picked up her phone and dialed Paisley's number.

"Hello, girlfriend," Paisley said from the other end of the line. "What's happening?" Simone could hear some pop music in the background.

"Where are you?" Simone asked.

"At some post-wedding bash," Paisley said. "My uncle's cousin-in-law's sister got married today."

Simone chuckled as she tried to figure out the connection. Paisley's extended family relationships were legendary. "You must have had fun."

"Hmmm, it was okay mostly, except when some distant aunt harped on and on about how I wasn't married yet, and that I needed to find me some nice boy."

"I bet she had a few in mind."

"How did you know? She kept dragging me around, introducing me to one young man or the other. It took everything in me not to scream and pull my hair out."

Simone laughed. "But did you meet anyone you liked?"

"They were cute boys, but oh so boring."

"I'm sorry."

"Don't be. I'm still holding out for my cowboy. Speaking of cowboys, how's Lover Boy doing?"

"He's fine. We're fine. Like really fine."

"Wait, you mean all is well in love land?"

"Yes. I told him the whole story, and we made up."

Screaming erupted at the other end of the line. Simone had to pull her phone away from her ear for a moment. "Girl, give me all the details," Paisley said. "I want to know *everything*."

Simone chuckled. "Maybe another day. That's not why I called you."

"What could be more important than Lover Boy's story?"

Simone told her the truth about her father. By the time she finished, she felt all wrung out.

"I'm so sorry," Paisley said. "It must have been a shock for you. Do you need me to come over?"

"I'm not at home right now. I'm at Jax's family ranch."

"It's great he's there to comfort you. But girl, I like your style. You move fast."

Simone couldn't help the laughter that bubbled out. Trust Paisley to lighten the mood. "Do you blame me?"

"I know, right? It's been five years in the making. I guess this means you won't be at work tomorrow."

"Already asked Dr. Guzman for some time off. I should be back by Wednesday."

"Take all the time you need. Consider it a vacation, one you haven't taken in a while."

"I will. Thanks, babe."

"My pleasure. Also, feel free to send a cowboy my way if you find an eligible one. I'm sure there'll be some hanging around there."

Simone chuckled. "I'll try."

"Alright. Have a wonderful night."

"You too. I'll talk to you tomorrow."

"Greet Lover Boy for me."

"I will. My regards to your parents and your wonderful distant aunt."

"I'll tell them. Not sure about the aunt, though. Might be best to avoid her for now."

"Alright. Bye," Simone said. Then she ended the call.

Simone dropped her phone on the night stand and stretched out on the bed. Talking to Paisley was always therapeutic for her soul, and she didn't know what she'd have done without her all these years. She sent a silent thanks up to God for bringing Paisley into her life.

Her thoughts turned to Jax. So much had happened to her in the last twenty-four hours, yet he'd been by her side through it all. She was sure he was already planning out ways to make her happy tomorrow.

As she drifted off to sleep, Simone couldn't wait for what tomorrow would bring.

CHAPTER 49

*J*ax left the small conference room at the ranch office on Monday morning and headed outside into the warm morning air. They'd constructed the single-story ranch-style log and stone building with large windows a few years ago when the ranch operations had expanded internationally.

He'd just finished the weekly finance meeting with his team to review the ranch's financial performance, budget, cash flow, capital investments, and other financial matters like vendor contracts and pricing strategies. Dex, as the head of ranch operations, had also attended the meeting. Thankfully, there'd been no major issues, and they'd even resolved the hidden costs he'd been worried about. But now he was looking forward to seeing Simone.

Jax had expected her to sleep in, so he'd asked Maggie to deliver a breakfast tray to her door on his behalf. He'd also left Simone a message that he'd pick her up at ten a.m.

It was now a few minutes to ten.

Jax had cleared the rest of his schedule for the day to spend time with her. He'd catch up on any outstanding work later tonight.

"Jax, wait up," Dex said from behind him.

Jax frowned. What could he want? Jax hoped it wasn't work that would delay him.

He paused on the building's patio and waited for Dex to catch up. "What's up?" he asked.

"I need to talk to you," Dex said. "Where are you off to?"

"I need to pick Simone up. Can whatever it is wait?"

"No, it can't," Dex said. "Let's step away from here." He looped his arm through Jax's and led him toward the main house.

Jax said nothing and followed him. Dex would talk when he was ready. Soon, they reached beyond the midpoint of the path, and Dex paused. "It's about Rex," he said.

The muscle in Jax's jaw ticked as he halted beside him. He loosened his arm from Dex's. "This isn't a good time for this."

"When will it ever be? You guys can't continue like this. It's time you made up."

"It's not my fault."

"I know, Jax. I never said it was. But this thing between you two is affecting everyone, even Maggie. We all have to tiptoe around you two when you're in the same space. It's even affecting the ranch operations. Do you know it's the reason Rex didn't attend this morning's meeting, when it's our policy that all owners have to attend financial meetings whenever they can?" Dex placed his hands on Jax's shoulders. "Can't you just extend an olive branch, for our sakes? Rex's trying. Can't you do the same?"

Not that Jax didn't want to make up with Rex. He missed him more than anyone could imagine. But the hurt had been deep, and it was just hard to see beyond that. "I'm not sure I can do that."

Dex let out a sigh, and his arms fell to his sides. "I was hoping you wouldn't say that."

"I know you mean well," Jax said. "But I don't know. Besides, now isn't a good time for this. I need to focus on taking care of Simone and making sure she's okay."

"How's she doing?"

"She'll be fine. She just needs time."

"Don't worry. We'll give her all the privacy she needs. Let me know if there's anything Zoey and I can do to help."

This was one of many reasons he loved his family. They were always ready to step up when needed. "Thanks for the offer. I need to go."

"Okay. Please send my regards to her. And please think about what I said earlier."

"I'll try." It was the least he could promise. Then Jax left his brother standing there and hurried down the path until he reached the main house's front door and stepped in.

He dialed Simone's number as he made his way through the foyer. The phone rang twice before connecting. "Good morning, sunshine," he said as he headed toward the kitchen.

"Good morning," Simone's sleepy voice responded.

"Did I wake you?" he asked.

"Not really. I was up earlier but got sleepy after taking a shower, so I took a nap. I didn't expect I'd be this tired."

"You had a long emotional day yesterday."

"That must have been it. Thanks for the

breakfast."

Maggie had delivered as usual. He made a note to send her some flowers later. "My pleasure. Well, it's almost ten."

"Okay. I'll freshen up and will be down shortly. Should I dress up in any particular way?"

"A pair of jeans and boots would be nice."

"Alright. Your wish is my command."

Jax chuckled. "If you say so."

"See you soon. Bye." The line went dead.

Jax couldn't hide the grin on his face as he packed the basket for the picnic he'd planned. Just hearing Simone's voice had been enough to put him back in a good mood after the talk with Dex. He looked forward to their time together.

"Uncle Jax," a sweet voice called out.

Jax turned to see Chloe burst into the kitchen, dressed in a sparkly pink top and jeans. Becca had homeschooled her this year, so Chloe had to be on her snack break. He lifted her into his arms. "How are you, sport?" he asked and tickled her nose.

Chloe giggled. "Mommy said I did great on my counting."

"That's fantastic. Give me a high-five."

They high-fived, and then Jax set her down. "What do you need?"

"A glass of orange juice and two cookies would be fine."

Maggie had already set out a tray for Chloe, so Jax carried it from the kitchen island to the smaller table in the kitchen's corner. "Here you go," he said.

"Thanks, Uncle Jax." Chloe settled in to eat her snack.

Jax hummed under his breath as he finished packing the basket.

"Uncle Jax?"

Jax turned in her direction. "Yes?"

Her startling blue eyes sparkled. "Are you going to marry Aunt Simone?"

So he wasn't the only one who'd thought about it. "Why do you ask?"

"Well, you kissed her like *that*. You have to marry her now," she said with the confidence of a girl who believed her word had to be obeyed.

"Thank you for your advice, Your Majesty."

"You're welcome," Chloe said and continued eating her cookie like she hadn't just dropped some sage words.

Jax poured a glass of water for himself. He'd thought about it all last night and had concluded that they both needed to take things slow for now. There were also other big details they'd need to work out first, like where they'd live. Jax was sure he wanted to remain at the ranch, but he didn't know if Simone felt the same way, even though she'd discussed the hospital partnership with Max. So the marriage discussion was best tabled. He took a gulp of his water.

"Uncle Jax?"

"Hmm?" Jax had his back to her.

"How do you know when a bull is ready to breed?"

Jax almost spewed the water in his mouth. He shook his head at the thoughts that passed through Chloe's head. How was he going to answer her? There was no way he was telling her how they measured the bull's scrotum.

"Um, we just have a way we use," a familiar voice said from the doorway. "It's too complicated for you."

"Daddy!" Chloe jumped up and into Max's arms.

Jax turned. *Thank you, Max, for the save.* "What are you doing home at this time?" he asked.

"I forgot some documents and came to pick them up," Max replied.

Chloe pulled on Max's shirt sleeve. "But, Daddy, I need to know about the bull!"

Jax chuckled. Chloe wouldn't give up until she

had an answer. Hmmm… Maybe there was a way Jax could explain it. "We do it by—"

The stern look Max gave Jax could have frozen all the water in the nearby brook. Maybe it was best to keep quiet and let Max take this one.

"Have you finished your snack?" Max asked Chloe.

"Yes, Daddy."

"Okay, let's go back to Mommy, and I'll tell you all about the bull."

"Okay. Bye, Uncle Jax. Thanks for the snack."

Jax smiled back. "You're welcome."

Max headed out of the kitchen with Chloe in his arms and could hear Chloe's chatter as they made their way down the hallway.

Jax shook his head in wonder as he finished his drink, picked up Chloe's tray, and did the dishes. He loved Chloe with all his heart, but he prayed God in His mercy would give her a more quiet sibling to balance things out. Otherwise, they were in for a whole heap of trouble.

A sound near the doorway made him turn as he placed the last dish on the rack. Simone stood there, a vision in a pink and white polo shirt over jeans tucked into boots. She'd pulled her hair into a ponytail and had a pair of sunglasses and a cute designer wristlet in her hands.

"Good morning, beautiful," Jax said. He replaced the dish towel and headed to her.

"Good morning," Simone said with a smile.

Jax pulled her into his arms. The familiar scent of fresh florals with notes of sandalwood tickled his nostrils, and he inhaled deeply. Jax didn't think he'd ever tire of having her in his arms. "How was your night?"

"I slept well. The bed was so soft and nice."

"I'm glad to hear it." He kissed her on the lips, and she nestled deeper in his arms. He broke the kiss after a moment.

"So what's on for today?" Simone asked, her beautiful brown eyes drawing him in.

"It's time I showed you my home, and then we can go for a picnic after that. Does that work?"

"Sounds like a plan."

Jax picked up the picnic basket. "Okay, let's go."

"Your home looks great, and I love the colors," Simone exclaimed as Jax led her into his home.

Jax had known she'd love it. He'd somehow had

her in mind when he'd decorated the place, which meant he'd always hoped to have her back in his life even then. "Thank you."

Simone moved to the kitchen area, her hand brushing the surface of the massive granite countertop, and Jax followed her. "This is a gourmet kitchen," she said of the high-end range and appliances. "I didn't know you enjoyed cooking that much."

"I get by. You can't live with Maggie and not learn how to cook."

"That's awesome, because you know I don't know how to."

"That's fine. I can cook for the both of us."

Simone flashed him a warm smile. "How did I luck out on meeting you?"

Jax pulled her to him. "I can think of one way you could appreciate me."

Simone swatted his chest. "You're incorrigible."

Jax gave her a quick kiss on the lips. Somehow, he couldn't get enough of them. "I aim to please."

"Why don't you show me the rest of the house?"

He'd rather keep kissing her, but showing her the home was important too.

Jax released her and then led her by the hand until they reached the door of his workroom. His special place. What would she think of it? It wasn't exactly a manly recreational activity.

He turned to face her. "I have a hobby. It's not any of the usual ones, and I picked it up after we parted. But I love it."

"Okay."

He punched in the code on the keypad. "Welcome to my workroom," he said as he pushed the door open.

The smell of beeswax, coconut, and jasmine hung in the air as he stepped in. Jax waited as Simone followed him in and watched as she scanned the room.

"This is amazing," she said as she studied the candles in the curing and experimentation areas of the workroom. "I had no idea you were this creative."

His shoulders relaxed. She liked it. "I didn't know either until after I started."

"What do you do with the candles?"

"I sell them to consignment stores. I also get several custom orders, too."

Simone continued moving through the space and then her eyes widened as she spotted a set of candles on a low shelf. "Is that what I think it is?"

Jax nodded. Simone had given him years ago the geometric piece she'd drawn after they'd first met, and he'd tried to recreate the pattern in a set of candles.

She moved closer and sniffed the air. "And it smells just like my favorite perfume!"

Jax had tried to duplicate the scent with the essential oils he had, even though her perfume had been custom made for her by a notable perfumer. "Because the candles are for you."

Simone whirled and jumped into his arms. It was all he could do to stop himself from falling over. "Thank you!" she said and kissed him all over the face.

Woah. He hadn't expected this reaction, but this was a thank you he appreciated. "I'm glad you like them."

Simone then rested her head against his chest. "Thank you, Jax. It's one of the best gifts I've ever gotten."

"I'll wrap it later for you to take home. Why don't we see the rest of the house?"

She gave him one more kiss on the lips and then hopped down. "Okay, let's do this."

Ten minutes later and they were done with the house tour and back in the living area. "So, what do you think?" Jax asked. Would she be willing to live here with him?

"Your home is lovely," Simone replied.

"Do you think it would work for you?"

"Are you asking me if I'd like to live here?"

Jax ran his hand through his hair. "Well, something like that."

Simone touched his arm. "Why do I get the sense you're nervous?"

"Me, nervous? No way." Yet he couldn't meet her eyes.

Simone chuckled. "Jax, look at me." She waited until he did. "I know you have some concerns, since I'm a billionaire and used to certain levels of comfort," she said softly. "But I want to make this clear: you, Jax," she tapped his chest with a finger, "are my home. If you want us to live here, then that's where our home will be. Is this what you want?"

He had to tell her the truth. "Yes." He could live in Boston if it came to it, but he loved this ranch and this home, and thought the change would be good for her, too.

"Then that's where we'll live."

Jax couldn't help the joy that filled his face. She'd agreed!

"But I'll need a bigger closet," Simone said.

He'd give her whatever she wanted. "I can

connect the master to the adjoining bedroom and turn that into your closet."

"And I'll need a studio. I'm jealous of your workroom."

"I'll build an extension to the house for it." He'd remodel the home, however she liked. What a weight she'd rolled off his shoulders. "Thank you, Simone."

"You're welcome. Now, how about that picnic?"

CHAPTER 50

"So, what do you think?" Jax asked Simone. They'd gone to the horse barn to pick some horses.

Simone glanced around the space. It was bigger than her own stable and had a second-level hay loft, but the aromatic scent of sweet hay, leather, and fresh pine was just as familiar. "It looks great."

"Let me take you to meet our favorite ladies." Jax led her down the aisle, past rows and rows of horses in their European-style stalls of steel and wood, until they reached the rear. "Simone, meet Bella, Lexi, and London," he said, pointing out each one by name. Both Bella and Lexi were beautiful thoroughbred mares, and London had the telltale inward-facing ears of a Marwari. All three poked their heads out at Jax's voice. "Bella is Max's horse and everyone's favorite, Lexi is Dex's, and London is Zoey's horse."

Simone's eyes widened as a thought struck her. "This is Bella, the horse I named back then?"

"Yes, she is," Jax replied.

Simone reached her first and rubbed her neck. She was as beautiful as Simone had imagined she'd be. Then she turned to the others. "Hello, ladies," she said and patted their necks. "It seems your family has a thing for mares."

"I know, right? But I prefer stallions." He moved a row up. "Meet King, my black Arabian stallion."

Simone studied the horse. From the flare of his nostrils, she could tell this one had some fire in him. "He's a handsome fellow," she said and patted his neck.

If looks could kill, Simone would be dead from the glare the stallion gave her.

She laughed as she patted him again. Feisty, just like Jax. She couldn't wait to ride him. "What about Rex's horse?" she asked.

Jax glanced at a stall two rows down that was empty. "Rex must have taken her out for a ride. But his other horses should be on their way to the DexGray Ranch."

Simone gave him a curious look. "There's another ranch?"

"Rex runs a horse-breeding business with his partners, Weston, Liam, and Cole—I'm sure you'll meet them one of these days—and they just built a new ranch not too far away from here."

"How are things with you and Rex?" Simone asked quietly.

Jax busied himself with grabbing two saddles and placing them on King and Bella. "I don't know," he said.

"I saw him briefly today."

"Who? Rex?" Jax didn't look at her as he asked.

"Yes. Near the kitchen entrance," Simone said. "I could see the longing in his eyes as he stared at you, yet he respected your space and didn't come in."

Jax said nothing in return. From what she could see, Rex was still a sore point for him, but Simone knew his heart needed his brother to be whole again.

She had to help him. "How about making up with him?" Simone asked as she leaned against the wall of King's stall.

Jax was silent for a moment. "I don't know, Simone," he then said.

She would have to nudge him a little harder.

"Could you please try?" she asked softly. "He means a lot to you, and he needs you just as much as you need him."

Jax finished saddling King and let out a sigh. "Okay, I'll try."

"Thank you," Simone said and gave him a back hug. Since he'd promised, she was sure Jax would make the effort. Maybe if they finally talked, the knot in Jax's heart would be unraveled at last.

Jax placed his hand over Simone's. "The things I do for you."

She gave him another squeeze from behind. "Thank you." Then she released him. "Okay, it's time for my ride now. I'll take King."

Jax turned to face her. "Are you sure? I wouldn't want him to throw you off his back. Bella might be a better choice."

Simone patted his shoulder. "Trust me, it'll be fine."

What had started off as a leisurely ride through fields, meadows, and streams had ended up as a race to a large oak tree Jax had pointed out in the distance.

They'd already passed a larger one earlier that Jax had called the Dexin Oak.

Simone arrived first and dismounted. "I won," she said with a big grin as Jax reached her side.

"You've been keeping something from me," Jax teased as he got off Bella and unloaded the saddle bags. Simone spread the blanket he handed to her at the base of the oak tree and helped him as he unpacked the picnic items. "When did you learn to ride like that?"

"I've been riding since I was a kid," she replied as she placed the food items on the blanket and the mouthwatering aroma filled the space. There was beef and grilled cheese sandwiches, homemade biscuits that were warm to the touch, potato salad, fresh fruits, trail mix, bottles of water, and a thermos of coffee. Simone couldn't wait. It seemed she'd become a glutton for food these days.

Jax's eyebrows rose. "Are you serious? No wonder you're so good. Do you have a horse?" He rose and nudged both horses on their side. The horses seemed to know what he expected, since they both headed to a nearby field to graze. Then he rejoined her on the blanket.

"Um..."

Jax gave her a curious look. "What is it?"

"Did I mention I own a stable of horses?"

Jax laughed. "Your secrets never end."

"Hey, I totally forgot about it. I promise, this is the last one."

Jax's eyebrow rose. "Are you sure? Maybe there's another secret hiding somewhere."

Simone's ears turned red, and she slapped his arm. "Jax Dexin!" He pulled her into his arms and she fought to get out of it. "Let me go, you annoying oaf."

"Hmm, you're feisty. I like that," Jax said. "If you stop struggling, I'll give you a kiss." She stilled in his arms. "Ah, you want that kiss, don't you?"

She stared at him unashamedly. "Nothing wrong with expressing what I want."

"A woman who speaks her mind. Well, I shouldn't disappoint the lady." Jax bent his head and kissed her hard enough to steal her breath.

The butterflies in Simone's belly popped like they were off to the races. Jax tasted sweet, like decadent chocolate one couldn't resist, and Simone couldn't help deepening the kiss as his hands caressed her face, sending sparks of electricity all over her skin. She wanted more, so Simone unapologetically looped her arms around his neck as she dove in, savoring the sweet love, longing, and joy that poured from his heart to hers. It was like heaven, and Simone didn't want to come back to earth.

When they came up for air and broke apart, Jax leaned against the tree trunk and pulled her to him.

Simone relaxed against his broad chest and stared out at the vivid and stunning horizon as cool, breezy air brushed against her skin. The broad leaves of the oak tree provided enough shade to block the overhead sunlight above, but the sky was at its brightest in deep blue colors fading to lighter blues in the distance, with the mountains providing a dramatic backdrop to the rolling hills and grassy meadows. A piece of heaven on earth. "My horses would love it here," she said.

"What kind of horses do you have?" Jax asked, the cadence of his low voice caressing her skin.

"Mostly thoroughbreds and quarter horses for the program I run for low-income kids and children with disabilities."

Jax twisted to look at her face. "When did you start this?"

"A few years ago. Since I don't ride as much as I used to, I figured I could use the horses to help kids who needed them. Horses can be very therapeutic, you know."

"It sounds fun."

"It is, and very rewarding, too. I have a brilliant manager who handles everything, so it's hands-off for me at this point. But I have two horses there that are just for my private use, though I hired a jockey to ride them regularly for their workout."

Jax stared at her disbelievingly. "You have a jockey."

Simone chuckled. The arrangement wasn't what he thought, though she could afford it. "He's not on my payroll or anything, just on a contract basis, to come by and put the horses through their paces."

"What horses are they?"

"An Andalusian stallion and a Fresian mare. I also have my eye on an Akhal-Teke I hope to acquire later in the year."

Jax whistled. "Those must have cost a pretty penny." Both the Andalusian and the Fresian had cost her over a million dollars because of their pedigrees, but Simone wasn't telling him *that*. "I see you have a thing for rare horses. I'm sure Rex would love to get his hands on those."

"Maybe that might happen soon," she teased him.

"Oh yeah? I see someone has been thinking," he teased back.

"I remember a certain someone mentioned marriage yesterday."

"Really? I don't recall that."

Simone tickled his side. "You don't remember?"

Jax fought to stay still. "I don't remember," he managed with a straight face.

She tickled him some more. "You're sure you don't remember?"

A grin broke on Jax's face, and he lifted his arms in surrender. "Okay, okay, I remember now."

Simone released him. "That's more like it." She relaxed again against him.

He looped his arms over her. "I'll get my payback for this."

Simone's lips turned up into a smile. "You're welcome to try."

They stayed that way for a while, enjoying the scenery, and then dove into the food they'd brought. Before long, with pleasant conversation and laughter between them, they'd eaten to their fill and packed up any remainders. Simone watched as Jax led the horses to a nearby brook for a drink. By the time he returned and tied them off, Simone was ready for a nap.

Jax settled in beside her and, with the calming and relaxing sound of running water in the background, Simone fell asleep.

She woke to see Jax had pulled a blanket over them. He'd flung his arm over her, and the weight was a reassuring presence.

Simone pulled her phone from her pocket and checked the time. It was a little after three in the afternoon. She didn't know she'd slept that long, but she felt better than she had in days.

She rested on her elbow and studied the profile of the man beside her. How could a man be this handsome? She ran a light finger over his eyebrows and then over the bridge of his nose. As she moved it over his lips, Jax caught it with his teeth as his eyes sprang open.

"Ouch!" Simone said as she pulled her finger from his mouth. "That hurts."

Jax reached for the finger and massaged it. "That's what you get for being naughty."

"Naughty? I was just touching your lips."

Jax gave her a half-lidded gaze. "You have no idea, do you, of what your touch does to me?"

Simone's cheeks warmed as the meaning of his words sunk in. "Oh."

Jax chuckled. "My innocent, darling Simone." Then a yawn escaped him.

"Do you need more sleep?" she asked.

Jax shook his head. "I'm good for now. Are you ready to go?"

All the talk of secrets earlier had reminded Simone of something she still had to do. Now was as good a time as any.

"I need to show you something," she said.

CHAPTER 51

"What's this place?" Jax asked as he glanced over the empty land with a little shack at the back. They'd returned the horses and come here to Main Street in Jax's truck. A gated wall of brick and metal surrounded the property.

It was the only empty lot on a street lined with trees, small businesses, a few local restaurants and shops, and a nearby park. Most buildings boasted a western architecture with brick facades, shutters, and awnings, but some modern concrete structures had made their way in too. Jax could hear the distant clip-clop of horses' hooves on the pavement mixed in with the sounds of passing vehicles.

"My clinic," Simone replied from beside him.

"I've decided to build it in Dexin and bought this land from Max."

The early evening breeze feathered Jax's skin as he eyed the space. The property could accommodate a large clinic with more than enough space for its own parking lot. No wonder she'd been quick to agree to live at the ranch. She'd decided to stay in Dexin Valley long before he'd asked her. "Why didn't you tell me?"

"I wanted it to be a surprise. Besides, I wasn't sure at the time if you'd want me back in your life."

Jax gave her a curious look. "What would you have done if I'd said no?"

"I considered the possibility, but hoped you'd agree. This was me taking a step of faith. Besides, I'd already decided I needed to get away from Boston, and Dexin Valley looked like a good place to plant my roots. So, what do you think of the property?"

"It's a great location. I didn't know Max owned this lot." The Main Street spot was perfect for easy access.

"I'm lucky he sold it to me," Simone said. "He also recommended a construction team he'd used for the hospital, and so I have a call later this week with both a licensed architect and a licensed contractor to review the draft plan the architect had drawn up. But I need a favor."

"What do you need?"

"Do you think you could oversee this project on my behalf? Max's team is excellent, but I'd love to have someone on the ground who'd check in every now and then. It's challenging for me right now to do so from Boston."

"I'll take care of it."

Simone broke into a grin. "Will you?" She crashed into his arms. "Thanks, babe."

"Anything for you, darling."

Her eyes locked onto his, and her sheer beauty took his breath away. Simone must think he was the best thing that ever happened to her, but he was the lucky one. Jax had never felt so complete as when he had her in his arms. Sometimes, he found it hard to believe that she was here, right now, in his life.

Her soft lips drew his gaze, and his breath quickened. Jax could kiss them all day, and even now, he couldn't resist. He bent his head to capture them.

A loud ring tone filled the air, breaking the tension.

"Hold on," Simone said and jumped down from his arms. She pulled her phone from her pocket and answered it. "Hello?"

Jax's thumb circled her free palm even as he waited for the call to be over to continue what they'd been about to start. A quick inhale from Simone assured him she was just as game for it.

Then Simone stiffened.

"What is it?" Jax asked. Her mood had changed.

She interlaced her fingers with his and gripped his hand tighter as she continued to listen to the person on the other end of the line.

Jax stroked her hand to get her to relax and waited for the call to finish.

A moment later, Simone ended the call and turned to him. Her face was now ashen with worry.

"What is it?" Jax asked. He'd move heaven and hell to get rid of whatever was the problem and make her smile again.

"It's my lawyer. Someone has been interfering with the partnership contracts I was hoping to sign with the Boston hospitals to send more difficult dermatological cases to them. They've all given one excuse or the other and are no longer interested."

Jax's eyes narrowed. Whoever it was would pay for the interference. "Does he know who's responsible?"

"It's my stepfather."

Jax felt sucker-punched. Her stepfather was

supposed to be her family, for goodness' sake. How could he even work against her? How terrible Simone must feel, if he, an outsider, was disappointed in the man this way.

He pulled her into his arms. "It's going to be fine. We'll figure it out," he said.

"How can he even do this? I worked so hard for this, and now I don't know what to do." Her forlorn tone pulled at his heart's strings.

There had to be another way. Given her stepfather's influence in Boston, it would be an uphill battle to fight him on those grounds. They had to look elsewhere. Jax wasn't familiar with hospitals, but he knew someone who did.

"I have an idea," he said.

CHAPTER 52

"I think it's a great idea," Max said to Simone and Jax as they sat across from him in his home office back at the ranch. "Let me call him now and ask."

Simone shifted, and Jax placed his hand over hers and squeezed it.

She gave him a small smile. Jax had told her about his idea before they'd brought it up to Max, and Simone prayed it would work.

Max made a call on his home line and placed it in speaker mode. The line rang three times and then connected.

"Hey, Max," a cheerful voice said from the other end of the line.

"Hi, Blake," Max said. "I have Jax and his girlfriend, Dr. Simone Addison, who's a pediatric dermatologist, on speakerphone."

"Hi, Blake," Jax said.

"Hello, Jax," Blake said. "Dr. Addison, it's a pleasure to meet you. Alicia has told me all about you."

"Same here, Dr. Dexington," Simone said.

"Please call me Blake. Any friend of Alicia's is a friend of mine."

"You can call me Simone."

"Simone it is. Max, to what do I owe the pleasure of this call?"

"Here's the thing," Max said. "Dr. Addison is moving from Boston to Dexin and is planning to open a new dermatology clinic in Dexin Valley."

"That's wonderful," Blake said. "I know you've been wishing for more specialized services in the area."

"True. However, she'd like to establish partnerships with teaching hospitals in nearby cities, which brings Dexington Medical to mind. Would that be something you guys would be interested in?"

"Absolutely," Blake replied. "Dr. Addison, I've heard about your work from Dr. Guzman, and it would be an honor for us to work with you."

Simone's shoulders relaxed. It was like a boulder

had rolled off her shoulders at his words. "Thank you so much, Blake."

"Why don't you send me the details of what you have in mind, and I'll discuss it with my team? But, I don't see any issues arising from it. From the time Alicia first mentioned you, I'd contemplated the possibility of a partnership and had even run the idea by my team to see what they thought, and they were onboard with it."

Simone's eyes widened. "You'd already considered it?"

"Blake's like that," Max chirped in. "He's a business owner through and through."

Blake laughed. "I'm just a forward thinker, that's all, especially when it concerns family, and you're one, since you're with Jax and all."

The idea she was family warmed her heart. "I'll send it in a few days," Simone promised.

"Perfect," Blake said. "Hold on." He muted the line for a few seconds and then came back on. "Sorry about that. It's Alicia on her way out. She sends her regards, by the way. She just mentioned Jasmine's family has been thinking about developing a line of cosmetics to complement their existing lingerie products for their cancer survivor customers. Some have complained their surgical scars itch when they wear bras, and they want to do something about it. But they believe dermatological research would be critical to the success of the line. Simone, would you be interested in a collaboration with them?"

This was so much more than she'd hoped for. "I'd love to," Simone said with joy in her heart.

"Perfect!" Blake said. "I can set up a call later this week with all the interested parties."

"That would be great," Simone said. "Thank you and thank Alicia for me."

"My pleasure, and I'll let her know."

"Thanks again, Blake," Max said. "We won't hold you up. Have a wonderful evening."

"You too. Bye, guys," Blake said and ended the call.

Simone slumped in her chair. "I still can't believe what just happened. This is a miracle." Then she turned and threw her arms around Jax's neck, his delicious scent of cedarwood and aftershave washing over her. "Thank you, thank you, thank you," she said and then kissed him all over the face.

"You're welcome," Jax said with a chuckle, his precious dimple making an appearance.

"Ahem," Max said, clearing his throat.

Simone's ears warmed. "Sorry," she said sheepishly. She'd forgotten about Max's presence.

"No worries. I understand." He winked at Jax.

Jax jumped to his feet. "I think this is our cue to leave, Simone, unless you want Max discussing our love life next."

Simone rose as well. "Thanks again, Max. For everything."

"I'm glad it worked out," Max said. "Let me know directly if you need anything else. After all, we're *family*."

"Time to go," Jax said and pulled Simone after him.

"Bye, Simone," Max called after them.

"Bye, Max," she blurted out before Jax shut the door behind them.

"That was close. Another minute in there and Max would have discussed our engagement. Our very *fake* engagement," Jax said as they made their way down the hallway of the wing and toward the French doors that led to the living area.

The engagement could be fake, but the relationship was now real. Still, it was best to avoid any discussions on it if they could.

"But I'm glad everything else worked out," Jax continued.

"Me too. Thank you, Jax."

Jax held her hand. "Your happiness means everything to me."

His words melted her heart. Oh, how she loved this man. She looped her arm through his. "And my stepfather won't be able to interfere with this."

"He can't. Blake's family owns the hospital, of which Blake is now the majority shareholder."

Simone had known Alicia had married a billionaire, but not that they were that *influential* in medical circles. Dexington Medical was a renowned medical institution on the east coast. "We should celebrate tonight." By now, they'd entered the living room and soon reached the bottom of the stairs.

"Of course," Jax replied. "Why don't you freshen up and then I'll pick you up in about an hour's time for dinner in town?"

"That'd be great." A celebratory dinner out in town sounded perfect.

Jax kissed her on the cheek. "I'll see you later then."

Simone beamed. "I can't wait," she responded.

Her heart was as light as a feather as she hurried up the stairs.

Today was Simone's best day so far, and even her stepfather's interference couldn't change that.

CHAPTER 53

*J*ax whistled as he left the main house and drove over to his home. Seeing Simone smile again had filled his heart with joy. Dinner with her would only be the icing on such a perfect day, and it seemed the weather agreed, with the cool, fresh breeze that fanned his face through the open driver's window.

He parked the truck in front of his home and hopped down. Now all he had to do was take a shower and get ready. Jax reached his door and inserted the key.

"Hello, Jax," Rex called out.

Jax froze. He didn't need this, especially not now.

He opened the door to step in, but a lean figure blocked his path. "Jax, please talk to me."

"Get out of my way, Rex. Don't think I can't lift you if I need to."

"Jax, please."

Then Jax remembered the promise he'd made to Simone, and he sighed. He'd keep his word, even if meant the death of him. "Let's talk inside."

Rex stepped aside and Jax entered his home. He hung his car key on its hook and then collapsed on the couch. Rex had shut the door and now settled on the love seat opposite him.

The silence in the room was deafening, even oppressive.

"Please talk to me," Rex pleaded.

Jax refused to look him in the eye. Where would he even begin? All the memories of Rex's betrayal came rushing back, causing the hurt to sit like a boulder on his heart. But he had to try like he'd promised.

He took a deep breath and let it out. "You hurt me, Rex," he began. "I can't just forget what you did."

"I'm sorry."

"Sorry?" Jax leaned forward. Those two words were not enough for what he'd gone through over the years. He wasn't sure if Rex understood the havoc he'd wrecked.

Jax ran his hands through his hair as his emotions surged. "You broke me, Rex. You were the other half of my soul, my twin, and you disappeared." They'd been inseparable since childhood, through the deaths of first their pa and then their ma, and made plans for the future, to conquer the world together. Then Rex had vanished. Jax hadn't understood why.

He stared out unseeingly as he recalled those horrible first days after Rex's disappearance. "I don't know how I survived those early days. I don't even remember them," he said, unable to keep the agony from his voice. "Dex said I was like a zombie."

Jax allowed himself to sink deep into the closed off, damaged area of his heart that had always belonged to Rex. The searing pain that tore through his insides as memories of the betrayal bubbled out was the reason he'd feared to go there, to expose his bleeding heart.

His hands gripped his head and he looked up at Rex, unshed tears brimming in his eyes. "You broke me," he managed in a whisper. "And you didn't even try to make it up to me as soon as you came back. I wasn't that important to you."

In a flash, Rex knelt at Jax's feet and crushed him in his arms. "I'm so sorry for hurting you, Jax," Rex whispered. "It scared me to approach you after what

I'd done. I wasn't sure if I could survive your rejection."

Jax had never thought he'd ever feel Rex's arms around him again in this lifetime, and the dam in him broke. Rex held him as Jax's shoulders shook as he sobbed.

He didn't know how long he cried, but by the time he was done, Jax's heart felt raw and light, as if his tears had flushed the diseased areas out. He looked into Rex's eyes and saw the tears and sorrow mirrored in them.

Jax reached out and wiped Rex's tears away. "Don't disappear on me again without notice," he said.

Rex sniffed. "I won't. I promise you with my life, I'll never leave you again."

Jax let his head fall on Rex's shoulder as Rex continued to hold him. Soon, he felt a part of his soul, a piece that had been missing, return to him. "Now you've made me cry and everything," Jax said with a chuckle.

"I'm sorry," Rex said. "Do you need a tissue?"

Jax punched his arm. "My nose isn't running, you oaf."

Rex winced. "You know that hurts, right?"

"It was supposed to. It's not my fault you've

become soft."

Rex raised an eyebrow. "Soft? I'll show you soft." Rex began to tickle him.

"Rex, stop," Jax cried out between chuckles.

"I won't until you tell me you love me."

"You're crazy. I ain't saying that," Jax cried out. "That's for Tara to say."

Rex stopped tickling him and leaned back on his hunches. "Shoot! I'm in trouble. I was supposed to video chat her about an hour ago."

Jax laughed. "I don't envy you. She's one tough lady."

"Hey! That's my wife you're talking about." Rex ran a hand through his hair. "But what am I going to do?"

Jax leaned back on the couch. "It's time for you to grovel."

Rex groaned. "This is insane."

Jax slapped him on the shoulder. "Welcome to the club, brother."

Rex rose to his feet. "I have to go." He headed to the door and then turned back. "Are we good?"

Jax gave him a crooked smile. "We're good."

Rex's face lit up, and he flashed a matching smile.

The suffocating weight on Jax's chest eased away.

CHAPTER 54

*J*ax had called Simone last night to let her know about his conversation with Rex. She'd applauded him and then suggested they cancel the celebratory dinner. She figured Jax needed some time alone to decompress following what had just happened, and the relief in Jax's voice had told her she'd done the right thing.

Simone had decided to head back to Boston the next day, a day earlier than she'd planned, to meet with her lawyers to discuss the partnership agreement with Dexington Medical and the cosmetics collaboration with IntimiRose, and Jax had promised to drop her off. She wished she could have stayed longer to further explore the ranch and Dexin Valley, but there'd be enough time for that in the future.

Jax opened the passenger side of the truck for her and helped her down.

"Thank you," Simone said as she alighted. He'd driven her back home, and they'd arrived at mid-day, just as the sun was at its highest point.

"My pleasure," Jax replied.

She waited until he'd retrieved her overnight bag from the truck's cab and then they walked side by side until they reached her private entrance.

"I'll take it from here," Simone said as she reached for her bag.

Jax held onto it. "I can handle it."

"I know cowboys love to take care of their ladies," Simone said. "But you have a face-to-face meeting with a supplier soon, and you'll barely make it back to Dexin Valley on time as it is." She gave him a kiss on the cheek. "I'll be fine."

"I'll take her bag upstairs," her concierge said from in front of them. Simone hadn't noticed when the slender, blond man had appeared.

Jax looked from her to the concierge. "Okay," he finally acquiesced and handed the bag to the man. "I'll call you later." He gave Simone a quick hug and a kiss and then strode to his truck.

Simone waved at him as he pulled out, and then, shortly after, he was gone.

"I'll take it upstairs, ma'am," the concierge said, and carried it ahead of her into the building.

As Simone ascended the initial building steps to follow him, her phone buzzed.

She pulled it out from her pocket and checked the screen.

It was an unfamiliar number. Who could it be?

She swiped the answer button. "Hello," she said.

"Hi, Simone," an unexpected voice said.

Ethan? What could he possibly be calling her about? He'd betrayed her six years ago, and they'd parted ways since then. What could he be up to now?

"This is an unexpected call," Simone stated.

"I know. I'm sorry about what happened between us, but I figured you should know the truth."

What was he talking about?

"Simone, I never cheated on you. Your father, Mr. Addison, threatened to ruin my life and that of my family if I didn't break up with you. He wasn't someone I could go up against, so I had no choice but to do what he asked. Vera overheard our conversation and offered to help. But that was it. There was never anything between us."

Simone couldn't help the pain that jabbed her heart, and she grabbed the handrail. Her stepfather was yet again behind another misery in her life.

When would it ever end? "So why tell me now? It's been six years."

"I wanted to before, but then I found out you'd started dating someone else, and I figured it was best to let sleeping dogs lie and let you move on with your life. But my fiancée, who's quite plugged into the Boston social scene, mentioned you were still single, and I wondered if your father had struck again and ripped you guys apart. I figured it was time you knew the truth."

"Okay, thanks for letting me know."

"Once again, I'm sorry for everything. I wish you all the best."

Ethan was now her past, and she wished him well. "You too," she said. The line disconnected.

Simone leaned against the outdoor handrail for support. So messing with her and Jax hadn't been the first time her stepfather had destroyed her relationship. How could a human being who called himself her father be so terrible? When would he ever stop?

But one thing was for sure: she had to put his interference in her life to an end once and for all.

Simone let out an exhale and took another step up the stairs. She'd think about what to do later. For now, she had a meeting to get to.

"Simone!" a voice called out, stopping her in her tracks.

She froze for a moment, then forced herself to turn.

It was her stepfather.

CHAPTER 55

Simone took a deep breath. "What do you want?" she asked in a bitter voice. It was hard enough holding back her anger at him.

"Can I speak with you for a moment?" her stepfather asked in a quiet voice.

This could be a trick, Simone thought, even though he'd never spoken to her like this. Her stepfather was not above using underhanded tactics just to win.

The skies darkened in that moment and thunder rumbled across the sky, as if it agreed with her.

Besides, she didn't have to tolerate him any longer in her life. "I have nothing to say to you." She turned and continued up the stairs.

"I'm sorry," her stepfather said.

Simone whirled around. "Sorry? Sorry for always trying to ruin my life? What did I ever do to you?"

Her stepfather took an involuntary step back. "I'm sorry I interfered with your contracts," he said.

"That's it? What about Ethan and Jax? What about the countless putdowns and manipulations? Was I some toy you could just toss around however you like? I'm a human being with feelings, for goodness' sake. You were the only father I ever knew!"

"I'm sorry, Simone."

"Why are you telling me this now?" She was pretty sure it wasn't from the goodness of his heart, even though there were bags under his eyes, and his tie was not in its usual perfect position.

He pulled at his shirt collar. "Your mother found out about the contracts and threatened to divorce me if I didn't apologize to you and change. And I can't live without her." He finally loosened the tie. "I'm sorry for everything," he continued. "I know I've hurt you in the past, but I'm going to do my best to be a better father."

So that was why he'd come. Not because he was sorry for what he'd done over the years, but because he didn't want to lose her mother.

Simone shook her head in disbelief. Her stepfather had always used the threat of divorcing her mother as leverage to get Simone to comply with his wishes. Who knew he'd been scared of it all along?

But he had a long way to go if he thought he was truly repentant for everything he'd done to her. In fact, Simone didn't expect things to change much between them.

Besides, it no longer mattered. *He* no longer mattered. Because as he stood before her, Simone realized she no longer felt anything—hatred, disappointment, need for approval—toward him.

She no longer needed his love and acceptance.

Simone had the love of her life back in her life. She had new friends, a new family that accepted her for who she was, and a new relationship with her mother where there'd been none before. Besides, her real father had loved and cherished her. She was happy with her life.

She didn't need Sebastian Addison.

"I have nothing else to say to you. You need to go," she said. "Mother will be waiting for you."

Simone didn't wait for his response. She entered her building and shut the door behind her.

CHAPTER 56

*J*ax tugged at his blue and brown checkered shirt as he knocked at Rex's front door. Rex had invited him over to meet his business partners, and after his meeting with the supplier and a series of follow-up meetings with his team, Jax had headed down to Rex's place.

He hadn't been here since he'd helped build Rex's home to ensure it met his specifications, but the place appeared unchanged.

The door swung open, and Rex stood before him in an identical shirt. "Come on in," he said with a broad smile.

"Thanks," Jax replied and entered Rex's home. The interior of the house remained mostly the same as he remembered it, with its various shades of greys and browns and the occasional burst of color. "But why are you wearing my shirt?" he asked. It'd happened a lot when they were growing up, but not since he'd come back. Maybe they'd synced up since the reconciliation.

Rex slapped his shoulder. "More like you're wearing mine."

"Hey, *twinsies*," Cole said as he waved from where he'd stretched out on the large couch. He was the youngest of the trio.

"Shut your trap, Cole," Rex said. Then he turned to Jax. "Now let me introduce you to my business partners. Weston and Liam Grayson." Jax had met them before at Blake's wedding.

"Nice to meet you both again," Jax said.

"Us too," Liam said from where he leaned against the wall. He was the quieter of the two.

"Hey! What about me?" Cole asked. "You left me out."

"You're the tag-along," Rex replied. "He doesn't count," he said to Jax.

"Ouch. That hurts," Cole said.

"It would hurt less if you bridled your tongue," Rex retorted.

Cole threw a couch pillow at Rex's head, which

he dodged. The pillow ended up on the floor, and Jax picked it up.

"Thank you for forgiving Rex," Weston said. He'd fit his solid frame into a single chair. "I didn't know he could be this nice. He actually made us breakfast."

"Hey! I'm a nice guy," Rex said. The looks the trio gave him said otherwise.

Jax chuckled. "You're welcome."

"Just know you're one of us now," Weston said. Liam and Cole nodded in agreement.

"I think the game's about to start," Rex said. Rex had mentioned their local football team was playing against the Dexington football team that evening when he'd called Jax earlier and invited him over. "Cole, bring the snacks and drinks."

"Why me?" Cole protested.

"Because you're the youngest," Weston said.

"I'll help," Jax said.

"Thanks," Cole said as he rose to his feet. "You're certainly the nicer half."

"I'd take back those words, Cole, if I were you," Liam said. "The profit-sharing exercise is coming up soon, and you don't want to get on Rex's bad side."

"Wise words," Weston said, nodding.

"Whatever," Cole said. He headed to the kitchen,

with Jax following behind. They grabbed the trays Rex had made up and returned to the living area.

By now, the eighty-something inch flatscreen TV was on, and the game had just begun. They dropped the trays on the coffee table and found seating spots for themselves. Jax ended up beside Rex. Cole dropped onto the couch and put his feet up.

"Hey, don't make a mess, Cole," Rex warned. "Tara and Hailey are coming back this weekend." They were transitioning from New York to Dexin Valley.

"My goodness, they've whipped you," Weston said.

"I don't mind," Rex said with a big smile. "Tara can whip me all day." He winked at Jax.

Jax chuckled. He understood what Rex meant. He felt the same way about Simone.

"Why does that sound nasty?" Cole said, turning up his nose. Rex threw a pillow at his head. "Hey, what was that for?"

"To get your head screwed straight. Tara is the best thing that ever happened to me, and that's why you scoundrels," he pointed to Weston, Liam, and Cole, "need women in your lives."

"No, thank you!" his friends chorused.

"No, sir," Cole said. "I've had enough whipping

from Grandma Grayson to last me a lifetime, thank you very much."

"How dare you speak about Grandma that way!" Weston said and grabbed Cole in a chokehold.

Jax chuckled as he watched the scene play out before him. This was what he'd missed over the years with Rex—the camaraderie, the teasing, and just altogether roughhousing.

But now he had that back in his life, and that was all that mattered.

CHAPTER 57

The opening night of her father's art exhibition at a gallery in the Boston's Museum of Fine Arts was going better than Simone had expected. She'd worked with her mom to curate the list of paintings and artwork, set up the art exhibition, and showcase her father's works.

Each work had boasted a summary of its story beneath it, and surprisingly, that had been a hit. Tonight's event was for members only—the artwork would be open to the public the next day.

There'd been some press too about the life of her father and his relationship with the Addisons, but they'd expected that.

Her mom had marked the pieces she could part with. Ninety percent of those had sold, and the night was not even over. Simone had convinced her mom to include her own paintings as well, and those had also been a favorite with the crowd.

Simone turned at the call of her name, her olive-green evening dress sweeping around her. Paisley hurried over, dressed in a black and white cocktail dress. "I made it!" she said. Paisley had been on call, but had gotten another doctor to cover the rest of her shift for her.

"Thank you for coming," Simone said as she pulled her into a hug.

"My pleasure. Anything for my bestie." She glanced around. "Where's Lover Boy?"

"Over there." Simone pointed to the far east section of the gallery where Jax was holding court in front of a painting, looking dashing in a black tuxedo, with the Grayson brothers beside him.

"Is that a cowboy I see? The one in a tux?" Paisley asked, even as she picked up a drink from a passing server. Weston was in a tuxedo, too, but had his cowboy hat on.

"He's one of Rex's partners."

"Is he single?"

"I believe so."

"I'm going to say hi. See you later, girlfriend."

Simone shook her head as she watched Paisley go. Some things never changed.

She looked around the space, seeing familiar faces from Boston's elite society, her family, and her friends. Everyone had come to show their support. The entire Dexin clan, as well as the Dexington family, had made it to the event.

Even her stepfather had shown up at the exhibition with her brother, Michael. Simone was still wary of him, but they'd been working on their relationship as a family. It was still a work-in-progress, but who knew what would happen in the future? Only time would tell.

Michael now called her all the time and spent time each week with her. He'd confessed the tension between her and her stepfather had kept him away, since he hadn't wanted to take sides, but he was glad he finally had a real big sister.

Simone had even introduced him to Jax, and Jax had taken him under his wing. It seemed her stepfather had approved, since Michael was now interested in taking over the Addison empire under Jax's guidance. It seemed Jax and her stepfather had found common ground because of his financial expertise.

Two hours later, the doors of the gallery closed

for the night. The event had been an overwhelming success, but Simone was now ready for it to be over.

Then the gallery lights went off.

Simone's heart pounded. What was going on? Thank goodness that hadn't happened during the actual exhibition.

"Simone," a low voice called out.

Simone whirled in the voice's direction. Jax headed toward her, holding an LED candle in his hand. "I'm glad you're here," she said with relief. "What's going on?"

Jax stopped in front of her. "Simone, I'd like to ask you a question."

"What is it, Jax?" She looked around. "Where's everybody?" They'd planned one big dinner after the event at a nearby restaurant, and Jax had made the reservations.

Jax placed the LED candle on the floor beside him, got down on one knee, and pulled out a box from his pocket.

Simone's heart thudded. Was this what she thought it was?

Jax opened the box to reveal a stunning diamond ring that almost blinded her.

She gasped. He was really doing this.

"Simone, you're the sweetest, most special

woman I've ever met," Jax said. "You complete me and push me to be a better man, and I can't imagine life without you. Would you do me the honor of being my wife?"

She'd never imagined he'd ask her today. How had she missed the signs?

But timing didn't matter. She'd fallen for Jax. Hook, line, and sinker.

"So what do you say?" Jax asked as he laid on a thick Western drawl.

Simone chuckled. He sure knew what buttons to press. "Yes," she said and extended her hand for the ring.

Jax slipped the ring on and then rose and swept her off her feet, giving her a sound kiss that sent electrical sparks all the way to her toes.

The lights suddenly came on as catcalls and clapping filled the air.

Simone broke off the kiss to see all their friends and families approaching them. Her cheeks warmed as she thought about what they'd witnessed. Congratulations filled the air all around them.

"I'm so happy for you, dear," her mom said, blowing her a kiss. The diamond choker at her neck sparkled in agreement.

Simone beamed. "Thanks, mom."

"I've heard about Jax's legendary kisses, and my goodness, it's as rock solid as they say," Cole said. "You've got to give me tips, bro."

Weston cuffed his head. "You don't know when to shut up, do you?"

"Hey! That hurts. Besides, *you* told me about the kiss."

"Gentlemen, can you just keep it down?" Paisley admonished, which started off a whole load of head-butting with Weston, like they'd been doing since they'd first met tonight.

Jax chuckled. "Why do I feel Weston won't be single for much longer?"

"Well, Paisley has always wanted a cowboy of her own," Simone said with a smile.

"I have one more gift for you," Jax said. He pulled out a small flat box and handed it to her.

"What is this?" Simone opened it to see a key nestled within. "A key?"

Jax's grey eyes twinkled. "The key to your private island."

Simone's eyes widened. "You bought me a private island?"

"I figured that's the one thing you don't have yet."

Simone laughed. Jax hadn't been kidding when

he said he had enough to take care of his family. "You're a hoot, you know that?"

Jax pulled her back into his arms. "Your own special hoot? Now, that I don't mind."

Simone stared into those grey pools she couldn't resist. "Thanks for the gift."

"You're welcome."

"Uncle Jax?" a childlike voice called out.

Simone and Jax turned to see the impish redhead in a beautiful, dark blue dress approach them. "Yes, Chloe?"

The little girl cocked her head. "I thought you were already engaged."

Simone's ears and face warmed. It seemed nothing could get by Chloe. She'd called them out on their fake engagement.

"We decided to re-engage," Jax said with a deadpan look on his face.

Simone couldn't help the laughter that escaped her. What was Jax even talking about?

"Like you guys were engaged in the first place," Dex mocked. "We all knew it was a lie."

"True," Max said. "A big, fat lie." Becca nodded in agreement.

"We all knew about it," Blake said. "Even in

Dexington." All the Dexington folks nodded their assent.

"I think that skillet is calling your name, Jax," Maggie said. "This isn't the straight and narrow you promised me."

"Guys, I was desperate. I couldn't help it," Jax confessed. "No more lies from now on, Maggie. I promise."

"You better," Maggie said.

"We'll be good from now on," Simone promised.

"Ah!" Chloe nodded with understanding. "Okay. Carry on."

"I guess this is the part where we give them more to talk about," Jax whispered with a twinkle in his eye.

Simone nodded as the corners of her lips quirked. "I absolutely agree. We can't disappoint them, can we?"

Jax pulled her closer. "I love you, Dr. Mrs-to-be Simone Addison-Dexin."

"I love you, Jax Dexin."

Then Jax bent his head and gave her the best kiss of her life.

EPILOGUE

SIX WEEKS LATER

*S*imone and Jax walked into the barn side-by-side as they carried large pastry boxes into the space where the next singles' mixer event was being held. The event was in full swing, and cowboys and cowgirls filled the space and mingled with one another that cool evening.

She'd signed the partnership agreement with Dexin Medical Center, Dexington Medical, and a collaboration agreement with IntimiRose, and was in town to check out the progress of the work on the clinic. Despite the busy weekend, Maggie had roped them in to deliver the pastries and desserts to Miss Prissy.

But Miss Prissy was nowhere to be seen.

"Why don't you wait here, and I'll go find her?"

Jax said. There was a nearby small table in a perfect spot away from the crowd, and they placed the pastry boxes on it.

"Sounds good," Simone said.

"I'll be right back," Jax said and left in search of her.

"Hello," a deep masculine voice said. Simone looked up to see a handsome cowboy at her side. "Would you care for a dance?" A new line dance had just begun.

"No," a loud voice boomed before she could reply.

Simone couldn't help the smile that flirted on her lips. It seemed the caveman had come back to claim his bride.

Jax's arm snaked around her waist and pulled her in. "She's taken," he growled to the cowboy.

"I think it's up to her to decide," the cowboy insisted.

Jax released Simone and stepped up to the cowboy. "I think this might be a good time to buzz off," he said in a low, dangerous voice. He didn't wait for the cowboy's response and pulled Simone after him toward the exit.

"What about the pastries?" Simone asked.

"Miss Prissy said I could leave them on the table."

"You didn't have to be so hard on the guy," Simone said. "He probably didn't know we're engaged, and this is supposed to be a singles' mixer." By now, they'd reached the exit.

"Really? Then I better make it clear you're taken."

Jax pulled her in right there and gave her a toe-melting kiss she'd never forget.

~

FOUR MONTHS LATER

Becca and Max had opted to hold a baby naming ceremony for their newborn son in the main house's living area, since the frigid winter weather prevented an outdoor garden event.

The whole Dexin and Dexington family had gathered, and Max had even invited a young dashing surgeon colleague of his, Dr. Roman Sinclair, to the event as well. It had been a lovely morning ceremony. The baby had ended up with six names—only two were official—and now it was time for breakfast and desserts.

Maggie had outdone herself with the dining farmhouse table piled high with delectable breakfast dishes, some of which Simone had never seen before. The family was now gathered around the table, and laughter and conversation flowed.

Simone bit into a croissant. It was buttery, luscious, and melted right in her mouth. She and Jax had gotten married about six weeks ago in an intimate wedding with only close friends and family and had just returned from their honeymoon at the private island Jax had bought for her as an engagement present. Simone had enjoyed their time together, but she'd missed Maggie's cooking.

She turned to Jax. "Do you want to try this?" she asked and offered him another croissant. "It's so good."

Jax's nostrils flared, and he turned away. "Why does it smell so fishy?"

Simone sniffed at the croissant in question. There wasn't any briny fragrance to it as far as she could tell. "It seems okay to me," she said. "Did you eat anything disagreeable?"

Jax shook his head. "No."

Rex had left during the ceremony to attend to an ailing horse and just returned after freshening up. He reached Jax's side and stole a mini cupcake from his plate.

"What do you think—? What's that awful perfume you're wearing?" Jax said and then gagged.

"Are you alright, darling?" Simone asked, but then noticed Tara and Zoey exchange looks. "What is it?"

Becca laughed from where she sat beside Max at the head of the table. "Sounds like Jax is pregnant."

Simone's eyes widened as she realized she hadn't seen her period since they'd gotten married. She put her hand over her mouth. "Oh, my goodness."

Zoey and Tara rose to their feet. "Come on." They led Simone out of the dining area to Becca's office, where she kept a medicine cabinet. They pulled a pregnancy test from it and handed it to her. Simone used the bathroom and then returned. The test held two glaring lines.

"Congratulations," Tara and Zoey said to her as they hugged her, one after the other.

"Thank you." She couldn't believe it. "I need to go." Simone hurried off toward the dining area.

She soon reached Jax and threw her arms around him from behind. "I'm so sorry," she said. It seemed Jax was the one that would suffer through the pregnancy symptoms.

Jax looked up at her. "Are we—?"

Simone smiled through the curtain of tears that now graced her cheeks. "Yes, we're having a baby."

Jax jumped to his feet and crushed her against his chest. "I love you, darling. You did good."

The sound of laughter that escaped from her lips echoed everywhere, mingling with the shouts of congratulations from her dearest family and friends.

Simone had finally come home.

As a Doctor Billionaire to her own special Cowboy.

Roman Sinclair glanced around the faces at the dining table. He'd lost his family—one he remembered only little of—at a young age and grown up as an orphan, and even though he'd eventually met a good family that had fostered him, it'd been nothing like the love, camaraderie, and boisterousness that he'd just experienced at the Dexin family house.

When Max, a fellow doctor he'd first met at Dexington Medical and now a mentor of his, had invited him for the ceremony, Roman hadn't known what to expect. But he hadn't anticipated the longing that sprung from his heart for a family of his own. He'd been content with his life over the years, grateful for what he had, but he hadn't known what he'd been missing.

Until now.

As he looked at the overflowing joy, peace, and happiness of the wonderful family around him, Roman hoped one day that this would be his reality, too.

That he would find the kind of love that lasted for a lifetime.

A love that was truly his own.

Thank you so much for reading! Want to know how Roman Sinclair found love (in a royal billionaire romance)?

Check out A LOVING THE BILLIONAIRE ROYAL DOC at https://dobidaniels.com.

Or want to know what happens next in the Dexington/Dexin world?

Sign up now at https://dobidaniels.com.

ACKNOWLEDGMENTS

Writing a book is harder and more rewarding than I could have ever imagined. And it would not have been possible without the support, love, and encouragement from my number one cheerleader, my dearest mom. My life would never have been this awesome and wonderful without you.

Of course, I have to thank my precious little DC for his smiles and antics. You brighten my day and give me the strength to keep pushing through.

Thank you to my sisters for encouraging me on this wonderful journey. And a special thanks to my baby brother (who is so not a baby anymore) for being super supportive and checking in on my progress. You guys are the best.

Thank you to my wonderful author friends. You know who you are. Your selflessness and willingness to share what you know has made my writing journey smoother and an exciting one. And a special thanks to my ARC readers whose support have made a difference.

Most of all, I want to thank God who gave me life, surrounded me with the most wonderful people, and loved me all the way. You make my life complete.

And finally, a special thanks to all my readers whose love of my stories spur me on to write more. Thank you!

ABOUT DOBI DANIELS

As a former physician and business executive in another life—with a childhood filled with reading multi-genre novels—Dobi Daniels loves to write sweet thrilling romance stories with heart. She enjoys dreaming up everyday characters who rise above unfavorable circumstances to overcome incredible odds and find joy along the way.

When not writing, Dobi can be found binging K-dramas and ice cream with her little sidekick by her side.

A Doctor Billionaire for the Cowboy is the third book in A Cowboy Loves the Doctor Series. Sign up at dobidaniels.com to be notified when the next Dobi Daniels book comes out!

Thank you!

https://dobidaniels.com
hello@dobidaniels.com
facebook.com/dobidaniels
bookbub.com/profile/dobi-daniels
instagram.com/dobidaniels